ALMOST CHOSEN ...

NEARLY SAVED

by

Jim and Cheryl Pahz

Almost Chosen...Nearly Saved is a novel and a work of fiction. Any similarity by the characters to people living or dead is coincidental and unintentional.

Stone Cottage Press
Mount Pleasant, Michigan

ISBN -13: 978-0-9824158-2-5
ISBN -10: 0-9824158-2-6

Prologue

Religion has always been a problem for me. It was a problem even before I was born. If I was telling the story of my life, that's the place my narrative would start: at an incident my mother had with anti-Semitism, and she wasn't even Jewish. She was a young woman, and she encountered it from a member of her own family. But she didn't pay much attention, or, as she told me years later, "I didn't give it no nevermind." That was because she and my father were in love. Each came to their marriage with their own religion; my mother was Baptist and my father Jewish. They were newlyweds and their love transcended theology.

Her family advised her "not to be unequally yoked." That is what the Bible said, and they reminded her that the Bible was the inspired Word of God. Parenthetically, she was also warned that her baby might be born with horns, like Michelangelo's statue of Moses. But Mom and Dad ignored the advice, and, luckily, I wasn't born with horns.

After my parents married they entered their days of prosperity. They became successful and acquired lots of stuff. It was the 1950s and religion was the least of their concerns. What they were interested in was a house in the suburbs and a Cadillac in the driveway. They were too busy to notice anything as ugly as anti-Semitism unless it hit them smack in the face, which it did when I was in fourth grade at the Woodlawn Academy. It was Easter week and one of my teachers, Mrs. Odykirk, asked me to recite one of those "funny Hebrew chants" in front of the class. I didn't know what she was talking about. But I knew I wasn't having fun. I guess that's when I first became aware of my interfaith dilemma—almost chosen, nearly saved, always troubled. I felt in-between and blamed all my problems on not knowing in which house of worship I belonged.

My mother told me our family "believed in tolerance." It was practically our family motto—tolerance. It was a nice ideal, and I embraced it with the same zeal as when one of the neighbor kids said I ought to be a Brooklyn Dodgers fan.

"Why?" I asked.

"Because," he said, "they are the best team, and the Yankees are the worst."

Of course, in fourth grade I didn't have the slightest idea what tolerance meant. All I understood was my mother believed in tolerance and Mrs. Odykirk evidently didn't. Today my mother would probably use different words. She might say something like, "We embrace diversity." That would be the politically correct way to put it at the start of the 21st century.

You could say I've been baffled by religion. Occasionally I found it. Not God, you understand, religion. There is a difference. I remember those Hare Krishna kids with their tambourines and finger cymbals, singing and dancing in airport lobbies. That's before the airports ran them out. They had plenty of religion. Then there were the street kids who used to panhandle in cities and called themselves the Children of God. They had an overabundance of religion, too.

I didn't actually realize I wasn't Jewish until I immigrated to Israel. That was a surprise. I was grown then, at least chronologically. When I went to the Holy Land, I wanted to commit to something bigger than myself.

It seemed a good idea at the time, especially after my stint at Theophilus College, an evangelical Christian institution. I marched to Zion to find "my people."

I've been lost, saved, and lost again—more than once. To be honest, I've had my fill of religion. But, despite it all, I'm still looking for God. I haven't given up on God yet.

Chapter 1

A Chance Meeting

Daphne Pearson was a good girl. In her small rural community of Signal Mountain, Tennessee, she was well-known for her green eyes and hair the color of a new copper penny. As a child she had been a tomboy; her father taught her to shoot, ride horses, and set a fence post. By 15 Daphne was too "grown-up" for such things, at least according to her mother, who thought it was time she settled down and became a young lady.

Daphne helped with the household chores and looked after her younger brother and sister. She found caring for Luke and Sissy a lot like dealing with horses. Everything went easiest if she was firm and decisive, never showing fear or frustration, never letting them do anything the wrong way. In her view if they did something incorrectly just once, it would take them forever to unlearn the behavior. She was fair but firm with her brother and sister, and the adults took notice. At her high school graduation ceremony, Sissy and Luke watched proudly as their pretty, smart sister marched up the aisle to graduate as valedictorian.

Daphne stood 5'6" without shoes. She had long, shapely legs and a firm, round backside that gave her a playful, coltish quality. Her rich, auburn hair fell in waves to her shoulders. Just short of beautiful, she was wholesome and pretty, without the tiniest speck of arrogance.

Her parents' one concern (at least her mother's) was that perhaps Daphne was too independent. Never one to follow the crowd or to do what everyone else expected, she refused to smoke cigarettes despite the fact that all the movie stars and most of her friends and relatives smoked. "I can't stand smoking," she would say. "The only thing worse than smoking is chewing the stuff." To the embarrassment of her mother, Daphne would make such statements in public. She was an opinionated girl.

But her mother wasn't that concerned about Daphne's position on smoking or even if some people considered Daphne's remarks rude. Mother was concerned about Daphne's future.

"All you ever talk about is traveling and getting a job," she said, waving her dishtowel like a distress flag. "Don't you want a husband and children?"

"Those things can wait. Mama, the Depression is over. It's the 1940s and I'm a modern woman."

That was partially true—Daphne did consider herself a modern woman. And she did want a career. What she wouldn't admit to her mother was that she also wanted a husband. The problem was that she didn't want a husband from Signal Mountain—or from Tennessee, for that matter. She wanted someone different from the boys she had grown up with, someone with mystery. And the only way to find him was to travel somewhere else. What better place to go than a big city? After Christmas, as a present to themselves, Daphne and her friend Virginia Jo traveled to New York City. High school was over and, to her mother's dismay, Daphne took this independent act. For Daphne, it was more than an act—it was her first step into the future she envisioned for herself. She had seen this future through her soft eyes, a trick she learned from her horses. She tried to see the world from a horse's perspective—with soft eyes. While riding a horse, Daphne would keep her eyes wide open to see everything around her, while, at the same time, focusing straight ahead toward her ultimate destination. As if by magic, the horse would go where she wanted.

It was hard to have soft eyes in New York City. She wasn't sure which way to go, and she found everything about the metropolis distracting. Even though she had no idea what the outcome of her trip would be, she loved every minute she and Virginia Jo were there. She was sure her future was waiting somewhere in this city of lights, with the Empire State Building, Times Square, and Broadway. Virginia Jo confided that she also wanted something other than Tennessee—something grander and more sophisticated. But she wasn't sure New York held the answers she was looking for. She found the city intimidating. Still, between sightseeing adventures, both girls read the newspapers and talked about the possibility of starting a new life in this exciting place.

One night, as they sat in their hotel room searching the classifieds for job prospects, Virginia Jo spotted an advertisement for the Starlight Ballroom and read it out loud. They looked at each other and laughed. Without a word they took out their suitcases and found their fanciest dresses—slightly rumpled but passable, since both girls would have looked pretty in a flour sack. They spent an hour and a half showering, painting their nails, and styling each other's hair, then hailed a taxi and set off on another New York adventure.

Daphne's eyes were still adjusting to the dim light in the ballroom and the glare from a rotating ball covered with tiny mirrors that hung from the ceiling. She had not even had a chance to fully examine her surroundings when a handsome young man with brown eyes, wavy, dark hair, and a serious expression approached her.

"You ladies look lovely. You must be tourists. You are far too pretty to be New Yorkers."

"We're from the South," Virginia Jo blurted.

"From Jersey?"

"No, I mean the real South. We're from Tennessee."

"Tennessee. You really are from Dixie."

Daphne could feel herself blush.

"My name is Abraham Fisher. My friends call me Abe. I just graduated from New York University, where I majored in business. I am polite and, by New York standards, a gentleman. At least I hope so. Anyway, that is my intention."

Daphne could feel Abe's confidence. It excited her.

"Are you always so forward, Mr. Fisher?"

"Usually, no. But I've just been drafted. I thought when I finished with school, I would be starting my own business. By now I was supposed to be making money—but no. Uncle Sam calls and where he leads I must follow. I only have a few weeks before I report for duty. So, you see, I don't have a minute to waste. And I don't believe I have ever met two such attractive ladies."

Abe's voice was soothing and melodic. He smiled easily and exuded a quality Daphne had not seen in other men. He was slightly taller than she, with a good build. Daphne found she was actually listening when he spoke, because, under his gaze, she found it hard to concentrate enough to speak herself, let alone be charming. And then, when the full intensity of his eyes met hers, she felt like she had been struck by lightning.

It's hard to endure after being hit by a lighting bolt. Daphne was not sure of herself. Her knees barely supported her weight. Two days later, when Abe proposed, Daphne didn't hesitate to accept. Maybe it was so sudden because the war was looming. Daphne wasn't sure. She only knew that when she looked into the face of this man, something special happened. After a one-week whirlwind romance, when Daphne was shown practically everything worth seeing in New York City, the two eloped across the river in New Jersey. Virginia Jo was a witness at the wedding. She lent Daphne her new pair of empire pumps and gave the couple their first wedding gift—a souvenir plate of New Jersey, the Garden State.

Virginia Jo cried. "Oh, Daphne. What will I tell everyone? How will they understand? I don't know if I can go back home by myself. Do you think I'll be all right?" Then she began to cry some more. Eventually, Virginia Jo did return alone on the bus to Tennessee, with no job offers but plenty of stories to share with the folks back home.

After their brief honeymoon in New Jersey, it was time to return to New York so Daphne could be introduced to Abe's parents. When the day arrived Daphne and Abe didn't speak as his car moved through the noisy city traffic. Daphne was nervous but gained strength each time she glanced at her new husband, who seemed confident and relaxed behind the wheel. She was only now beginning to sense the immense changes in her life that would result from this impulsive marriage to a man she scarcely knew, a man who, in a few weeks, would be sent to Camp Campbell, Kentucky and then off to fight in a war thousands of miles away. But when she looked into his serious brown eyes, she knew that she had had no choice. She belonged with him.

She was nervous about meeting Abe's parents but curious and excited too. So much about Abe was still unknown that she looked forward to any event that would provide more information. At the same time she was worried about what his parents would think of her. Had Abe been a typical boy from Tennessee or Georgia, Daphne would have felt confident about receiving his parents' approval. But from the little she had learned, Abe's family was not at all like the typical Southern families she was familiar with. Abe tried to reassure her as best he could. Stroking her hair and pulling her close, he said, "They will love you. How could they not? You're perfect." But Daphne sensed that he himself didn't exactly know what to expect when he broke the news of their marriage.

Over breakfast at the Mayflower Restaurant on Second Avenue, Abe explained that his family had emigrated from Romania before he was born. His father, David, had arrived at Ellis Island in the early 1900s. "He came to America on the steamship Hudson when he was twenty-one and earned a living selling milk and cheese from a horse-drawn cart, going from house to house. I know this will sound strange, but his marriage to my mother was arranged by his parents before they left the old country."

Daphne looked at him, not knowing what to say. "You mean they... they didn't love each other?" she blurted.

Abe smiled reassuringly. "That's a difficult question. I'm not sure I know the answer. But they learned to love each other, I guess. Oh, they argue all the time—pretty loudly sometimes—but they've managed to stay together all these years and put three kids through college. I believe that qualifies as love."

Daphne seized her chance to change the subject. "My parents have three kids too, two girls and a boy. Cecilia—we call her Sissy—is fifteen and Luke is fourteen. Are you the oldest like me?"

"I have a brother and sister too," Abe said, "but I'm the youngest—the baby of the family, in my mother's view. She still wants to tie my shoelaces, and I'm already out of college!"

Daphne just looked at Abe and smiled, not quite sure how to interpret this bit of information. She considered changing the subject to her own family again but decided against it. "Oh, look. The food's here," she said instead.

Abe took the hint and they finished the meal without much conversation.

As they drove the few miles to the Fisher home, Daphne felt her stomach tighten. She couldn't remember ever being so nervous and wondered if she might faint. She thought of Tilly, the goat her uncle Tillman had on his farm in Rossville, Georgia. Tilly was a Tennessee fainting goat. Whenever Tilly got nervous or frightened, she would collapse. It was great fun to sneak up on Tilly and give her a good scare. She would just keel over on her side, with her legs stretched out stiff. That's what Daphne imagined herself doing, right in front of David and Hannah Fisher. By the time Abe rang the doorbell, she was so anxious that she could hardly breathe.

An elderly man answered the bell. He was thin and gaunt in appearance. His skin looked gray and had a translucent quality. Though shaved, he had a stubble of beard. Abe gave Daphne a gentle nudge, and she stepped inside a comfortable-looking living room with lots of books and an aqua couch that clashed with the lilac drapes. She didn't faint, but even if she had, she doubted if anyone would have noticed. Abe introduced her. "Dad. Mom. This is my wife, Daphne."

They briefly acknowledged her presence and directed her to the couch. Daphne sat down just as the storm approached. The three began moving around the room in an agitated fashion, flailing their arms, pointing their fingers, shaking their heads. They spoke some words in English, but mostly, the words were from another language, one with which Daphne had no familiarity. *Maybe they're gypsies,* she thought. She heard one word— *shiksa*—repeated several times. Then everybody would stop talking for a moment and look at her.

At one point Hannah stood in the doorway of the kitchen, swaying in a small circle, with her hands covering her mouth as David strode from one end of the living room to the other with his head down, back and forth, as if searching the floor for a treasure. Hannah was a short, stocky woman. Her hair was pulled back in a bun. She had a round, rose-colored face. Daphne noticed her ankles looked like fat sausages, and she wore thick support stockings. She reminded Daphne of the woman on the can of Old Dutch Cleanser. *Yes,* Daphne thought, *it's conceivable. I can imagine her driving a gypsy wagon.* Abe turned from one parent to the other, apparently explaining and answering the gypsies' questions. Occasionally, all three would stop moving and look at Daphne in contemplation, as if she were an item for show-and-tell.

All Daphne could think about was Tilly. She felt like laughing and crying at the same time. Once, when they were staring at her, she realized she was giggling to herself like a 10-year-old. She quickly adopted a blank expression, and the three resumed their conversation. She heard that word again—*shiksa.*

Eventually, things settled down in the Fisher living room. To Daphne's astonishment, Hannah sat down beside her and took her hand. David told her in heavily accented English what a pretty wife she was. "You are most welcome into our family, my dear." Hannah dabbed her eyes with Kleenex and sighed. Then Hannah pulled Daphne off the couch and led her into the kitchen for coffee and streusel. The men followed dutifully—or hungrily. Daphne wasn't sure which.

Although Hannah and David had been in the United States for over 30 years, their accents were heavy, and Daphne had to listen carefully to understand them. Often, they would both talk to her at once about completely different topics, as if oblivious to one another. At other times they would break into the strange language that Daphne assumed was Romanian, holding their own private conversation and ignoring Daphne and Abe completely.

By the time they left Abe's parents' house, Daphne was exhausted, but Abe seemed excited and pleased. "Don't worry, honey," he said. "It was only the suddenness of the marriage that upset them. They're from the old country and just need a little time to come around. They already like you. I just know they're going to love you once they get to know you."

"Abe, what does *'shiksa'* mean?"

"Gentile. It means a gentile girl—a woman who is not Jewish. It doesn't mean anything. I mean, it means something but not really. You shouldn't be concerned. They are just old people, speaking in the language with which they are familiar."

"Abe, are your parents gypsies? Don't gypsies come from Romania?"

"Actually, I'm not sure where gypsies come from. But no, they're not gypsies; they're Jewish."

"I see." Daphne was thoughtful. *If Abe's parents are Jewish then Abe is too. What does that mean for us? What religion will we be?* Then she thought of Abe's words and wondered, *How can something have meaning and not have meaning? At home there is more precision. A thing either has meaning or it doesn't.* Daphne realized she must seem as strange to Abe's parents as they to her. She silently vowed to accept and love them in the way she hoped they would someday learn to appreciate her. *Whatever our differences may be, we will adapt.*

Chapter 2

Tennessee

The next hurdle was introducing Abe to her family. Daphne had telegraphed her parents shortly after Virginia Jo got on the bus for home, realizing that, however shocked and angry they might be at the sudden marriage, they'd be even more upset if she didn't break the news to them herself. At least they could be prepared for the gossip that was sure to follow once Virginia Jo arrived home.

Abe had never been to the South, and he was excited about the trip. At the same time he was apprehensive. Daphne thought it touching that he was concerned about what shirt to wear and which shoes would make the best impression on her family.

"Stop worrying," Daphne said. "My folks will like anything you wear. They are not any more sophisticated than your parents. They're simple people. Most of my relatives are farmers. Their chief concern is weather."

But, secretly, Daphne was worried about facing her parents, especially after the reaction of Abe's family. As she and Abe boarded the train and headed south to Chattanooga, Daphne felt a bit like she was leading the Biblical Daniel into the lions' den. Abe was different from the boys she had introduced to her parents, mainly because he wasn't a boy. He was six years older than Daphne, and being with him made her feel like a woman, not a girl of 18. He had the mystery she had been looking for. But he was also Jewish, a new experience for Daphne. What would her parents think of him and, more importantly, of her? When she got off the train in Chattanooga, would they accept her as a married woman or scold her like a naughty little girl?

Getting married was easy, she thought. *Being with Abe is easy. It's explaining it to everyone that's going to be hard.*

As the train snaked its way south, she and Abe passed the time dozing, joking, and gazing at the scenery. They passed several advertisements painted on the side of barns, such as "Chew Brown's Mule Tobacco." But, by far, the most frequent advertisement was, "See Rock City." That was painted on the side of barns and buildings, as well as an assortment of birdhouses that appeared first in Maryland and continued until they arrived in Tennessee. Daphne and Abe talked about their dreams, shared their histories, and named all six of the children they decided to have once Abe returned from war.

Daphne insisted on naming one of their sons either Tripp or Daniel, after her great-great-grandfather, Daniel Tripper, who had served in the Civil War. "My hobby is genealogy," she explained. "I found his discharge papers when I was looking through old letters and other family documents that my mom saved." She told Abe the sad story of how Daniel and his brother William had enlisted in the Confederate Army in March 1861 and were sent to Richmond, Virginia. Shortly afterward, Daniel developed dysentery and was sick for 30 days. In July 1861 he was discharged from the Army after having served just four months. He was so weak that he was sent home in the back of a wagon and died on the journey just a few miles from home— almost home. "I thought if I ever wrote a story about him, I would entitle it 'Almost Home.' Anyways, his widow and sons continued working on the farm, eking out a living as best they could. Gradually, the family grew and prospered through hard work and perseverance until today, the descendants are spread throughout Georgia, Tennessee, and the Carolinas. One of those descendants is my grandfather, Phinnaeas Tripper."

"Tripp Fisher sounds okay. I think Daniel sounds better," Abe said. "It sounds Biblical and has dignity. I don't like the sound of Phinnaeas Fisher. It sounds too fishy." They both laughed and spent the next few hours naming and renaming their imaginary children.

"Don't forget," Abe said, "before I return home, I want to see Rock City, whatever that is."

Daphne's father, Ralph, met them at the train station in Chattanooga. It was January and the weather was chilly. He gave Daphne a big hug and shook Abe's hand enthusiastically with both of his hands.

"Kind of cold," Ralph said. "Do they have weather like this in New York?"

"Yes, sir," answered Abe. "It's cold in New York too."

Ralph didn't respond. As he loaded the suitcases in the trunk, he turned to Daphne. "Your mama's made dinner in your honor. All the kinfolks will be there." He turned to Abe and grinned. "Some of them are callin' you 'the Yankee.' I hope you won't take offense. Never had no Yankee in the family before. Some folks are still a bit upset about the war."

"The war?" Abe asked. He hadn't even left yet for his military service.

"The big war." Mr. Pearson said, "The war between the states."

"Oh…that war." Abe nodded and smiled, looking slightly amused.

Daphne's mother, Virginia, welcomed Abe warmly, with a broad smile and a quick hug. The rest of the family introductions were equally uneventful. Everyone was polite and friendly toward Abe. Daphne was relieved but not really surprised. Southerners were taught to be polite. Being outwardly rude meant that you were low-class. Only when someone was overcome with grief or responding to another's outrageous behavior were the rules of proper etiquette tossed into the trash.

Daphne had feared that her unexpected marriage might qualify as "outrageous behavior." What people really thought was seldom obvious in the South, but Daphne knew that if she waited patiently, she would glimpse the suspicions beneath the superficial politeness.

Her first glimpse occurred beside the burn pit, a large hole in the ground where the family burned brush and debris. It was dug about two hundred yards behind the back of the buildings so as not to be an eyesore, yet close enough to the house to be convenient. As a girl Daphne had spent many fine mornings at the burn pit with her daddy, who enjoyed burning whatever he could put in the pit: brush, tree limbs, baling twine, and, sometimes, manure from the horse stalls. Stillborn foals and calves wound up in the pit once they could be separated from their despondent mothers—otherwise, the farm dogs would be endlessly dragging bones to the kitchen door to gnaw on. As Daphne later explained to Abe, "Life on a farm is living in harmony with nature. Birth and death are part of the cycle.

The burn pit, though not aesthetically pleasing, is necessary. To Daddy, who is sort of a firebug, burning things is fun."

"It sounds pretty scary to me," said Abe. "Wouldn't dead animals smell?"

"No," answered Daphne. "Not really. They are burned right after death under lots of wood. They haven't started to decompose, and there is no smell, except maybe a hint of barbecue." She smiled sheepishly.

"Actually," Daphne continued. "Mama's not partial to the burn pit. She doesn't like to go there. If there's trash to burn, she leaves it for Daddy to take care of. It's one of his chores."

On the morning after the celebration dinner, there was a lot of trash to burn. Many relatives had bought wedding gifts for Daphne and Abe, and a bag filled with torn wrapping paper stood beside two other trash bags by the kitchen for Dad to collect. Her father, her brother Luke, and Abe had left for town after breakfast in search of a tractor part—one of Daddy's favorite activities, which Daphne knew from experience would keep them away till lunch.

Drinking coffee and chatting with Sissy while their mother puttered at the kitchen counter, Daphne was suddenly overcome with a sense of warmth and comfort. The kitchen faced southeast and, on this morning, it was bathed in sunlight. How often had she sat at this table? She realized with a jolt that this cozy, familiar kitchen—this home, this farm—were no longer hers in the way they had been before she left for New York. She would now make her own home somewhere else, with someone new. Daphne didn't doubt her love for Abe, but she felt a strange tightness in her chest. She stood up, intending to leave the kitchen and collect her thoughts.

"Mama, I'll take the garbage to the burn pit for you," she said as she took her half-empty coffee cup to the sink.

She was surprised when her mother answered, "I'll go with you." It was the first time the two women had been alone since Daphne's return. They strolled side by side between the chicken coop and the barn toward the burn pit, where smoke hovered like mist above the ground. Something was still smoldering from Daddy's earlier burn.

Her mother seemed nervous, like she was trying to find the proper way to ask a question. She hesitated for a few moments and then blurted out, "Honey, are you all right?"

Daphne nodded, a little confused. "Sure, Mama, I'm just fine."

Her mother persisted, looking uncomfortable but determined. "You can tell me, honey. I won't be upset. I promise. I just need to know…is there some reason…" She paused, gathering strength. "Daphne, are you pregnant?"

Of course, Daphne thought. *That's exactly what people would think.* She laughed and tossed the two bags she had been carrying into the pit. "No, Mama. At least I don't think I am, although I guess I could be now. But, Mama, that's not why Abe and I got married. We just fell in love. I knew that if I didn't marry him, I'd lose something important. It was like a train pulling out of the station. If I didn't catch it then, I'd miss it forever. So I jumped on board. I love him, Mama."

The two women hugged. "I'm happy for you, honey—so happy for you." Her mother's face was covered with tears but she was smiling. They held hands as they walked back to the kitchen. At this moment—not her first lovemaking with Abe or even later, with the birth of her first child—

Daphne knew she was a woman, walking the same path as her mother, her friend.

The second glimpse of what some people really thought about her marriage came just before she and Abe were to leave Tennessee for New York. Once again, Abe was not present. In fact, it was probably because he was not present that a truth emerged. Her uncle Tillman, owner of the fainting goat, had stopped by with his wife and mother-in-law to say good-bye.

Daphne and her mother were sitting with them on the front porch drinking iced tea— sweetened, the way you didn't get it up North. It was an unseasonably warm January day. Everyone was speculating on the winters in New York, and Tillman asked if she had seen the Empire State Building.

"It is the tallest building in the world. It's also the building from which the airplanes shot King Kong!"

Daphne wondered if Tillman failed to realize that the big gorilla wasn't real. She didn't say anything, however, because she was preoccupied with other concerns. She wasn't sure whether to stay and work in New York while Abe was gone or come home again. There were so many things to figure out in the little time left, and Daphne was getting anxious. Suppose she couldn't find a job in New York? Suppose her mother was right and she was pregnant?

She was startled out of her reverie when Uncle Tillman turned to her and bluntly asked, "So, why did you marry a Jew?"

Daphne felt herself redden under his gaze. "I married a man," She replied. "I didn't marry a religion."

"What do you know of Jews?" persisted Tillman.

"Nothing. What difference does it make?"

"Some people say Jews are born with horns."

"That's stupid, Uncle Tillman. You should know better."

"Haven't you ever seen Michelangelo's statue of Moses? He has horns."

"Maybe he does, that's his problem. People aren't born with horns."

"You don't know. There are secrets—rituals. Maybe they could have them removed at birth—like a calf. They could be de-budded. All I'm saying…"

"Good gracious, I never heard such nonsense," her mother snapped.

"Well," continued Tillman, "how many births have you attended? And what if you have a boy? Are you going to clip the tip?"

"What?"

"The weenie…are you going to…circumcise your baby? Give him the mark of the covenant?"

"I don't know."

"Have you thought about how you'll raise children? What religion will you practice?"

Her mother came to her defense. "Tillman, that's enough. Daphne is a long way from having children. She has plenty of time to decide such things."

"I reckon," Tillman replied as he and Mother exchanged glances.

Daphne presumed that the issue of her suspected pregnancy was put to rest.

"I'm sorry, Daph," remarked Tillman. Turning to Daphne: "I don't mean to be meddlesome, but it's a cruel world out there. I don't think you know what you're letting yourself in for, girl. I just don't want to see you hurt."

"Abe and I have discussed it," Daphne said half-truthfully, thinking of the naming game they had played on the train to pass the time and realizing that she would have more to explain to little Tripp or Daniel than how he got his name. "We'll cross that bridge when we come to it."

"The Good Book says be not unequally yoked," Tillman said. "Are you goin' to become Jewish too?"

At that remark Tillman's wife kicked him in the shin. "Tillman, you know better than that—bothering this child with such things. Don't you pay him no nevermind, Daphne. He's just being ornery."

With that, Uncle Tillman shrugged sheepishly, and the conversation turned away from the topic of Daphne and Abe. But Tillman's remarks stung. As crude and blunt as they were, Tillman's words gave Daphne something to think about. In their rush to get married, she and Abe had skipped over some details, naively assuming that everything would work itself out. Their answer was simply that they were in love and love would suffice. But now, Daphne thought, *Maybe love is not enough.* They were left with some catching up to do and little time. She didn't want Abe to leave for war worrying about things that they could work out after he returned—if he returned.

Every time she started thinking seriously about important matters, Daphne would stop to pray. "Please, God, keep him safe. If it be Thy will, bring him home to me in one piece. He's a good man and we deserve to be happy. I will attempt to be a faithful servant. In Jesus' name I pray. Amen."

After Abe left for war in February, Daphne returned to her parents' house to wait for his return. Nine months later she gave birth to a baby boy. She named him Daniel. Baby Daniel was perfect. He had all 10 fingers and 10 toes. He didn't have horns.

* * *

Abe Fisher missed the birth of his first child. He didn't get to hold Daniel until seven months after the baby was born. God had heard Daphne's prayer and returned Abe home safely.

It was 1945 and Abe didn't want to talk much about the war. He seemed quieter and more somber than Daphne remembered. When he did talk it was about baseball and his days at Camp Cambell playing catcher. But gone were the jokes and the levity, as well as the cavalier attitude she had seen at the Stardust Ballroom.

She and Abe were awkward the first days together, each one trying too hard to make the pieces of their marriage fit. Baby Daniel was the bridge between them. Both would sit smiling at Daniel and watching his every move while they nervously glanced at one another.

Daphne had feared that Daniel would be afraid of Abe. He might cry or refuse to go to him. Fortunately, Daniel showed only a few minutes of shyness and quickly warmed up to the attention of his father. The first night together she and Abe made quiet love and then clung to one another like two survivors on a life raft. Daniel cried in the middle of the night, and Daphne brought him into bed between them.

Abe had a nightmare on his second night home. The bad dreams continued for a few weeks. Usually, they were dreams about being lost in a foreign land where he didn't know anyone and couldn't speak the language. He couldn't remember where he was or how to get home. Sometimes Abe and Daphne would get up in the middle of the night after one of his dreams to have a cup of tea and talk until they were tired enough to go back to sleep. One afternoon Daphne awakened from a nap with Daniel. He had been cranky from teething, so Daphne curled up beside him on the couch to help him sleep. When she opened her eyes, she saw Abe kneeling on the floor beside them, crying softly. Startled, she shot straight up into a sitting position, nearly knocking Daniel on the floor. Before she could ask what was wrong, Abe whispered, "I'm okay. It's just that I love you both so much. I'm so happy to be home with you."

Daphne couldn't speak because she started crying too. While Abe was gone she hadn't fully known how much she missed him. Now that he was back, she was having a delayed reaction. Perhaps that had been a blessing, a small gift from God. That night she thanked God for her blessings— including the ones she didn't know about.

* * *

At first, Abe and Daphne settled in an apartment in Brooklyn, near Coney Island, in a part of the city named Sheepshead Bay. Abe went into business with his cousin Mordechai, who had previous experience working in a metal fabrication shop. Together they began to manufacture their first product—tweezers. Mordechai was in charge of production, while Abe was the sales force. Next, they expanded into dental equipment and assorted small hand tools. As the business and his young family thrived together, the nightmares stopped and Abe learned to smile again.

When Daniel was three years old, Daphne and Abe bought their first home, a two-story clapboard house with a fenced backyard and a sidewalk out front. It was on a tree lined street where the houses were filled with other young families and television sets. Daphne and Abe could afford to eat out each Friday night at Lundy's famous seafood restaurant. Lundy's had given Daphne her first experience with steamed clams, and she couldn't get enough. Every Friday night she and Abe would order a large basket of clams and Daniel would get a hot dog. The couple would laugh about the events of the week and make plans for the future. The clams were always delicious. The economy was booming and Abe's business was thriving. Daphne found out she was pregnant again. Life was sweet.

Chapter 3

The Quetzal Bird

By the time Daniel was six years old, the Fishers were moving again. This time it was to a quaint village on Long Island. Abe's business was prospering and Daphne was pregnant again. Mikey (short for Michael), their second son, was already two years old and such a little tyrant that even Daniel hoped that the next baby would be a girl. Mikey was always breaking Daniel's toys and ruining his art projects. Daniel liked to draw and color, but every picture that Daphne put on the refrigerator ended up being torn by Mikey. She finally resorted to taping them high on the walls, just below the ceiling, so Mikey couldn't get his hands on them.

"It's a phase," Daphne explained to Daniel. "This is what little brothers do. He'll get over it soon; I promise."

Daniel suspected that a baby sister wouldn't be so troublesome. He was supposed to be the big brother, helping to take care of Mikey, but, in his view, Mikey was not so much a brother as he was a dangerous pet that dominated the house. Mikey refused to obey Daniel and would destroy any toy that Daniel valued and left unattended. In fact, Daniel had begun to call Mikey "The Destroyer," which got him into trouble with Mom and Dad. Lately, Mikey had taken to biting—he would bite if he was displeased or even just bored. Sometimes he would bite for no reason at all.

Mom would laugh. "Isn't he cute?" she would say. "He's become a biting baby."

Daniel didn't see anything cute about Mikey, especially after he'd been bitten by little brother. If Daniel retaliated, he wound up in trouble.

"Big brothers should know better," Mom would say. "He's just a baby, Daniel. You need to have patience with him."

Daniel couldn't wait to move to the new house, because, there, he would have his own room. The family planned the move so Daniel could start second grade in his new school, and everyone would be comfortably settled before the baby arrived.

Everything went according to plan, and when Anna Tripp Fisher was born December 9, 1952, Daniel was relieved that he didn't have another brother. Daphne and Abe were thrilled to have a daughter, even if she was bald. The little hair Anna had was so fair and fine that it was invisible, but her eyes were startling—so deep and dark that they gave Daphne goose bumps when she gazed into them. Daphne couldn't wait for tea parties, dress-up, and baby dolls. She and Abe now considered their family complete.

The new home was quite a step up for the Fishers. Sometimes Daphne felt uneasy about the opulence of her new lifestyle, but the business was doing well, and they could afford it. Their new neighborhood had spacious homes with large yards. The streets bore names like Misty Lane, Deerfield Drive, and Fox Manor Court. Some of the families had maids to keep house and gardeners to tend the lawns. Abe's business remained in Brooklyn, and, like the other husbands on Deerfield Drive, he drove to work in the city each day, a stressful one-hour commute. Daphne stayed home with the three children. If she became bored, there was the country club or the garden society or charity work where she could volunteer. At least once a month, she and Abe attended a dinner party at the country club—a grown-up event without the children, where she and Abe would dance and she could wear a cocktail dress.

Although there were beautiful churches and synagogues close to their home, the Fishers never attended any of them. They had no need. Religion was an unopened door in their home to a room they never entered. Yet Daphne and Abe considered themselves spiritual people, and they believed they were enlightened because they respected all faiths. To others who questioned their approach, they stated, "We believe in tolerance."

Neither Daphne nor Abe was comfortable with the religions they had grown up with. They both felt the strict rules too limiting. They had outgrown their parents' religions and felt the world was too complicated for the simplistic approach that had worked for earlier generations. They wanted their children to accept both Christianity and Judaism as moral foundations. When they met complaints from either side of the family, Daphne and Abe calmly explained, "Our children are free to discover their own path to God, whatever that path may be."

Their children, however, were far too busy being children to notice, much less discover, any such paths. So, in the Fisher home the two religions merged haphazardly, forming a crazy quilt of ideas and practices. Hanukkah, Christmas, Passover, and Easter, Santa Claus, the Easter Bunny, Jesus, and Moses were all part of the same colorful tapestry, with Tinker Bell and the Tooth Fairy thrown in for good measure. Judaism and Christianity were equally—and superficially—acknowledged.

This approach worked while the children were young but proved insufficient as they grew older. The interfaith dilemma first became a problem when Daniel was 10 years old. He and Mikey were enrolled in the Woodlawn Academy, a private elementary school for boys. Woodlawn was associated with the Episcopal Church. The boys wore a uniform that consisted of a white shirt and red tie beneath a blue blazer. On the left pocket of the blazer, over the heart, was a white shield divided into quarters by a conspicuous red cross. In each corner, above and below the cross, were intriguing symbols. Daniel was in fifth grade and his brother Mikey in first.

Daniel had been working on an assignment for school. He was supposed to investigate birds and write a report on one he particularly liked. He researched his assignment by examining *National Geographic magazine* and several others, including *National Audubon Society Birder's Journal.* It was a difficult choice. He thought about the American eagle because it was the national bird. The robin was a contender because it heralded spring and he had just found a dead robin in his driveway. Eventually, he chose the quetzal bird because he thought it was the most beautiful bird in the world. This bird was special. When he first gazed upon a picture of the quetzal, it seemed to call to him from the pages of the magazine. It was as if he recognized it, even though he had never seen a quetzal before. So, on a Wednesday afternoon a few days before Easter, Daniel was ready to present his report on the quetzal bird to the class. When his turn came he proudly stood in front of the room with his exhibits. He had drawn and colored an impressive quetzal bird on poster board alongside a crude map of Central America. The poster leaned on an easel beside him as he addressed the class. He held his written report in his hands. It was not necessary for him to read it because he had committed it to memory.

He looked out at his classmates and took a deep breath, as his mother had advised during practice sessions at home. Then he began.

"The quetzal is one of the most beautiful birds in the world. It is the national bird of Guatemala. The ancient people of Guatemala were called the Maya. They thought a lot about the quetzal. It is a pretty bird with shining colors. His blue and green and red feathers have a sheen and glitter that make him very beautiful. The Mayan chiefs thought the quetzal bird was their spiritual protector. In Guatemala it is against the law to hunt the quetzal. The bird can't live in captivity. If you confine a beautiful quetzal bird to a birdcage, it will die. That is why this bird is a symbol of freedom. It must be free to live. The quetzal lives in the cloud forests of Central America in the countries of Guatemala and Costa Rica. What is the future of the quetzal bird? I don't know. Some scientists say it's in danger of becoming extinct. That means it may die. It's disappearing because man is cutting down all the trees and destroying the natural habitat of the bird. I hope the quetzals don't all die, because they are beautiful birds."

Daniel was proud of his report and relieved when he finished the presentation without any mistakes. At its conclusion the teacher, Mrs. Odykirk, stood at her desk and said, "Thank you, Mr. Fisher. Does anyone have any questions for Mr. Fisher?"

Daniel liked Mrs. Odykirk, a short woman with a happy, round face. She always wore pink lipstick and lots of costume jewelry. As usual, her blond hair was pulled neatly back from her face and twisted into a bun. Today she wore a collection of Bakelite bangles on her wrists that rivaled the quetzal in their color and brilliance. As she spoke to the class, gesturing with her hands, Daniel could imagine a quetzal flitting around the room. One hand waved at the back of the class, and Mrs. Odykirk called on Brian Miller.

"What color are the quetzal birds' eggs?" Brian asked.

Mrs. Odykirk turned to Daniel, her eyes wide with curiosity. "An excellent question. Can you tell us anything about the quetzals' eggs, Mr. Fisher?"

"Yes," Daniel replied, thrilled to be able to provide the answer. "The quetzal lays two blue eggs."

"How lovely," Mrs. Odykirk said. "That reminds me of the Easter eggs some of you will be hunting on Sunday. Thank you, Mr. Fisher. You may sit down now." Daniel grabbed his quetzal poster and headed to his desk, while Mrs. Odykirk began to tell the Easter story.

Mrs. Odykirk was a good storyteller. Although she was small, she was dynamic, with an expressive voice and face. Now that Daniel had finished his report, he could relax. He vaguely knew about Easter but had stopped believing in the Easter Bunny, so instead of listening to Mrs. Odykirk, he was reliving the success of his report and watching the quetzallike bangles on her wrists swing back and forth as she flung her arms for emphasis.

"Of course," she said, her voice now lowered to gain her students' full attention, "not everyone believes in Easter." She paused to let this idea sink in. "Not everyone believes that our Lord and Savior arose from the dead. Some people don't believe in Jesus. Does anyone know which people don't believe in Jesus or that he arose from the dead?"

Silence. No hands were raised.

"Well, I will tell you. Jewish people don't believe that Jesus was God. That's one group. Jewish people pray differently. They read and write backward. They even speak in a different language when they pray in their church. Their language is called Hebrew." She smiled and looked around the room cheerfully.

"Actually, we have a Jewish boy in our classroom. Daniel Fisher is Jewish, I believe. Isn't that right, Mr. Fisher?"

The sound of his name broke Daniel's reverie, and he stiffened in his chair, suddenly aware that all eyes were on him—and not in appreciation for his quetzal report. He tried to think of the correct answer, but Mrs. Odykirk didn't wait for a response.

"Can you speak to us in Hebrew?" she asked. "Or maybe you can recite some of those funny-sounding chants?" She smiled widely.

Daniel could feel himself blushing and realized that he must be turning red. He wanted to jump up and dart from the room, but he felt like he had been nailed to the seat and wasn't sure what to do. Was he Jewish? He didn't know the answer. He knew that his father was Jewish, and Papa Dave and Nana Hannah were Jewish. They were from Romania and spoke with an accent. Sometimes they spoke Yiddish, with musical words that Daniel liked—words like *tchotchke, meshugenuh,* and his favorite, *a bisele mayzla.* These were "old country" words. Was Yiddish the same as Hebrew? He didn't know.

His mother's family was different. They were Baptist, which he knew meant that they were Christian and believed in Jesus. But what religion did this make him? He realized he had to say something. Everyone was now looking at him as they waited for his answer. He felt like a bird trapped in a cage. On the verge of desperation, he realized that, in addition to everything else that had gone wrong, he was beginning to sweat. Then, in his head, he heard his mother's voice stating the answer she always gave when relatives talked about religion, and he repeated her words.

"We believe in tolerance."

That answer seemed to break the spell. His classmates then turned their scrutiny to Mrs. Odykirk, who had lost her smile and stared at Daniel as if trying to comprehend what he had said. Daniel could breathe again and the prickly sensation was going away, but he was still troubled. He didn't fully understand what had just happened, but he didn't like Mrs. Odykirk so much anymore. She really wasn't a nice person, although her quetzal bracelets were pretty. He was going to ask his parents about tolerance when he got home. He needed to know whether tolerance was Christian or Jewish.

*   *   *

When Daniel arrived home that afternoon, he told his mother about his troubling episode. He told her how good he had felt about the quetzal report and then described as best he could how Mrs. Odykirk had asked if he was Jewish.

"She wanted me to chant, but I didn't know how," he said. "I was scared because I didn't know what to say, so I told her that we believe in tolerance."

"What did Mrs. Odykirk say to that?" Daphne asked casually.

Daniel shrugged. "Nothing. She said we needed to get into our science groups because we didn't have much time to finish our projects." He paused, looking at his mother intently. "What is tolerance?"

"We'll talk about that when your father gets home." Daphne was putting milk and cookies on the table, and Anna had just wandered into the kitchen. "Can you get The Destroyer?" Daphne asked Daniel. "Go and find your brother."

While Daniel was gone Daphne tacked the quetzal poster on the wall in the breakfast nook, where it could be appreciated while they had their afternoon snack.

That evening, after Abe arrived home, Daniel's parents talked for a long time. Daniel was asked once again to describe what had happened at school. Daniel told them, adding his suspicions about Mrs. Odykirk.

"I don't think she's a nice person," he said. "I think maybe she doesn't like me because I'm Jewish like you, Dad." His parents smiled sympathetically and his dad gave him a hug.

"Daniel, you're lucky because you can be whatever you want to be. You can be Jewish if you want, or you can be Christian. Nobody, not even Mrs. Odykirk, can decide that for you."

"But I don't know what I want to be."

"That's okay. You can take all the time you want. Some people spend their whole lives trying to decide."

That wasn't what Daniel wanted to hear. He would have preferred a quick answer. Even having someone like Mrs. Odykirk telling him what to be seemed better than trying to decide for himself.

"Daniel," his dad continued, "your mom and I think that maybe we can find a better school for you and Mikey—a school where people are more tolerant."

"What does that word mean?" Daniel asked.

"It means that the teachers will be nice. They will treat you better. Not like Mrs. Odykirk."

"And, Daniel," Daphne added quickly, "we think it's time we get a dog."

Daniel couldn't believe his ears. He had been asking for a dog for more than two years and was always told, "No, a dog is too much work."

"You're older now. If you'd be willing to help care for it, we think you and your brother Mikey are ready."

"Wow! Thank you, Mom." *What a confusing day,* he thought. After all that had happened, he was getting a dog, and, in a weird way, he had Mrs. Odykirk to thank for it.

Mom and Dad kept their word. The following week Daniel and Mikey were enrolled in Public School 109. When Mikey first heard the news, he was upset.

"I like Woodlawn," Mikey said, "especially the uniforms. They don't have uniforms in public school." Even so, Mikey wanted the dog as much as Daniel. Changing schools was a small price to pay for a real dog.

The puppy was waiting for them when they got up Easter morning.

"Did the Easter Bunny bring him?" Mikey asked.

"No, sweetheart. He's a gift from your dad and me," Mom said.

The puppy was a Cocker Spaniel with wavy, black hair and a cold, wet nose. In an instant Daniel knew the puppy's name. It was Buddy.

Chapter 4

Camp

D aniel had just finished the fifth grade. He was ten years old and the whole summer lay ahead of him. It was Friday and he was spending the night at his friend Melvin's house. He knew Melvin well and the two boys were talking to Melvin's older brother, Art, a handsome teenager who kidded with Melvin and Daniel, treating them like pals. Speaking with authority on cars, music, and sports, he made a good impression on Daniel, who thought it must be great to have an older brother.

"How old is Art?" He asked Melvin when they were alone.

"Seventeen," answered Melvin.

Daniel was impressed. "Boy! That's really old! I can't imagine being that old. It must be great."

"It is," answered Melvin, smiling. "It's terrific. You can do practically anything you want when you're seventeen."

The following morning, Daniel walked home from Melvin's house thinking about Art and what it would be like to be seventeen. He couldn't wait to be old enough to drive, stay out late, and date girls.

As Daniel approached his house, he saw an ambulance parked in front. He rushed inside in time to hear his mother in the hallway at the top of the stairs. She was explaining in a breathless voice to a paramedic what had happened. Daniel waited at the bottom of the stairs, listening closely.

"I found a large bug in the bathroom," she said. "A nasty bug. I stomped it and tossed it into the toilet bowl. But it wouldn't die. I flushed it, but it wouldn't go down. I was worried it might escape so I sprayed a can of insecticide into the toilet. I shut the lid on the toilet bowl thinking the bug would die. A few minutes later my husband came home from work. He went into the bathroom. He was smoking a cigarette. Apparently he took a puff of his cigarette and dropped it between his legs into the toilet. The cigarette ignited the fumes. I heard him yell 'shit' and then I heard a thud. He must have leapt into the air or was blown off the toilet. Anyway he landed on the tile floor. By the time I got to the bathroom, he was lying in a fetal position and moaning. I think he must have burned Mr. Johnson and the twins. I covered him with a towel and called emergency."

As Daphne reached this point in her story, one of the paramedics carrying Abe down the stairs began to laugh. He lost his balance, spilling Abe off the stretcher. Daniel watched in horror as his father bounced down the stairs, landing at the bottom with another thump and a cry of pain. Daniel looked down at his dad who was wearing a shirt and tie, but no pants.

Abraham Fisher had fractured two ribs and spent the next two nights at the hospital. When he was released, he was confined to bed at home, with Daphne spending her time tending to him. His ribs hurt so badly he couldn't lie flat, so the Fishers had to order a special hospital bed that could be cranked up into a sitting position.

Shortly after the accident, which was referred to in the Fisher household as "the incident," the boys were sent away to camp. Abe's need for quiet rest was given as the principle reason, but their parents also said that the boys would love camp; it would be an experience they would never forget.

* * *

At ten years of age, Daniel Fisher was a skinny, tow-headed boy who played with imaginary friends. Unlike his brother Mikey, Daniel disliked athletics. He preferred fishing, or drawing, or taking walks alone, collecting stamps, or just about any non-competitive activity.

Camp Thunder Bay, located in New York's Adirondack Mountains on beautiful Raquette Lake, advertised itself as an athletic camp. It emphasized team sports and promised to build strong character in boys. Every day, weather permitting, the campers played games. Daniel's athletic incompetence soon became apparent at Thunder Bay, and he was either teased or ignored by most of his fellow campers. No one wanted to pick him for a partner in any event, and whenever he missed at bat or didn't catch the ball, the other kids would snicker.

"Fisher, you are the worst," they would say. "The worst softball player, the worst basketball player... you're terrible... you can't do anything. Maybe you can fish. That must be why your name is Fisher. So, go fish, Fisher."

Sometimes they called him "chicken arm" because he couldn't throw a ball straight. "You throw like a girl," they would say. They also called him "sneaky" because he was never around when he was supposed to be.

The taunts were painful, but Daniel had no choice but to endure them. One survival trick was to slip away from camp when nobody was looking and wander through the forest. Most of the time he walked alone, but occasionally other boys, who didn't exemplify the attributes Camp Thunder Bay tried to encourage, accompanied him.

Nelson Peters was one such boy. He was called "Mad Dog," but Daniel had no idea why. Maybe it was because he physically resembled a bulldog—or because he acted like one. A bow-legged, stocky kid with a flattop haircut and a hair-trigger temper, he would frequently start fights with campers who were bigger than he. He usually got the crap beat out of him, but he never backed down from a fight. Everybody kept a respectful distance from Mad Dog. One day Nelson confided to Daniel that he had a secret, which he kept in a blue trunk at the foot of his bed. He promised he would share the secret with Daniel when the time was right.

Another companion of Daniel's was Bruce Lipschultz, a small boy with freckles and red hair. Because of his small size and lack of interest in sports some campers referred to him as Brucie Baby. He wore thick-rimmed glasses and always seemed to be the last, or second-to-last (depending on whether Daniel was present), picked for any game. Bruce was a loner, and even though the other boys said he was a loser, he didn't seem to mind. He always had his face in a book and seemed oblivious to what the others thought or said of him. When Daniel asked him why he didn't care when other boys teased him, Bruce would answer, "Consider the source."

Both of these boys, like Daniel, were Thunder Bay misfits. The other campers said of them, "When one of these guys is on your team you might as well be baking a cake." Daniel wasn't sure exactly what they meant, but he realized he would, in fact, have preferred baking a cake.

Daniel and his two friends came together for companionship or to complain about camp. Most of the time, these boys remained apart. Each endured the indignities of camp life in his own personal way.

One day when the three were together, Nelson asked Daniel and Bruce if they'd like to go with him on a safari. Daniel didn't know what Nelson was talking about until Nelson revealed the secret he kept in his blue trunk—an army surplus rifle lay hidden beneath his pants and shirts. Nelson had bought it with a coupon he'd cut from the inside cover of a comic book. He also had two bullets, each about three inches long, and Daniel could easily imagine the devastation they could cause.

"Thunder Bay is part of Adirondack National Park," Bruce said. "Hunting is prohibited."

Mad Dog just smiled in his devious mad-dog way, and the boys agreed to go with him on safari.

With a little luck and planning, it wasn't difficult to sneak away after lunch when the campers were supposed to remain in their bunks and rest for an hour. Luckily, Daniel's counselor was away from the cabin, doing whatever counselors did during rest period. The other two boys also managed to escape unnoticed. They met up behind the maintenance garage.

They hurried away from camp and into the forest. Nelson, carrying his rifle, took the lead. Walking behind and talking to one another the other boys followed.

"Why do they call it a bay?" asked Daniel. "They call it Camp Thunder Bay, but where's the bay? Can a lake even have a bay?"

"You make an excellent point," Bruce said. "Oceans have bays, not lakes… I think. There isn't even an indentation in the shoreline, so where is the bay? In fact, you could consider the whole damn lake one big bay. Why name a camp after a bay that doesn't exist? It doesn't make any sense."

Suddenly Nelson stopped. He turned his head and put his finger over his mouth, indicating they should stop talking. Then he pointed straight ahead where a deer stood in their path about twenty yards in front of them. The deer stood motionless, looking directly at them. The boys froze. Nobody spoke. Nelson slowly lifted his gun and fired. The deer went down, but it wasn't dead. It thrashed about, pawing at the ground as it struggled to regain its footing.

"Holy shit!" said Bruce.

Nelson immediately threw the gun on the ground and ran directly past the deer into the forest.

Daniel and Bruce stared at each other in amazement, then saw Nelson change direction and run back toward them, wide-eyed and hysterical. His hands were shaking.

"What am I going to do? Oh, boy. Oh, boy. Shit! What am I going to do?"

The deer was still thrashing on the ground, its motions becoming slower and more erratic. Blood dripped from its mouth. Nelson turned again and ran back into the woods.

Daniel felt his heart pound, but he resisted the impulse to bolt and follow Nelson. His friend's bizarre behavior fascinated him, compelling him to wait and see what Nelson would do next.

"We'd better put it out of its misery," Bruce said calmly.

"What do you mean?" asked Daniel.

"It's dying. We should shoot it in the head or something. We can't just leave it to suffer."

Nelson returned, still shaking. Tears were running down his cheeks, and he was muttering unintelligibly.

"Nelson," snapped Bruce. "Calm down. Do you have the other bullet?"

Nelson stopped mumbling and reached into his shirt pocket, but his hand was trembling so much that he dropped the bullet on the ground. Bruce picked it up and loaded it into the rifle. Walking to where the deer lay, he aimed the rifle and fired directly at the deer's head. The animal jerked and then lay still.

Bruce lowered the gun and turned to Daniel. "We'd better hide the evidence," he said calmly. "Get some branches and cover the deer."

Again, Daniel wanted to run, but he deferred to the authority in Bruce's voice, recognizing him as a leader. Nelson, by contrast, was acting like a squirrel in the highway, trying to decide which direction to run.

"Don't tell anyone," Nelson stammered desperately, still crying. "You won't tell?"

"We won't tell," answered Bruce. "Will we, Dan?"

Daniel shook his head no. *How is it possible,* Daniel thought, *that this strange little boy who likes to start fights with bigger boys could be acting like such a baby?*

"We could get in a lot of trouble for this," Nelson continued. "We could go to prison. We could all go to prison. Swear you won't tell."

"I swear," said Daniel. "I won't tell anyone."

"Me, too," Bruce answered calmly. "Now, help us find some brush and cover the animal."

When they had concealed the body as well as they could, the three boys walked back to camp in silence. At the edge of the forest, Nelson hid the gun under some brush by a large sugar maple. They reached camp in time for the next activity without attracting any attention, and then they went their separate ways.

Daniel felt terrible about the deer incident. For the next few nights, he didn't sleep well. His depression added to his overall distaste for camp life. He had already been feeling sorry for himself, knowing how the other campers regarded him and wished he could just go home. It was humiliating to be the last one picked for every activity except fishing. Worse, he knew that the insults were true. He was not an athlete. He didn't want to be an athlete. He would have preferred being a musician or a scuba diver, or a cake decorator or anything else in the world. He'd never asked to come to this stupid camp. No one asked him when his parents reached their decision. He knew his parents loved him. He also knew his father needed time to heal from his accident. But, really, was there ever a dumber accident? Why should Daniel and his brother have to pay because his father had barbecued his testicles?

He missed everything about his life at home, including his dog, Buddy. During the school year, he hardly gave Buddy a second thought, except to complain that the dog made the house smell bad. But this summer, he couldn't stand to be parted from Buddy. It didn't matter how the creature smelled. Buddy was his best friend.

A week after the deer episode, Daniel lay in his bed, waiting for the bugler to blow reveille and start a new day. He was feeling miserable. The other boys in his cabin were sleeping, but Daniel couldn't stop thinking. He felt badly about leaving his dog behind, feeling sure that Buddy was as lonely as he was and waiting anxiously by the door for Daniel to return home. He also felt bad about the terrible thing he had done with Nelson and Bruce. He was an accomplice to murder, and he didn't know if he could keep the killing a secret for the entire summer. He felt compelled to confess.

Suddenly, Daniel had an idea. He would leave camp. How easy. How obvious. Why hadn't he figured it out earlier? He would just go.

He climbed out of bed, got dressed, and crept out of his cabin. Going to another building and entering quickly, he tiptoed to the bunk where Mikey was sleeping. He woke his brother and explained they needed to return home.

"I had a dream about Buddy. In my dream he told me to come home. I know that Buddy misses you, too. I think we should listen. Come with me, Mikey. We can run away together."

Daniel knew that Mikey was only six years old, that he loved camp and didn't miss the dog. Nevertheless, he was startled by Mikey's response.

"Go away," the six-year-old said. "Get out, or I'll call the counselor."

"What about Buddy?" Daniel asked.

"Fuck Buddy."

Daniel panicked. He ran from the cabin, straight into the Adirondacks. His only thought was to leave camp forever, to flee this terrible place and return home to his parents and his wonderful dog. He might have made it, too, if the camp hadn't been on an island in the middle of Raquette Lake. With nowhere to go, he wandered aimlessly through the woods until a search party discovered him, exhausted, tearful, and covered in scrapes and bruises, later that afternoon. As the counselors led him back in shame to camp and brought him to the infirmary, he resolved he would not betray Nelson or Bruce. He wouldn't tell about their crime, even if tortured.

An attractive young nurse named Charlotte with long blonde hair and a friendly smile treated his cuts with a greasy, white ointment.

"Here," she said. "Binky Cream. It will take the pain away."

Daniel forgot about Buddy, the deer, or his humiliation. He fell in love with the camp nurse and wished he could stay in the infirmary for the rest of his life and have Charlotte rub Binky Cream all over him. Unfortunately, his stay was brief. He had to return to his cabin so he could be ready for softball.

*   *   *

That summer, Daniel never revealed the secret of Mad Dog Nelson shooting the deer. The three boys never spoke of it again, not to each other or to anyone else. As far as Daniel was concerned, it never happened. When the summer ended, Daniel and his brother Mikey returned home. By then his dad was healed, but Buddy still made the house smell terrible.

Chapter 5

Big Chief Six Cats

After their first year at Camp Thunder Bay, the Fisher children began the tradition of going to camp every summer. Initially, Daniel hated camp and regarded his summer experience as an obstacle course with his goal being to survive the season with as few humiliations as possible. However, over time he came to like camp. Even though it was an "athletic camp," it was not all sports all the time. There were other activities like hiking, and canoeing, drama and glee club. There were nature walks in the forests and arts and craft sessions in a building designed for this purpose. Some of these activities were enjoyable to Daniel and he looked forward to them. One of his favorite regular events was pig night. Each Thursday evening instead of eating in the dining hall the campers were responsible for cooking their own dinner at a campfire in front of their cabin. Each camper was given a T-bone steak to grill. They could dress however they wanted and didn't even have to wash their hands before eating. All the boys loved pig night.

Friday nights at dusk were reserved for religious services. Sundown would bring in the Sabbath and each camper would shower and put on clean clothes. They would march according to their designated group to the social hall. The camp director would serve as rabbi and one of the counselors would be the cantor. The campers would recite prayers and sing hymns in Hebrew like *Ein Keloheinu* and *Adon Olam*. The words of the hymns were written phonetically in English and Daniel wondered if anyone knew what the words meant. But it didn't matter. It was a spiritual time, a time of quiet meditation and community. Since almost everyone at Camp Thunder Bay was Jewish, Daniel now thought of himself as Jewish; it seemed natural.

After the first season, wandering through the forest lost some of its appeal. When he did venture in, Daniel avoided walking near the spot where they had hidden the deer. The memory stayed strong and the ghost of the deer continued to haunt him.

When Daniel was twelve, he became acquainted with Big Chief Six Cats, a counselor who frequently participated in the Friday night services. Daniel didn't know how old the chief was, but he was old. He looked ancient. Big Chief was famous at camp because he was supposed to be a real Indian. He wore short pants, was usually shirtless, and, except for Friday nights, mostly ran around camp barefoot. He was a short, bow-legged man, whose skin was tan and his face craggy from too much time in the sun. Sometimes Big Chief Six Cats wore war paint even though the only war at camp was color war—the highlight of the summer. For color war the camp was divided into the White Team and the Green Team. It was an organized competition with contests in athletics, singing, and other activities. Everyone looked forward to color war. Daniel especially loved the singing.

During color war, Big Chief Six Cats took center stage, putting on a feathered war bonnet and wearing war paint. After the evening meal, he would stand on a chair in the dining room and whoop and holler. Then he would recite a war chant. It sounded like gibberish, but it was an authentic

Indian language, or so everybody said. Like a conductor, the chief would lead the body of campers in camp songs. Everybody liked Big Chief Six Cats.

One day, during rest period after lunch, the chief came to visit Daniel. Although Daniel knew who Big Chief Six Cats was, he had never had a conversation with Camp Thunder Bay's only Indian. The chief explained to Daniel that Daniel's parents had made a request. They had decided he should have a Bar Mitzvah. Daniel was surprised at this news because his parents had not discussed it with him. He knew several Jewish boys at camp who would be having a Bar Mitzvah, but he never thought he would have one because his family didn't attend synagogue and they were not religious. He asked the chief why his parents wanted him to have a Bar Mitzvah and Big Chief Six Cats answered, "Big responsibility of every Jewish boy." He also confessed he was being paid by Daniel's parents to get their son ready for the big event. Daniel explained that he'd never had religious training. He couldn't read or write Hebrew and didn't have the slightest idea what the words to the hymns meant on Friday night.

"No matter," Big Chief Six Cats replied. "Me teach you everything you need to know. You can listen and recite what I say after I read it. We practice same reading every day. Not necessary to know how to read Hebrew, just how to recite it. By time camp finished, you'll have words memorized and sound great. Have heap big Bar Mitzvah party."

Daniel spent a large portion of his third summer at Camp Thunder Bay reciting Hebrew. Each day, the chief would appear during rest period, and he and Daniel would go to the social hall to practice reciting Daniel's Haftarah, the portion of the Torah that Daniel would read on his thirteenth birthday. By the end of camp season, Daniel was ready for his celebration, which was only one month away.

*   *   *

Throughout his adolescence Camp Thunder Bay on beautiful Raquette Lake was an integral part of Daniel's life. As he grew older, life at camp improved as the emphasis changed from athletics to camping and conservation. One day, when Daniel was on a hike he requested a roll of toilet paper and went off into the woods to have a bowel movement. For this accomplishment and act of courage he was inducted into the Squeegee Tribe. A ceremony was given in Daniel's honor, officiated by Big Chief Six Cats.

By age fifteen, most campers were more interested in girls than baseball. Boys who had been outsiders a few summers ago were more highly regarded if girls liked them now. Others, former shining stars that could throw a ball as straight as Big Chief Six Cats could shoot an arrow, were beginning to lose some luster. There was a reshuffling of the deck.

From Daniel's point of view, the best thing to come out of his camp experience was Sarah Koppelman. On the first and third Saturday nights of every month, a boat would take the oldest campers, the seniors, across Raquette Lake for a weekly social at Thunder Bay's sister camp, Camp Pine Needles for Girls. On the second and fourth Saturdays, the boat would bring the girls to Thunder Bay. The socials started at seven p.m. and ended at ten.

It was the first social of the summer. Daniel was fifteen years old. He was standing with the other boys against the wall watching the girls from across the room. The girls were watching them while Bill Haley and The Comets were wailing over the loud speaker. Nobody was dancing.

They were all waiting to see who would make the first move. Daniel's eyes moved right and left, considering each girl. Then he spotted a girl with reddish-brown hair. She was standing with another girl who was even prettier, but the first girl was different. Her hair hung long and almost covered one of her eyes giving her, Daniel thought, a somewhat wild and sultry look. She reminded Daniel of a movie star he had seen from his parent's generation—Veronica Lake, who his dad told him, was known as the Peek-a-boo Girl. The girl across the room had full lips and large breasts. She was wearing a powder-blue, V-neck, sweater that was pulled tightly across her chest revealing a noticeable cleavage. She reminded Daniel of a flower blossom from his mother's garden that was just about to burst forth into full bloom. This girl looked like a woman while most of the other girls against the wall looked like girls. Daniel looked at her and then he looked at her friend—the pretty one. Which was better? Then the sexy one smiled at him and the scales were tipped.

Daniel could feel his heart beat and the palms of his hands were sweaty. Despite his fear of being rejected, he began to walk across the room. It was a long walk.

"Hello," he said. "I'm Daniel. How are you?"

"Fine," the sexy girl replied. "I'm Sarah. Pleased to meet you Daniel. This is my friend Melody."

"Hello Melody," Daniel managed to say. His mouth was dry. He was running out of words. "Nobody is dancing," he muttered.

"I noticed that." Sarah smiled once again, a broad toothy smile and she took him by the hand as her hair swung and almost covered her eye. "It is probably going to take a real man to break the ice and show the others that a dance is meant for dancing. Do you think you could be that man, Daniel?"

"Well… sure." Daniel stammered. The pressure was on. His knees felt weak, but at the same time he felt exhilarated.

"Good, then let's go and show them how it's done." And then Sarah led him to the dance floor and they began to dance to Johnny Mathis' song *Chances Are*.

It was all fine after the first moments. All the others needed was a leader. The campers followed them to the dance floor. Daniel and Sarah spent the remainder of the night talking, dancing, and laughing. Daniel found his lost words and he, Sarah, and Melody talked about many things, but mostly about how wonderful camp was.

"Don't you just love it here?" Melody was animated. "It's just the most wonderful place on earth."

"Yes it is," replied Daniel.

They all laughed a lot that night, and, somewhere between *Chances Are* and the *Twelfth of Never*, Daniel fell in love.

Each week he looked forward to the next Saturday so he could see Sarah again. Camp was brighter after meeting Sarah. Any past disappointments of everyday camp life were forgotten. Sarah was all that mattered. She was enough to get him by from week to week.

"Daniel," Sarah said, "you're sweet. You're not like other boys. You have made my summer great. I don't think I would have enjoyed camp half so much if you hadn't been here. And Daniel, I've decided to return next year as a staff member. So will Melody. We love camp."

Daniel didn't, but he was liking it better and he wanted very much to see Sarah again, so he decided that he would return the next season. And for the following two summers, Daniel returned to Camp Thunder Bay, first as a counselor in training and then as a full counselor.

When does one stop being a kid and become a man? When I was thirteen I had my Bar Mitzvah. I was called to the Torah to address the congregation. It wasn't really our congregation, we had never actually attended synagogue there. But it was somebody's and they were willing to have us. I guess it was rented. Anyway, on that day I was ready to assume all the rights and responsibilities of a Jewish man. The only problem was I wasn't Jewish, not technically. Nevertheless, I gave a good recitation and my parents were proud. No parrot anywhere could have performed better. But was I a man?

At that time all my religious training came about because of my experience at camp. If it wasn't for Big Chief Six Cats, who taught me what I needed to know, I would never have been able to have a Bar Mitzvah. I got a lot from camp. I stayed every summer from age ten until seventeen. It was toward the end of my camp experience that I learned that Big Chief Six Cats was not a chief at all. In fact, he wasn't even an Indian. His real name was Lester Katz. He and his wife were childless, but they did have six cats: Hence the name.

I remember when I left camp for the final time. During that last summer I worked as a counselor. I led other boys as I had once been led. Only I wasn't mean. I didn't make campers play baseball if they couldn't throw a ball straight. I respected the nerds and geeks and every other kind of oddball you found there. I was tolerant.

In later years, camp came to represent something special to me–an idealized fantasy-land. Raquette Lake for me was like Never Never Land was to Peter Pan. It was a place of adventures, to be in touch with nature, and also to fall in love. There was little expected except to have a good time.

Seventeen was an important age. I remember what Melvin's brother had said years earlier: "Seventeen is old. You can do practically anything when you are seventeen." But Melvin's brother was wrong. I didn't feel old. I felt like I was just beginning. If possible, I would have stopped the clock at Camp Thunder Bay and remained there indefinitely. I would have done this even though I threw a ball like a girl and other kids teased me. Of course, I couldn't remain and you can't stop the passage of time.

I remember my last night on Raquette Lake, that final year, as we boarded the barge that took us across the lake. It was sunset and the light was fading. As I looked over the side of the barge at the shimmering moonlight reflected on the water and the silhouette of the pines on shore, I had the realization I would not pass this way again. I thought to myself: This is my last night of camp. Remember what this moment feels like. Notice the colors as they play on the surface of the water. Remember the smells of the forest and the sounds of the night air. Remember how it feels to be making this final trip across Raquette Lake.

Soon the barge arrived at the Antlers Hotel, and we boarded school buses to be driven to the train depot in the town of Thendara. Later that night we arrived at the train station and got on a sleeper train for the final portion of the journey. Through the night, the campers and staff slept as the train chugged through the Adirondack National Park and surrounding countryside. When we awoke in the morning, we had arrived at Grand Central Station. Camp was over.

My parents had once said that Mikey, Anna, and I, would have fun at camp. "You'll love camp," they told us. "You'll never forget the experience." Well, Mom and Dad were right. As I grew older, I came to remember my camp experiences as some of the sweetest times of my life.

Camp Thunder Bay represents my childhood. It was the Peter Pan time.

I realize memories are selective. In my mind the bad memories of camp athletics and even the incident with the deer have faded. The good memories remain; the ones of nature and camping, of color war, and especially of Sarah. I'll always have these and I guess when I'm old and grey I'll be rocking on my porch and singing green team fight songs from color war. Camp was great. It was high school that sucked.

Chapter 6

High School

Although Daniel had a driver's license, he wasn't allowed to use the car to drive to Sarah's house because his parents felt a drive from the North Shore of Long Island to Brooklyn was too far and dangerous for a beginning driver. But sometimes his mother would drive him to Brooklyn, dropping him off at Sarah's while she went shopping, ran errands, or visited friends. A few hours later, she would pick him up. Since this was inconvenient for everyone, especially Daphne, Sarah's parents suggested that Daniel come and stay the night. That way his mother could drop him off on Saturday and pick him up Sunday. This arrangement worked well and Daniel stayed many Saturday nights at Sarah's. Her parents allowed Daniel to hang out with her family and participate in family activities. When the two could slip off alone, he and Sarah would make out, hugging and kissing for hours. These opportunities for affection didn't occur often—about once a month, sometimes less—but their infrequency made them all the more enjoyable.

When Daniel wasn't spending time with Sarah, things weren't going well for him. He regarded school as a waste of time and this attitude drove his parents crazy. All Daniel wanted to do was go to Brooklyn and see Sarah. A person reading Daniel's school records might have concluded the boy was cognitively challenged. He wasn't, but Daniel amassed an impressive record of absences from school. When he did attend, he was frequently late. He didn't do his homework assignments and when asked why, would answer, "Because I don't want to!"

His first suspension was for disrespectful language toward a teacher. The school guidance counselor told his parents that Daniel had a bad attitude; his mind was on things other than school. "I don't know what it is, but it's not academics. We believe he's troubled… emotionally delayed…a late bloomer."

When Daniel misbehaved, his excuse was "I was only goofing."

"What does that mean?" his exasperated father demanded one night.

"It means having fun, playing around." This conversation occurred when Daniel was in tenth grade. He and some friends had stolen a school bus. After they returned the bus to the school Daniel and his parents were called into the principal's office.

The principal inquired of Abe, why his son would do such a thing. Abe didn't know how to answer. "I don't know," he said. "The boy knows better."

"We just borrowed the bus," Daniel said. "We were goofing around."

Later at home Abe talked to his son. "Having fun?" Abe's face was scarlet. He looked like his head was about to spin off and explode. "This is your life Daniel! Don't you realize that? Do you want to have any sort of a future? What kind of trajectory are you setting for yourself? Just where do you think you'll end up?"

Daphne intervened. "Please try to stay calm. Remember, dear, you have hypertension."

"Calm? How can I stay calm with a kid like this? Being disrespectful to teachers, stealing school property—that's his idea of fun; it's not mine. He wasn't raised to be like this."

Daniel and his parents talked. "What are your plans?" they would ask. "Do you have any plans?"

"I don't know. I guess...maybe."

"Well what? Be specific. Do you want to become a gangster? Is that your goal?

"No."

Throughout high school, they talked at each other, and nobody seemed to hear what the other person was saying. Daniel was incapable of appreciating his father's wisdom, and his father could not, in any way, empathize with his son, whom he loved but was beginning to regard as an ungrateful moron.

In the eleventh grade, there was an episode with a mannequin. One night, when Daniel and his friends were cruising around town, they stopped at a traffic light. In the backseat, one of Daniel's buddies pretended to be stabbing a woman. He jumped from the car, tossed what could easily have been mistaken for a lifeless body into the trunk. When the light changed, the boys sped off. The people in the cars behind them witnessed this event and someone called the police.

About five minutes later, several police cars, with sirens blaring and lights flashing, stopped their car. They approached the boys with revolvers drawn and demanded they place their hands on the car and spread their legs. Next, they ordered the driver to open the trunk. When he complied, the officers found the mannequin, splattered with catsup.

The police didn't find the prank funny. They took Daniel and his friends to the station and detained them for four hours. Their parents were called and Abe brought his attorney. The boys were reprimanded. Finally the prosecutor agreed not to press charges if the boys promised never to do anything so stupid again. They promised.

Daphne and Abe clung desperately to the hope that their son really was just a late bloomer. Soon, they reasoned, he was bound to grow out of this obnoxious and immature phase and become a man. But it was taking a long time for Daniel to bloom.

At the beginning of Daniel's senior year the police summoned his parents again. This time their son had been detained for stealing a Babka, a coffee cake made with raisins. According to the police, a seventy-five-year-old woman was leaving a bakery with her purchases. It was dark and she couldn't see well. Suddenly, four young men whom she described as "hoodlums" leaped from behind a tree. She was frightened, fearing she was about to be assaulted and robbed. In a high-pitched, squeaky voice, one of her assailants yelled, "Gimme that Babka!" and snatched the bakery box from her hands. The terrified woman dropped her other parcels and screamed. The four boys ran off. A block away, the police apprehended the culprits calmly walking down the street, stuffing pastry into their mouths and giggling like children.

Once again, Daniel's parents were called to the police station to retrieve their son. This time, charges were filed and Daniel's parents had to post a bond before taking him home.

Abe had reached his breaking point. "How did you get to be such a fuck-up?" Abe shouted. He seldom cursed, but this time he was furious. "You make me ashamed. You bring dishonor to our family. You act like a schmuck and are proud of it. What is wrong with you? You could have given that lady a heart attack. Didn't you see how old she was? Do you want to go to jail? Are you really that stupid?"

His father's words stung. Daniel hadn't anticipated being arrested, but he thought the Babka episode was funny. It was a classic goof. He wasn't being malicious; he was just having a good time with his friends. If his dad didn't appreciate how clever Daniel was, his dad didn't have a sense of humor. Daniel's feelings were hurt. What kind of a thing was that to do—call your son a schmuck? So Daniel delt with his stress the way he usually did; he became sullen and belligerent. He stomped upstairs and slammed his bedroom door. Alone in his room, Daniel turned on his black light and gazed at the psychedelic posters that lined his walls. When the house became quiet and he was sure his parents had finally gone to bed, Daniel smoked a joint of marijuana and went to sleep.

*　*　*

That was the night Daphne lay in bed and wept for her son. She hadn't been a religious person since childhood, but that night she prayed: "God, please help him. Daniel's a good boy. He's bright but he's confused. And these friends of his are bad influences. Please help Daniel. Speak to his heart. Help him to find his path."

As she finished her prayer, Daphne decided she would start attending church. She hadn't been to church in many years and maybe that was the problem. She hoped her children would go with her, but if not, she would go by herself. Being a liberal thinking mother in an interfaith family had once seemed a good idea. Now she wasn't so sure. Certainly, nobody could fault her and Abe for advocating tolerance, but maybe tolerance wasn't enough. It didn't seem to be helping her son. Daniel seemed to be growing worse by the day. The flame of her faith had burned low, but it had never gone out completely. It just needed some fuel, and the perfect fuel, she thought, had been Babka.

The following morning, Daphne woke Daniel, Mikey, and Anna. They were not used to being awakened on Sunday morning, and they were all grumpy as she herded them to the table for breakfast.

"Come on, kids," she said. "It's time for church."

"What?"

"It's time for church. God knows; we can use it."

The three youngsters were puzzled. Daniel thought he might still be stoned.

"Since when do we go to church?" Mikey asked.

"Since today," Daphne responded. "As the saying goes: 'Today is the first day of the rest of your life.'"

"But I don't want to go to church," Anna whined. "I'm tired. Besides, I don't know anything about church. I want to go back to bed."

"Me, too," said Mikey.

"I'm not going." Daniel added defiantly: "I don't care if it *is* the first day or what day it is."

"Suit yourselves," Daphne said. "I can go alone. Maybe next week, one of you might be kind enough to accompany me. And Daniel, until you come with me, you will not be driving our cars. And I will not be chauffeuring you to Brooklyn. Do you understand? You are grounded until further notice."

"What?" Daniel was furious. "How will I see Sarah?"

"That's your problem. Take a bus. Ride the train. Walk. But I won't be taking you to see her—that is, until you start going to church."

"I'm not going. You can't make me."

"Really? We'll see." And with that, Daphne got dressed and went to church. She continued to go every Sunday. Three weeks later, Daniel accompanied her, reluctantly.

* * *

Before graduating from Wheatley High School, Daniel applied to three universities. He received one rejection and two acceptances. One university was in Boston and the other acceptance from a school in Ohio. His family and friends were surprised any university would accept Daniel as his grades were so poor. Daniel decided to attend the shool in Boston. It wasn't ivy league, but it was an accredited and respectable university. Sarah, who had applied to colleges closer to home, decided to go to C.W. Post College on Long Island.

Daniel's first semester passed in a blur. Most of the time, he was stoned or sleeping. He seldom attended class. He wasn't even sure in which building some of his classes were held. He was lonely and depressed—a stranger in an alien city. He might as well have been attending college in Moscow, Russia. He missed Sarah and thought about her all the time. Then he would smoke a joint or go out and get drunk to ease the loneliness. But it was only a temporary fix. When he received his first semester's grades he saw he had failed all his classes. He shrugged it off. One night shortly after his grades arrived his parents called:

"How did you do, son?" They asked.

"Fine," he lied. "I didn't do great. I mean, not spectacularly, but I did all right."

But of course, he hadn't done all right.

He began his second semester thinking that he would try a little harder. He also began to consider transferring to C.W. Post so he could be closer to Sarah again. He made a feeble effort to attend classes, but he didn't get started right and the few times he did attend were frustrating. He was so far behind he had no idea what his assignments were or what was going on in the classroom. So he returned to his room and smoked a joint and put on records by Bob Dylan or Phil Ochs. When he received his grade report for spring semester it was accompanied by a letter that said he had failed out of school. Daniel was disappointed.

"Oh well," he said. "I'll return to New York. I'll see Sarah and do better next time."

He headed back to Long Island. He apologized to his parents and offered a feeble explanation. His parents didn't say much, but they let him move back into his old room. Daniel applied to C.W. Post, but because of his terrible record, the school would not grant him regular admission. He was allowed entrance as a non-matriculated student. The letter he received said that if he could complete fifteen hours of coursework with passing grades, he could apply for regular admission. Daniel wasn't concerned. School was not a priority. His only goal was to be back on Long Island in familiar surroundings. He registered for classes and began commuting daily from his parents' home to school.

At C.W. Post, he pledged a party-house fraternity composed of students who could have been carbon copies of his friends from high school. He told no one he was not a regular student. It probably wouldn't have mattered. These students didn't care about academics. Lacking either goals or ambition, they spent their time in the cafeteria drinking coffee and telling lies. At night they smoked pot and partied. For the most part, they were kids from Long Island whose parents paid the bills. Daniel immediately lapsed into the high school type behavior that had caused so much grief to his parents. They were not around to witness most of his goofs and there were no telephone calls from the principal. But Sarah was around.

When Daniel arrived at C.W. Post, Sarah had already been there two semesters. She was comfortable with her own group of friends. She left them in the cafeteria to sit with Daniel, but after becoming acquainted with his fraternity brothers, she moved back to her former table. When Daniel objected, Sarah explained simply: "I don't like your friends."

Sarah's friends were athletes and spit-heads. Daniel hated athletes. They reminded him of his early years at Camp Thunder Bay. He would rather she was sitting with lepers than athletes. So, every day at lunchtime, Daniel sat with his buddies at the other side of the cafeteria and glared at Sarah, who was becoming increasingly distant. When they talked, they argued. They never laughed as they once had. One day in late October, Sarah approached Daniel.

"Look," she said. "We've known each other for a long time. We grew up together. I've had fun with you. But it's over. We're finished. Please don't call me anymore. And please don't bother me in the cafeteria. You embarrass me."

"What do you mean, it's over?" Daniel stammered. Hadn't he left Boston for Sarah? Hadn't he come to C.W. Post specifically for Sarah? Her rejection was difficult to comprehend.

"Why?"

"Daniel, you're a nice person. But you're a loser—a jerk. You're never going to amount to anything. You don't know what you're doing or where you're going. But I know. You're not going anywhere. You're like a child screaming at his parents: 'Look at me…look at me.' Well maybe they looked. I don't know, but I have. I looked hard. All this semester I've been looking at you, and I don't like what I see. You're not the person I thought you were. Everything is a joke with you. All you want to do is get stoned and act silly. You're a child trapped in a man's body. I don't need a child and I am too young to be your mother. As I said, you embarrass me. I can't afford to waste any more time waiting for you to grow up. So, please, Daniel, don't call me anymore."

Waste time? Won't amount to anything? A child? What is wrong with her? Can't she see how clever I am? I'm funny, irreverent, a comedian. Is she blind or just stupid?

Daniel left the campus and got into his car. Still fuming about the things Sarah had said, he drove fast and recklessly. Since it was the end of October, the leaves had fallen from the trees. Along the sides of suburban streets, the dead leaves had been raked and piled so the city truck could remove them. Daniel deliberately hit one of the piles, scattering the leaves in all directions. Smash! He knew that someone had worked hard to rake those leaves. He felt inconsiderate, but he didn't care. It was fun. Smash!

A second pile went flying. How could she do this to me? Was today the Twelfth of Never? *What about all the good times we had? What about camp?*

Spotting an especially large and inviting pile, he drove directly for it. And then something quite extraordinary happened. It was a faint whisper inside his head. *"Don't do it. Don't hit those leaves."* Daniel hesitated, thinking of a cartoon he had once seen on television, in which Donald Duck had a devil on one shoulder and an angel on the other. "Do it. Don't do it." Now it was Daniel's turn to hear those voices. He was getting closer to the pile. *Fuck it.*

At the last possible second, he swerved away from the pile of leaves. After he passed it, he glanced in his rearview mirror. Two heads popped up from the center of the pile, just like a jack-in-the-box. Two small children had been playing in the leaves. Daniel felt his heart pounding. His vision blurred. Trembling, he stopped the car at the side of the road and wiped the tears from his eyes.

After failing out of college I didn't do much of anything except get stoned and play records. I liked Phil Ochs at the time. He was a message singer. Most of his songs were about the Vietnam War. I guess that's when I began to realize I was in trouble. I mean, I was a 20-year-old man, still living with my parents in the same home I grew up in. I slept most of the day and stayed out late at night smoking dope with my friends from the neighborhood, kids I went to high school with. What we had in common was we lacked a sense of purpose. We lived only for the moment and had no ambition. It was as if we all had a question mark on our backs. Interestingly, I could see it on the others, but not on myself. But, to be honest, sometimes I felt the weight of something unexplainable pushing me down. When I sat with my friends (Larry, Mel, or Lenny) trying to determine which music would be best to get high with, I felt something was wrong. I could feel that nothingness and it was growing heavier day by day. The choice of music was important. Music and drugs were the salve in which I immersed myself. Music was my Binky Cream, a temporary fix, soothing like the ointment nurse Charlotte rubbed on me the day I tried to run away from Camp Thunder Bay.

I was angry and I wasn't getting along with people. I was criticized because of my hair, which was long and, okay, maybe a little greasy and unkempt. I decided to grow a beard. I bought my clothes at the army surplus store and wore sandals. Even in winter when there was snow on the ground I wore sandals. I tried a couple of times to get a job, but of course no one hired me. Hell, I wouldn't have hired me. People said I looked like a hippie, but I thought I looked Biblical, like a prophet or something. I walked around with a wounded expression like I was carrying the weight of the world on my shoulders. My parents hardly spoke to me any more unless they had to. Even my brother Mikey and my baby sister left me alone. I think Anna was afraid of me. I pretended not to mind and said I liked my privacy. I didn't expect to be understood; because I fancied myself an artist and artists seldom are appreciated. Van Gogh wasn't understood and neither was Bob Dylan, back then. What my family didn't realize was how noble I was for not giving in. I refused to "sell out." Sometimes I thought: What if I am drafted and have to go to Vietnam? They will feel sorry for me then. The thought of being sent to Vietnam terrified me. Would I run to Canada like so many others had? I wasn't sure. All I knew was it was cold in Canada and what would I do there? I didn't even ski.

Oh, I went through the motions of acting happy, but life was unrewarding, even when I was high. When I look back upon those times it seems I was in a perpetual fog. I was only vaguely aware of the passage of time. I didn't know what was happening in the real world because I never watched the news or read the newspaper. I hadn't heard of Barry Goldwater or that he planned to challenge Lyndon Johnson in a run for president. I didn't know about the war on poverty. When I wasn't high with my friends I felt sorry for myself and wrote poetry. I thought I might become a conscientious objector, even though I wasn't sure exactly what that meant. But the world was passing me by and people didn't appreciate the gifts I had to offer. My parents were ashamed of me and to be completely honest I didn't blame them. I was frequently depressed, so I would get high and go to sleep. I slept a lot during those years.

One night while on LSD with Mel and Lenny, I started thinking about how deficient my life had become. In a moment of clarity I told Lenny how pathetic I felt. "I'm not smart," I said. "I've flunked out of two universities. I don't think I'm especially good looking and nobody wants to date me. I don't blame them, but I'm practically celibate and that's not good for my health. My old girlfriend won't even take my telephone calls. I don't have musical or artistic ability. I'm not funny any more, although sometimes I still think I am. I'm a bad athlete. They used to call me 'chicken arm' at Camp Thunder Bay. I think Sarah was right—I am a loser."

Lenny, who was also tripping, responded: "Yeah man, dig it. You are a big zero. Who's Sarah?"

Later that night my LSD trip turned bad. Maybe it was the revelation of my inadequacies and the cold hard facts of my empty, meaningless, existence. Perhaps the dosage was too high. Whatever the reason, the trip evolved into an unpleasant anxiety experience. I was afraid and could feel my heart pound. It was as if a thousand ropes were tied to my body and each was pulling in a different direction. I thought I was about to explode into a million fragments. Believing my death to be eminent I decided I should try to get home where I could die beneath my psychedelic posters. Lenny's house was only two streets away from mine, so I attempted to walk home. That was a mistake. I became disoriented and didn't know where I was. The night seemed wrapped in a shroud of mystery. The colors were murky greens and purples. In the background I heard the sound of a duck quacking at irregular intervals. I was sure that duck was mocking me, but I didn't know why. I wandered for minutes or hours. I'm not sure because I lost all track of time. Eventually I got home and dragged myself up the stairs to my room. I took two Thorazine tablets which I had been saving for such an occasion. Then I collapsed on my bed and slept until late the following afternoon. When I awoke I remembered everything from the night before; all the thoughts and fears I had that plagued me and made me feel like a loser. I kept wondering about the duck. Who was that duck? Did he have special significance?

That was the day that I realized I needed to change my life. I wasn't the righteous dude I was pretending to be; I was just some shmuck with his head up his ass. But I didn't know how to change. All I knew was there was an ache inside, an emptiness that was growing.

Then something extraordinary happened—something unbelievable. Moses had his burning bush and I received my acceptance letter from Theophilus College. Of course I hadn't applied to Theophilus College. In fact, I had never heard of the school. No matter. I jumped at the opportunity of resuming my academic career. But I was mystified. I remember checking the envelope to make sure the letter really was addressed to me. It was, though it seemed odd. I had no recollection whatsoever of applying to this school. But I realized a lot had happened since Sarah dumped me. My memory was fuzzy. I had done a lot of drugs and I guess they made me more stupid than I already was. Maybe, I reasoned, I'd read about this school in a magazine or on the back of a book of matches. But then I figured, what difference did it make? I was accepted. That was all that mattered. As they say, don't look a gift horse in the mouth. Besides, life is full of mystery. Sometimes the most extraordinary things happen and we don't have a clue as to why. For me this was one of those times.

JIM & CHERYL PAHZ

Chapter 7

Theophilus

Theophilus College was located in Nashville, Tennessee. The more Daniel thought about going to school in Tennessee, the more excited he became. He decided to clean up his act and leave for Nashville as soon as possible. He would reinvent himself and do whatever was necessary to change his life in a positive direction.

At this point in time, Theophilus College was probably the only institution of higher learning that would take him—and they only accepted him on probation. That was okay; Daniel was used to probation. It wasn't that the school didn't have standards. Their policy was to give those who hadn't succeeded another try.

Theophilus College was run by the Richland Avenue Baptist Church, the "Church of the Green Light." The school claimed to be one of the largest independent Baptist congregations in America. It was an Evangelical, Christian institution, which probably explained why all the students in the brochure looked so odd—like they had just stepped out of a Dick and Jane reader. But they also looked happy. Daniel liked that. He wanted to be happy also.

When he told his parents about his good fortune, his mother was supportive. His father was positive, although skeptical.

"Sure you should go," he said. "But try not to fail again. You don't need another failure on your record."

Before leaving for Tennessee, Daniel read and reread the church newsletter and other material they sent him. He thought it might help him get ready for the big change he was soon to make. However, nothing could have prepared him for Theophilus College. He had occasionally attended church with his mother while he was in high school, but Daphne's church had been quite different. The services were short and dignified. You were in and out in one hour, and that was just fine with Daniel. That's the way a service was supposed to be. At least that's what Daniel thought. But at Theophilus, the services were long and seldom subdued. The audience joined in whenever the mood hit—especially when the speaker said something particularly inspiring. Worshippers would shout, "Hallelujah… praise the Lord," or "amen." During the first few services, Daniel squirmed awkwardly, feeling completely out of place. He thought of the movie *The Invasion of The Body Snatchers* and was certain that at any moment people would turn to him and point while shrieking "Jew-boy"—exposing him as the imposter he felt he surely was. But others paid no special attention to Daniel, who had cut his hair and shaved his beard. He wore khaki pants, a white dress shirt, loafers, and a blue blazer. Daniel looked just like one of the odd, old-fashioned-looking kids in the Theophilus brochure, and he went about his business largely unnoticed.

The church newspaper was called *The Life Line,* and according to it, there were about 600 people attending Sunday school. Each week the number rose. It reminded Daniel of the number of hamburgers sold in America by McDonald's. The number kept going up.

On Sunday mornings, yellow buses would venture forth from

Richland Avenue to gather worshippers for church and Sunday school. It was a sight to behold as the fleet arrived with their human cargo. From the expression on the faces of the passengers, one might conclude some people didn't fully understand what was going on. Unloading the buses caused pandemonium. Children were separated from parents. Babies cried. Some people were herded into the tabernacle and up to the balcony, which reminded Daniel of the monkey section at a zoo. A lot of commotion went on in the balcony. These bus people were not supposed to sit downstairs because the downstairs area was reserved for the regular members of the church and the students from the college. The first two rows of the balcony inside the tabernacle were reserved for the mission bus. These people came from the flophouses and lion-dens. They were the unfortunates. Sometimes the unfortunates had trouble sitting upright. Occasionally, one would lean over the balcony and become part of the sermon.

After the first two days of observing Theophilus, Daniel panicked. He had enough. He wanted to leave Theophilus College, which he believed would have been better named Pandemonium College. He forgot about his previous resolve to change his life. The whole atmosphere of the institution was bizarre. Daniel had never seen anything in his entire twenty years like this place or these smiling people. He was ready to make sacrifices, but this was too much to ask. He had already given up smoking pot and was trying to go cold turkey. He wondered if he hadn't really crossed dimensions and fallen into an episode of *The Twilight Zone*. He almost expected to hear Rod Serling on an audio track talking. Rod would have said, "You've entered a new dimension…somewhere between sight and sound, between heaven and hell. You think you're in college. You are. You just enrolled in the College of The Twilight Zone." Then the creepy music would play.

On the third morning of school, after only attending for two days,

Daniel walked out. It was the middle of chapel service and Daniel had reached his limit. He left the building and walked around the corner looking for a public telephone. His plan was to call a taxi service and go to the bus station. He wanted to return to New York. He was miserable and badly needed to get high. His mouth hurt from smiling. Then something strange happened. He was standing in the phone booth getting ready to dial the telephone when he glanced up and noticed something green and white moving against the building across the street. Curious, he looked harder. A large piece of canvas had come loose and was flapping in the wind. It was the movement that first drew Daniel's attention. The canvas had words on it, but it was hard to read because of the cloth's movement. Daniel looked harder. Straining to see, he finally read the banner. It said: "To the weak and the timid, all things seem impossible…"

Daniel stood there contemplating the words. He asked himself, *Is that me? Is that why I'm leaving…because I'm weak and timid? Am I running away? Is that why I always screw things up, because I always take the easy way out?* Sarah's last words replayed in his head, "You are a loser—a jerk. You are never going to amount to anything." He replaced the telephone receiver. *Do I fail because I am a loser, or am I a loser because I fail?* As he considered this puzzle, he heard another voice in his head. It was the same voice he heard a few years ago when he almost smashed the pile of leaves in which the children were playing. It was just a whisper, so faint it would be easy to ignore. But Daniel had listened then, and he had been right to listen. This time the whisper said: *"Don't run away. Stay. Be a man."*

That was a significant moment in the life of Daniel Fisher, one of the turning points. He resolved he would return to the tabernacle, even if he felt uncomfortable. He would complete this day—this one day, without running away. If he wanted to leave, he could go tomorrow. Not today. Today he would go back to the strange school run by crazy people who liked to shout "halleluiah" and "amen." Today he would not be weak. He would listen to his inner voice. So he returned to the assembly inside the tabernacle building.

* * *

Days turned into weeks, and then the weeks into months. Daniel took each day, one at a time, gradually realizing how repetitive and predictable the routine was. It was like swimming in a pool, you just had to get used to the water. His life began to follow a pattern. Classes were held in the academic building and were offered between the services, which seemed to be going on all the time. There was always a service in progress: morning services, evening services, chapel services, prayer meetings, and special assemblies. Attendance at these events was mandatory, and students had to sign a form at a monitor's station before taking a seat. Trust was unknown at Theophilus College.

In addition to the regular services, there were special events. At any given time there was usually a conference running: The Third Annual Missionary Conference...The Twenty-Second Annual Bible Conference... The Fourth Annual Sword and Spirit Conference. These were highlights of the school year, and students were required to attend. The conferences usually featured an individual with some particular talent or accomplishment they could use for the Lord's glory. Some were regulars on a circuit, such as Larry Kong, a jujitsu expert who toured the country in a Winnebago on his "Jujitsu for Jesus" campaign; Sister Sarah Louise who recited the book of Psalms from memory; and Aaron Axelrod, the Hebrew Christian, who wore a yarmulke wherever he went on campus.

The weekly assemblies were mostly for providing information and allowing student groups to speak or perform. However, sometimes there was a special assembly called to draw attention to an infraction of school regulations. On one occasion, shortly after Daniel's arrival, two young men had to address the student body and give a public apology. They had been seen leaving a movie theater in downtown Nashville. Even though it had been a Disney movie, by seeing the movie they had broken the school rules. Students were not allowed to go to the movies, any movie. Now these two boys had to atone for their transgression by making their apology. *Poor guys,* Daniel thought as he watched his fellow students being humbled.

The minister, Brother McPherson, singled out one of them. "This boy," he said pointing to an athletic-looking student, "this is Tommy Tuttle. Of all boys, Tommy should have known better. His father has a ministry in Central America, and is a frequent speaker at Theophilus. Tommy is a Christian boy. I can't understand how Tommy could do this to his family, not to mention, to you, the students of this great institution. But the devil is beguiling. He has his ways. He will snare you if you lower your defenses, if you let your guard down. Remember students; your life is your testimony. At Theophilus, we must be guardians of truth. You are each an individual guardian. You are a role model for others." There was absolute silence while the two boys, with their heads hung in shame, mumbled apologies and slinked off the stage.

The climax of every service was the invitation to be saved, followed by the baptisms. Behind the back wall of the tabernacle, an indoor pool had been constructed. The mural behind the pool depicted the River Jordan. The baptistery had a curtain in front, and prior to the baptism, the curtain would open. The church lights would dim, background music would play, and the river would start to "flow." Steps led from the sides where the person to be baptized would enter with Brother McPherson. The proselyte wore a white sheet and bathing cap. Brother McPherson wore a black, double-breasted suit. It wasn't fashionable, but looked good when wet.

Brother McPherson would lead the person into the water, and then hold his or her nose and tilt them backward until the individual was submerged. Baptism by emersion represented birth, death, and resurrection. When the individual emerged from the water, their sins were washed away. The person was clean inside and out, and he or she was ready to start life anew. Leaving the baptistery, Brother McPherson would click a switch. The Jordan would stop flowing, the baptismal lights would go out, and florescent lights would leave an effect like moonlight.

While at Theophilus, Daniel was baptized twice. The first was a formality, a prerequisite for being accepted as a student. Although Theophilus College was a non-discriminatory institution, it regarded most incoming freshmen and transfer students as unrepentant sinners. Theophilus wanted (expected) the students to be "born again." Daniel didn't object. He didn't think it was a big deal. He never objected to saying the Pledge of Allegiance or for having a Bar Mitzvah when he didn't even think he was Jewish. He figured there were times when one needed to conform to the wishes of others, just to get by. It made life easier for everyone. This was one of those times.

The second baptism was different; it was for Grace Spindler. He met Grace during his second year at Theophilus. To Daniel, Grace was amazing. She had long honey-colored hair, a creamy, flawless complexion, and a warm, easy smile. It was as if she was made of sunshine. Grace lit up a room with her presence. She was different from Sarah; she was attractive, but not in Sarah's overtly sexual way. Daniel saw something special in Grace. With her broad smile, when Grace laughed it was a magical moment. What astounded Daniel most about Grace were her eyes. While they seemed to laugh, they also bore into Daniel's heart. Her eyes saw through all his pretence and insincerity. Yet those eyes were never condemning.

Grace radiated a sense of peace and spirituality that Daniel found comforting. But so it seemed did everyone else. She seemed genuinely happy, a person who loved life. Because of this attitude, coupled with her physical beauty and serenity, Daniel found her irresistible. He thought she might be an angel, come to earth on a secret mission. He tried to be with Grace whenever he could. Unfortunately, Grace was frequently occupied with other activities and other people. She wasn't impressed by Daniel Fisher, but that made her even more desirable to him. He was ready to commit everything to Grace, and he told her so on more than one occasion. When he proposed marriage, the first time, she warmly, but firmly declined.

"Daniel, you can't be serious. You don't even know me! Besides, I can't marry you. Your life is not a testimony to Christ. All you really want to do is hug and kiss me." Then she looked at him with her all-knowing, laughing eyes, and said, "You want pleasure, Daniel, that's all. But I can't give it to you. I know you're a good person, but you're not a Christian. You're too much of this world." She smiled and shook her head. "It just wouldn't work. And you know what, Daniel? You'd come to hate me. Really, you would."

There was no question about it; Grace wasn't interested. Daniel needed to convince Grace he was a Christian and to demonstrate his sincerity.

"It's not just pleasure I'm after. I've stopped walking the railroad tracks looking for hemp to smoke. I've stopped listening to rock-in-roll music. I don't drink alcohol, and I've even given up tobacco. Grace," Daniel said, "just think about it. I have stopped doing almost everything that is normal and fun."

"Daniel, you just proved my point. All those things you describe as fun are not fun. They are only fun to a tormented soul, a soul in pain. You do them because you are in distress, and they help blot out your misery. Your soul is healing, but it is still wounded. It is Jesus you need to commit to, not me."

No matter what Daniel said, Grace was not persuaded. Daniel reasoned he had to show her he was sincere to win her heart. So one night in a grand gesture, Daniel professed his faith once again to the whole congregation and was baptized a second time. But even that didn't work. Grace only laughed and told him she could see into his heart.

"You did it for me," she said, "and that doesn't count. You must do it for you, Daniel, not for me. Do you know what the word Theophilus means?" She asked.

"No," admitted Daniel in defeat.

"It means friend of God, not friend of this world. And it doesn't mean friend of Grace. Grace is not in the equation. Grace doesn't matter and I am not important. Your mind, Daniel, is not on spiritual things. You have a long way to go."

Daniel was frustrated. Grace was probably right. He did have a long way to go. Could she really see into his heart? Was he so transparent? Perhaps, but he believed he loved her. Shouldn't that count for something? The more he was with her, the more convinced he was he wanted to marry her. If only she would give him a chance. He resolved not to give up. He would try harder.

Although he was not gaining any ground with Grace and probably not progressing spiritually, Daniel was getting excellent grades in his academic subjects. This was a new experience for him. He enjoyed his classes and liked the feeling of success. As if to make up for lost time, he spent most of his free time studying. His religion courses were hard. They included such subject as homiletics, eschatology, Bible prophecy, and practical evangelism. The Bible was incorporated in every course at Theophilus, from biology to physical education. He found the Bible confusing. But, there was an endless stream of guest preachers and speakers to help make the task of understanding the Bible easier. They spoke at the various conferences, and Daniel paid attention.

Doctrines such as "evolution" were proclaimed as a modern day heresy. Preacher after preacher explained that mankind had really been "devolving," not "evolving." Man was, "going down hill, traveling in reverse." This process had been going on since the time of original sin in the Garden of Eden. Interracial dating was frowned upon. It might be gaining acceptance by society, with the civil rights movement, but it was "not Biblical" and not accepted by those at the helm of Theophilus College. Another thing condemned was sex. Sex represented the mystical union between Christ and His church. In the context of marriage, sex was wonderful. That's what the preachers said. In all other regards, sex was bad—a device the Devil used to ensnare people into sin. There were other objectionable practices, such as abortion and rock-and-roll music.

"Our nation," a speaker proclaimed, "though once a great nation, has lost its moral compass. Now, it is a nation in decline – too much sex, drugs, and violence. We are on the verge of becoming a nation in which anything and anyone is welcome except God. It is a time of Godless hedonism." According to the speakers, unless there was a nationwide revival, they feared for the future of America.

Once, when Daniel was having a difficult time with Biblical doctrine he went to Grace for advice. Besides being beautiful, Grace seemed to have a quick mind. She confided that Jesus never really turned water into wine. It was grape juice. If this truth could be understood, other truths would likewise emerge. The Bible was certainly confusing. Daniel thought, *if Jesus turned the wine to grape juice, why wouldn't the Bible just say so?* Grace was uncertain about the answer, but she praised Daniel for giving so much thought to the subject. It showed that he was truly seeking spiritual understanding. She confessed there was a lot to the Bible that she didn't understand, but she firmly believed all would be revealed at the right time. She advised Daniel to pray and be patient.

Unfortunately, patience was an attribute Daniel didn't possess. So one day he went for counseling to Brother McPherson. It was the grape juice question. Brother McPherson was an awe-inspiring, giant of a man. He stood well over six feet tall and had broad shoulders and a snow-white mane of hair. He was always dressed in a black, double-breasted suit. When he spoke, he was passionate—regardless of the topic. He was an inspiring and entertaining speaker. However, his intensity cast a long shadow, and many students were uncomfortable with a close-up encounter because they found him to be intimidating.

Other than his baptisms, Daniel had never approached Brother McPherson with a personal concern. He felt nervous as he stood in the office and explained he was having trouble understanding doctrine. Daniel reasoned if anyone could explain the grape juice question, he was sure it was Brother McPherson. To his relief, he was warmly received. Brother McPherson suggested Daniel sit down and relax. He offered tea and candy from a box on his desk. While Daniel explained his dilemma, Brother McPherson sank back into his brown leather chair, with his eyes closed and face upturned toward the ceiling, as if awaiting a divine message. When Daniel finished talking and posed his question, silence flooded the room. Brother McPherson remained in his contemplative position, and after several seconds Daniel feared the man might have fallen asleep. But no, he suddenly straightened up in his seat and opened his eyes. He leaned forward with his elbows on the desk as if about to reveal a great secret. Then he smiled and explained there were things in the Bible that Daniel might find confusing. It took years of study to comprehend the Bible.

"Young people are always so impatient," he said. "The important things in life take time. For now, you should read your Bible like eating fish." He continued, "Whenever you come to something you don't understand, treat it like a bone when you are eating fish. Put it on the side of your plate and forget about it. If you can do this, you won't have trouble understanding doctrine."

This explanation did not suffice as far as Daniel was concerned. He left the office feeling unsatisfied. Grace must be right. Daniel was too much of this world, and he had a long way to go. But he wasn't getting much help—just a lot of talk about grape juice and fish bones. He kept hearing that he needed to be more patient, but why? Even the patient people didn't seem to know much. It was like the *Catch 22* book he had just read. Be patient and everything will be revealed at the right time. But if you ask too many questions it means you are impatient so nothing will be revealed. If something hasn't been revealed it means the time was not right because if the time was right it would have been revealed. It was enough to drive you crazy, which Daniel suspected was why so many of the people at Theophilus appeared crazy.

Yet even with such thoughts, the idea of leaving Theophilus and returning to New York was no longer an option. Daniel remained at Theophilus College and held fast to his philosophy of "one day at a time." He never forgot those words he first read on the banner that was attached to the tabernacle. "To the weak and the timid, all things seem impossible." Daniel didn't want to be weak or timid; he didn't want to be a jerk and fail again. Most of all, he didn't want to confirm Sarah's opinion of him as a loser. So he studied hard and gave academics his best effort. And one day he noticed something surprising. He wasn't depressed anymore, nor was he unhappy. He was busy, but his life had purpose. He felt good about his accomplishments at school and all the things he was learning. So he continued to work hard, aiming for graduation, or The Rapture, whichever would come first. All the while he continued trying to convince Grace that she should marry him.

* * *

By the time Daniel was a senior, it looked like this time he was actually going to graduate. One night, after services, he met Grace by the Jordan River in the Baptistery. He had asked her to meet him and told her he had something important to say, a secret. Church was over and the Jordan River wasn't flowing. It was a quiet setting, spiritual, but at the same time, romantic. The stained-glass windows glowed around them, and Daniel felt as if he was inside a fairy tale world. He was feeling positive, overwhelmed with the joy of the moment. He knelt down and looked up at Grace.

"Grace," he said. "I have to tell you something. I love you. I've always loved you. I want to marry you. I know I've asked before, but please, Grace, will you marry me?" This time, she didn't laugh, and her eyes welled with tears. She took his hand in hers and leaned forward, giving him a soft kiss on his forehead. Daniel was too thrilled to question the sadness in her eyes. He thought that this was finally the reward for his patience. Or, maybe it was a reward for getting saved a second time. He didn't care which. Then Grace firmly pulled back.

She squeezed his hand and looked into his eyes. "I can't marry you, Daniel. Please don't ask me again."

"Why not?"

"Because I'm engaged."

"You're what? Engaged?" Daniel couldn't believe it.

"Yes Daniel, to a very fine man…a Christian man. He graduated last year. We're getting married and then we're going into mission work together."

"Who?" Daniel stammered. "What man?"

"Tommy. Tommy Tuttle."

"Tommy." Daniel was trying to remember. It took him a few moments. "You mean that guy from South America? The guy who got caught at the movies three years ago?"

"Yes, him. He's not from South America. He's from Ohio. The movie incident—well, we all make mistakes, don't we? Tommy backslid, that's all. He was a sophomore when it happened, and the movie was a Disney movie for goodness sake. It's hard to believe everyone made such a fuss about it. Anyway, he's been on track ever since, and he's right where he should be. He's working hard to save money so we can go to missions together. Look." She held out her hand. "This is my engagement ring."

Daniel thought he was going to be sick. He was afraid he might throw up into the Jordan. He didn't know Tommy personally. He had seen him once or twice talking with Grace the year before, but he thought they were just friends. Everyone talked to Grace. Tommy was a good-looking fellow. He was one of the school's star athletes, a *Fighting Friend.* Daniel didn't think he would like Tommy. He was still not partial to athletes. Probably Tommy would not like him, either.

"I see," Daniel said. "I didn't know you two were even dating. I suppose I should congratulate you. If you and Tommy marry, I hope you will be happy."

"Thank you Daniel. I'm sure we will be. And I hope that you and I can always remain friends. I've enjoyed our friendship so much."

"Of course," he replied. Then feeling like he had been pierced through the heart, Daniel arose and gave Grace a perfunctory hug, then slowly turned and walked away from her and out of the tabernacle building. As Daniel descended the stairs and headed for his car he had to concentrate on his breathing. He didn't want to cry, but he felt wounded. It was a different feeling than when he had broken up with Sarah. At that time he felt angry. Now he carried a heavy sadness with him.

That night Daniel walked away from his angel and left church behind.

Chapter 8

Work

Daniel felt good about himself when he graduated from Theophilus College in June of 1969. Mom and Dad attended the ceremony and watched their son receive his diploma. It was a sweet day, and Daniel was proud of his accomplishment. Yet he couldn't help but feel a bit anxious. He had come to a juncture in life where he needed to choose a path, and there were no signposts to direct him. The only thing he knew for certain was wherever he went, it would be away from the protective cocoon of Theophilus. He was heading into the unknown, and that was unsettling.

Grace would not be a part of his life. She would marry Tommy and move—probably to Guatemala. Their friendship survived the goodbye in the baptistery, though the pain lingered. During his last few weeks at Theophilus, Daniel had reluctantly listened while Grace talked about her wedding plans and the mission she and Tommy would go to in Guatemala. She intended to accomplish great things, and Daniel believed she probably would. Grace had a certainty Daniel never possessed.

One afternoon, prior to graduating, she presented Daniel with a gift. "I got this for you, Daniel. It's not a graduation present; well, it sort of is, but really it's more of a keepsake. I want you to remember me."

Daniel opened the small white box and found a silver key chain—the ones sold in the Theophilus gift shop. It had a small medallion attached to it with a cross engraved. Beneath the cross was written the name of the college, *Theophilus,* and beneath this were the words *Friend of God.* On the reverse side was engraved, *To my friend Daniel. G.S. 1969.*

Daniel stammered, "I don't know what to say… Grace, I'm sorry, but I didn't get anything for you."

"You weren't supposed to. I just wanted to give you something, so you wouldn't forget me. I want you to know how special you have been to me."

"How could I forget you, Grace? Knowing you has been a privilege. I would have left this place a long time ago if it hadn't been for you."

After the ceremony on graduation day, Daniel overheard his mom talking to his father. "He's changed! I think he finally bloomed."

His father didn't answer.

"Maybe it's a miracle?" Daphne continued. "God works in mysterious ways."

"Doesn't He?" Abe answered. "I just hope it's not a temporary miracle, like the calm before the storm. A permanent miracle would be nice. But let's be thankful for small blessings. At least he's cleaned up and doesn't look like a shaggy dog anymore. He's actually smiling."

Daniel gave no sign that he had overheard his parents talking or that his father's words stung. Instead, he offered to give them a tour of campus.

"Mom, Dad, I have decided not to return to New York. There are too many memories there, environmental cues. I'm afraid that around my old friends and familiar surroundings I might slide back into my old ways. I answered an ad in the newspaper about a job with decent pay and good benefits. It has free training, room for advancement and travel opportunities. It's with an insurance adjustment company based here in Nashville but with branch offices throughout the South. They will train me to be an adjuster, and when the training is complete, I can decide which office I want to work from."

"It sounds like a good opportunity son," Abe said. "It makes sense."

"I am so proud of you and the man you've become." His mother beamed. "But remember, Daniel, you can always come back to New York—if you want to...when you're ready."

"Thanks, Mom. I know I can. But for now, this feels right. A person has to grow up sometime."

*   *   *   *

Daniel's job training started the following Monday after his parents returned to New York. It took about a month to complete. Then Daniel spent an additional month traveling throughout the state with different adjusters so he could get a feel for the work. When it was time for him to select a home office, there were four possibilities: Memphis, Tennessee; Chattanooga, Tennessee; Mobile, Alabama; or Biloxi, Mississippi. Daniel opted for Chattanooga. He had relatives near Chattanooga, and it was only a few hours from Nashville. The first weekend in September, Daniel packed all his belongings into the new VW station wagon his parents bought him and headed to Chattanooga. He signed a lease at Germantown Village, a new apartment complex where he rented a one-bedroom apartment.

Initially, Daniel liked insurance adjusting. He handled claims, and with each case he learned something. His territory was eastern Tennessee and northern Georgia. In the back of his station wagon he carried a large briefcase filled with forms, a Polaroid camera, a small tape recorder with cassette tapes, and two boxes crammed with stationery, envelopes, brochures, manuals, maps, and reference books. There was also a packed overnight bag that went with him everywhere, just in case. Sometimes cases took longer than expected, and sometimes Daniel liked looking around an area once he was there. Besides, there was no one he needed to hurry home to.

Daniel enjoyed driving, especially through the rural countryside. The mountains and trees often reminded him of Raquette Lake and his summers at Camp Thunder Bay. At each destination he was welcomed by someone who was eager to see him and have a claim settled. He had taken to stopping at the small antique shops that he passed along the way. In fact, one of his first claims involved an antique shop in Cleveland, Tennessee. An elderly woman had accidentally driven her car through the storefront's glass window when she hit the gas pedal with the car mistakenly in drive instead of reverse. Daniel took pictures of the window and damaged items. Then with the assistance of an antique appraiser and receipts from the owner, he determined the amount of the loss and settled the claim.

The whole process took a couple of days and during that time the appraiser gave him a crash course in antiques. Daniel found the subject fascinating. He had always been a collector. First it had been stamps, then coins, and then almost anything. Antiques presented a new frontier. He purchased a couple of reference books and kept them with him on travels. He especially liked the small town stores where people sold antiques out of their homes. These owners were usually talkative and happy to share their knowledge. Eventually he began buying items, and before too long his apartment resembled a small warehouse. One afternoon he took three boxes of lob-top bottles he had purchased outside of Knoxville to an antique shop in downtown, Chattanooga. He bartered, leaving the shop with a round, oak table and a new friend. It was the first of many visits. Eventually Fred (the shop owner) began telling Daniel of particular items he was on the lookout for. Daniel found it fun and profitable to scout around for Fred.

Weekends were tricky for Daniel. It was easy to be lonely if he didn't plan his days carefully. Daniel had no trouble meeting women at a popular dancehall called the Carousel Club. Unfortunately, these women were lacking compared to Grace. Instead of long hemlines, the women wore miniskirts. Most of them smoked, drank, and were on "the pill." They proclaimed their independence, and most denounced the paths their mothers had taken. They wanted careers, not commitment; marriage and family would have to wait. They were gloriously hedonistic with no strings attached.

But after a few weeks, a change would occur. His apartment, which they initially liked, would suddenly need a woman's touch. They all had decorating ideas and sometimes would even move furniture around when he went out for food or the morning paper. They would box up his antiques and tell Daniel he needed to find a place to store them—"too much clutter." Sometimes Daniel would return from work and find a potted plant had been added. After a month the woman (whichever woman) would leave personal items. "It's only for convenience," she would say. Next it would be hints about a permanent living arrangement. At some point the woman would conclude that Daniel needed someone to "take care of him. Men are so helpless," she would say. He was deemed too messy, too careless, too clumsy. He didn't eat right or know how to coordinate his wardrobe.

Daniel saw what was happening. He would try to extricate himself, but by then it was complicated. He was stuck with the tar baby, and she was holding on. Usually the tar baby would cry. Eventually, when Daniel finally got free, she would stomp out of the apartment, accusing him of being insensitive. He didn't disagree, which made matters worse.

"You don't care! What do you want?" she (whoever) would shriek and make a terrible scene.

Daniel tried to be polite. But he couldn't tell her the truth, which was he wanted Grace. He wanted someone soft and special—someone he could bring home to Mom and Dad. He wanted an angel.

Daniel continued to date women, but the relationships were unrewarding. In fact, he preferred hunting for antiques or having a beer with Fred. Lately he began making visits to the relatives he had only rarely seen as a child but always knew of. His grandmother, Virginia, lived with her two sisters who were Daniel's great aunts, on the family farm on Signal Mountain. All three of the women were now elderly widows. The farm was only thirty minutes from his apartment, but it seemed like another world, a place where time stood still. A single road snaked up the mountain, with steep drop offs and one really sharp, hairpin turn called the double-S turn. Right at the turn a handmade sign read: *The Signal Mountain Ku Klux Klan is Watching You.* Every time Daniel passed that sign he felt offended. Still, he resisted the urge to stop and pull it down because he was afraid they really might be watching him.

Daniel often had Sunday dinners with his grandmother and her two sisters, Aunt Gretchen and Aunt Letty. He called them "the three musketeers," and they seemed to enjoy the visits as much as he did. The three women listened intently to his insurance stories, such as the one about Mr. Claiborne who tried to make a living by slipping in hotel bathtubs.

"My word," Aunt Gretchen would say, shaking her head in indignation.

"When I told him," Daniel said, "we could only pay one hundred dollars for the claim, he was outraged. The man said, 'but I got five thousand dollars for my first claim.' Yes, Mr. Claiborne, I know, but you have fallen on three previous occasions. He said it was because he was clumsy. Now I know clumsy," Daniel said to the three older ladies. "I was clumsy as a child. But three times in one year! I told him if he didn't sign the release and take the money I was offering, I would have to call the police. Needless to say, he took the hundred dollars. I think his slip and fall days are over."

"My, my," Grandma Virginia said, shaking her head from side to side. "What is the world coming to? Imagine, people lying and cheating just to get money."

"People do that," said Daniel. "Have I told you about my racehorse claim?" He knew he had, but he also knew the old ladies really liked the story, so he proceeded to tell it again. "I was called to determine the identity and cause of death of a racehorse. There was a fifty thousand dollar policy on the animal."

The aunts and Grandma Virginia appreciated horse stories because they had grown up with horses on the farm. Horses were something they understood.

"So I was able to verify the horse was the right animal because of the tattoo number on the inside of the upper lip. But the veterinarian wouldn't autopsy the horse. It was too decomposed. It had been laying out in a field in ninety-degree weather for the better part of a week. It smelled bad. The vet simply refused to open the animal to determine if the death was accidental or not. When I asked him what the insurance company should do, he replied, 'get another veterinarian.' I tried, but nobody else would touch it, either. In the end I sent my report, and I guess the company just had to pay the face value of the policy."

"My, my," Grandma Virginia repeated again. "I reckon it's important work you do, Daniel." The other ladies gave a nod in agreement. "Just think of all that money you're responsible for."

Initially they quizzed him about girlfriends and asked why he wasn't married yet. Eventually he told them about Grace and his futile attempts to replace her.

"You know," Daniel said, "you don't find angels at the Carousel Club."

"No you don't. Grace was right with the Lord," Aunt Letty said: "That is what you need Daniel, a good Christian girl who is right with the Lord."

"He needs an easy-keeper." Grandmother added, "You'll be a lot happier that way."

"What's an easy-keeper?" Daniel asked.

"That's horse talk," Aunt Gretchen explained. "You should ask your mother. Daphne knows about horses. She rode with a soft eye." Aunt Gretchen paused to reflect a moment and then continued, "There are some animals that just seem to know how to be horses better than others. Generally, you put a horse in a field, throw a little hay and grain, and they do just fine. Some, however, do spectacular—they thrive and blossom way beyond the other horses without any special care at all. Those are the easy-keepers. We had a few of those. Just the finest horses you could ever want. Then there are the others that are puny and sour no matter how much feed or vitamins you throw at them. Some are just plain rank or crazy. People are the same way. Most are average, a few are fools, but some are easy-keepers. I bet Grace was an easy keeper."

"Do you remember that crazy horse that kept going through fences?" Aunt Letty began to laugh.

"You mean that one that ended up stumbling and falling into the burn pit?" Aunt Gretchen added. Now they were all laughing.

"Yeah, that's the one. What was that fool's name?"

They laughed harder and tried to remember the name of the horse. Nobody was certain, but Aunt Letty thought the horse's name was Dakota. The incident must have occurred a long time ago when they were just girls.

When they finished reminiscing, Grandma Virginia settled down and continued, "Find an easy-keeper, Daniel. You'll be happy if you do."

Daniel smiled. "I'm trying, Grandma. But it's not easy. I don't know how many easy-keepers are available."

Daniel always enjoyed hearing stories from the three musketeers about his mom and early life on the farm and tales about Joseph Tripper or Uncle Tillman's fainting goats. He preferred to steer the conversation away from insurance business because the truth was his job didn't always seem something to be proud of. It was a game, with the outcome often determined by who was the better player. Many people who didn't deserve settlements won because they knew the rules and the insurance company couldn't prove they were lying. The guy with the racehorse was one such customer. In some cases deserving people got less than fair treatment because they were trusting. Daniel, working as an advocate for the insurance company, would see people settle for less than they deserved, simply because they were honest. He couldn't really advise them to demand more money or go see an attorney. His job was to buy the claim off as cheaply as possible, but then he felt guilty. The more Daniel was praised by his employer, the worse he felt. He didn't confess his feelings to "the musketeers." The fact was, he was no longer happy with his job. After two years the company asked to transfer Daniel to Atlanta. He used the transfer as the reason for his resignation. Although it would be a promotion, Daniel knew it was really just more of the same—only in a bigger city with a better car. He was ready for a change.

The next job Daniel was able to get was as a substitute teacher at a high school for troubled adolescents. It began as a temporary position in the fall of 1972, but after the resignation of one of the regular teachers, his job became permanent. Technically, Daniel was supposed to teach social studies and geography. In reality, he was a babysitter along with all the other teachers at the school. It made no difference that Daniel didn't have a teaching degree. The students were so out of control and academically deficient it really didn't matter. Some of the students reminded Daniel of himself as a teenager—rebellious and without direction. They seemed to be goof-offs who liked to drink or just be lazy and complain. Most of these kids ended up at "the academy" after getting caught at some minor infraction. Either it was for shoplifting or truancy or merely running away from home. When he thought about it, Daniel was surprised he hadn't wound up in such a place when he was their age. He could relate to the students, and for the most part he got along with them. However, there were a few whom Daniel considered to be extremely troubled. These students were in the minority, but there were enough to make life difficult for Daniel and the other teachers. He wouldn't admit it to anyone, but he was afraid of the ones the teachers referred to as the "truly disturbed." Daniel tried talking to Mrs. Banks, the therapist, about the two kinds of students. He wondered if she saw it the way he did. But no, apparently she didn't. According to Mrs. Banks, all the students at the school were disturbed. They had to be or they wouldn't be in the program. The therapist said that "disturbed" just meant they had problems. Daniel pointed out there was a difference between someone stealing a tie from a department store and someone killing the family cat or pointing a loaded gun at their parents. "Not really," he was told. It was only a matter of degree. "And remember, it's not their fault. They are children and many of them come from terrible homes." Mrs. Banks pointed out that she had a Master's Degree in counseling and adolescent behavior was her specialty.

So Daniel ignored his instincts and followed the therapist's advice. He tried not to distinguish between the students, treating them all as equal. He was determined not to be intimidated by any of these maniacs. Then one April afternoon in his second year of teaching, as he walked out to the parking lot to leave early for a dental appointment, he was shot with an arrow. He felt a searing pain in his thigh and was thrown completely off balance. He fell backward and saw the shaft of an arrow with feathers sticking out the end lodged in his leg. He could hardly believe it, or the blood he saw oozing from the wound. In a matter of seconds his whole pant leg was soaked. As he grasped the reality of his situation he fainted and later gained consciousness in the ambulance as it sped off to Erlanger Hospital, the same hospital in which he had been born. He later learned a student (one he had always regarded as a psychopath) had been sitting on the roof, waiting for a teacher, any teacher, to ambush. He had stolen the bow and arrow from the equipment closet. Daniel learned this when Mr. Wright, the school administrator, visited him in the hospital.

"It's most unfortunate," Mr. Wright said.

"How does an emotionally disturbed sixteen-year-old have access to the equipment closet? And why do we even have bows and arrows?"

"We don't know where he got the key from. But it's important our students are treated like other teenagers. Archery is one of the favorite activities. You know our boys have problems with self esteem."

"They're not just other teenagers," Daniel said. "You can't fix their problems by giving them a weapon. I never had bows and arrows in high school. Did you?"

"Nobody gave Patrick the weapon. He stole it from the equipment room. The important thing, Mr. Fisher, is your recovery. Naturally there will be paperwork to sign, and a promise not to sue or to report the event to the media."

Daniel agreed, and the next day was sent home with crutches. Patrick, the boy who shot Daniel, was given fifty demerits.

Chapter 9

Hershel's Plan

During his convalescence, Daniel wasn't sure he wanted to return to work at a school where students shot their teachers with arrows. *No wonder this job was so easy to get,* he thought. It was while he was on his leave of absence waiting for his leg to heal, that Daniel realized what he really wanted to do—nothing. *I want to retire,* Daniel thought.

During this time Daniel spent a lot of time in the park reading and thinking about retirement. On one particular day he was just starting *The Autobiography of Malcolm X,* when a young man approached him and handed him a religious tract.

"Thank you," Daniel said, putting down his book to take a look. It turned out to be a crudely drawn picture of people being consumed by hellfire. The caption read: Where Will You Spend Eternity?

Daniel glanced at the young man, who was now about fifty feet from him. He was going up to people and handing out pamphlets. Daniel wondered if the man was a student. It seemed every major city in Tennessee had a church affiliated college or university, and Chattanooga was no exception. *I wonder if he is taking a course in practical evangelism?* It had been six years since Daniel's graduation from Theophilus, but he could still remember that course. As an assignment for this class, students had to stand on the street corner in Nashville and hand out religious tracts. If the person accepting the tract was receptive the student was supposed to witness. That meant they would ask if the person had a personal relationship with Jesus Christ and if they knew about God's plan for salvation. It had been Daniel's least favorite course. He never liked the idea of trying to sell God to others or speaking as if he were an authority on the subject.

Daniel knew that however many courses he took, he was no authority on God. How could he credibly explain God's plan for others when he wasn't sure of God's plan for himself, or even if God had a plan? It was like recommending a movie you never actually saw. Of course, at Theophilus he was not supposed to see movies, but Daniel managed to sneak away and see them anyway. When he was taking that course and handing out pamphlets, most people accepted politely and said, "Thank you." But not everybody was so courteous. Some people didn't want to be bothered—and why should they? They were on their way to the doctor's, or to meet someone for lunch. Besides, they had heard this all before. Daniel understood completely when the people he approached behaved poorly and said unpleasant things. People could be rude and disrespectful to messages about God and His plan for salvation. Some people would just ignore Daniel and keep walking or take the pamphlet and move away as quickly as possible. Daniel felt badly about this assignment, so after a few days he began to cheat. He would pick up a handful of tracts and head off to a nearby park where he would scatter the pamphlets on benches, in the men's room, and by the water fountain. Any leftovers were thrown away. Once he had confessed he had discarded pamphlets to Grace and she was livid.

"That's terrible!" she said. "You are supposed to be soul-winning. If you don't do this assignment correctly, something bad will happen to you.

God will not be mocked, Daniel. Be warned."

The pamphlet Daniel had just been handed was similar to the ones he'd passed out. He wondered if anyone, other than Grace, ever read them or took them seriously. Daniel placed it on the bench and returned to his book.

He had just resumed reading when another person approached the bench. This time it was an older fellow with a black beard. This man was wearing a black coat and hat. He had side curls and was wearing a prayer shawl beneath his jacket. He reminded Daniel of the Amish he had seen in Pennsylvania. Then Daniel noticed the edges of a yarmulke underneath the man's hat. *He is not Amish, he must be a Hasidic Jew.* The man looked so out of place, that Daniel wouldn't have been more surprised if a penguin had approached him. He was, after all, in Chattanooga, Tennessee. Daniel realized he must be staring, but he couldn't help himself.

The man stopped in front of Daniel and nodded. "Do you mind if I share your bench, young man? I am a little tired."

"Of course not," Daniel replied, gathering his wits. "It's a lovely day, a nice day to be in the park."

"Yes, it is," the man replied, sitting down next to Daniel.

The two men sat in silence watching the antics of a nearby squirrel. The man reached inside his black jacket and pulled out a cloth bundle. From the corner of his eye Daniel could see it was a handkerchief in which pieces of bread were folded. The man picked out pieces one at a time and tossed them to the squirrel. They watched together as the squirrel gathered the courage to investigate the white pieces of bread. Soon the animal was bravely darting up to the man's feet begging for more. The two men laughed.

Daniel gave up the notion of reading; the stranger next to him seemed more interesting. He cleared his throat and turned toward his companion on the bench.

"I don't mean to be rude," Daniel said, "but I am curious. Are you a Hasidic Jew?"

"How did you guess?" The man gave Daniel a mischievous smile, and then turned back to the squirrel.

Daniel chuckled, appreciating the stranger's sense of humor. "Maybe it was the clothes that gave you away. Your yarmulke is showing. But I'm wondering, how in the world did you wind up here in Chattanooga?"

"My name is Hershel Kirzner." The man extended his hand, and Daniel accepted the handshake.

"I'm Daniel Fisher. I'm pleased to make your acquaintance."

"As am I, young man. I have not seen you here before, and I come here often. I am a member of the Lubavitch Court, temporarily on assignment in your beautiful city." The napkin was empty, and Hershel folded it up and placed it back in his coat pocket. Then he leaned back and picked up the pamphlet that lay on the bench between him and Daniel.

Daniel was surprised to notice that he felt embarrassed. "Have you read that pamphlet?" he inquired.

Hershel nodded. "Yes, as a matter of fact I have. I got one last week, I think from the same gentleman."

"What do you think of it?"

"Not much, I am afraid to tell you. I don't like people trying to convert me."

"Why is that?" Daniel asked.

"Oh, as a matter of courtesy, I suppose." Hershel had a slight accent, which sounded familiar to Daniel; it reminded him of his grandparents who had died while he was in high school. Hershel spoke a formalized English. "We do not proselytize them, so they should have the courtesy not to try and convert us. We should all accept one another for who we are. We don't believe you have to be Jewish to find the path of God. The Torah of Moses is there for everyone, Jews and non-Jews alike. All people are endowed by the creator with the same divine spark."

Daniel nodded, thinking of Michelangelo's painting of God and Adam on the ceiling of the Sistine Chapel. Hershel continued. "Of course, for most of our history we were not allowed to proselytize, so that could have something to do with why I feel the way I do. We have lived for thousands of years among Christians or Muslims or whomever, not permitted to seek converts—even if we wished to. Yet other people, especially Christians, have always wanted us to believe like them. Sometimes it was demanded. In Spain for instance, in 1492, Jews were offered the choice of conversion to Christianity, expulsion from Spain, or death at the hands of the inquisitors."

"That's interesting," Daniel said. "I didn't know that."

"Yes," Hershel said. "Our history is interesting but tragic. This is not a new thing, trying to get us to change our beliefs. It has been going on for a long time. Fortunately, now they cannot demand it. They can't put us on the rack or peel our skin off. We are in America where there is freedom.

So, they have to find other ways to persuade. Now they pass out pamphlets like this one." He glanced again at the drawing of the unfortunate sinners burning in hell. "I guess they are still trying to scare us into conversion."

"But don't some Jews convert because they want to? Not just because it is forced?" Daniel remembered Aaron Axelrod, the Hebrew Christian he had met at Theophilus. Aaron embraced Christianity. What about the chapter in the Book of Romans? The one that talked about salvation and said "to the Jew first and then to the Greek?" How many times did Daniel hear that verse in chapel? Daniel thought about mentioning the passage, but he didn't want to be discourteous.

"Oh, yes. Of course—the *meshumadim.* I can give you an example of one." Hershel paused, stroking his beard then continued. "Yes! His name was Heinrich Heine, and he was a famous nineteenth-century poet, very talented and successful. He converted to Christianity so he would be accepted in society. He said it was his 'ticket of admission.' That was the phrase he used. He wanted what he considered to be a better life, and by converting he was able to get it. That was his choice. Just as it is the choice of every Jew—for me, for you. I am assuming you are Jewish by your name. Am I correct?"

Daniel was caught off guard, not certain how to answer. He thought it best not to mention Theophilus College or his two baptisms. Mr. Kirzner probably wouldn't understand or be sympathetic. Daniel thought it better to be evasive. He hadn't been called "sneaky" at Camp Thunder Bay for nothing.

"Actually, my father wasn't observant, so I wasn't raised with any formal training—except for my bar mitzvah."

Hershel clearly took this response as a yes. "A man such as you," Hershel continued, "you should go to Israel."

"You think so? Why?" Daniel asked.

"Have you been to Israel?" Hershel responded.

"No."

"Ah, yes." Hershel nodded. "You should go. Every Jew should go."

And so it began. Most afternoons, Monday through Thursday, if the weather was nice, Hershel and Daniel would meet in the park. They would throw popcorn and crumbs to the squirrels while they chatted about different things, but Daniel never shared his experiences at Theophilus. Often Hershel tried to persuade Daniel to go to Israel. One day Hershel walked up to the bench where Daniel was sitting.

"Well, well," said Daniel. "It's the man in black." When Hershel gave him a quizzical look, Daniel explained, "You know, Johnny Cash, the country singer. You do know who Johnny Cash is, don't you?" Hershel shook his head, looking confused but interested. "He's a singer who always wears black clothes. Like you. He's known as 'the man in black'—a very cool guy."

Hershel grinned. "Oh, I see. That's funny. Yes, I am a man in black. I am cool. But tell me, Daniel, this Mr. Cash, he is Jewish?"

"I don't think so," Daniel said. "But he does wear black. You know, Hershel, I've always wondered, why do you dress the way you do? I mean, you do stand out in a crowd. Doesn't that make you uncomfortable?"

Hershel shrugged. "What can I say? This is how we dress in our community. It is our custom. Anyway, why should I want to look like others? This is who I am."

"I don't know," Daniel replied. "It just seems life might be easier if you weren't so…so identifiable. It's like you're trying to draw attention to yourself."

"No. I'm neither trying to, nor not trying to. It's just the way we dress. In my community you would stand out. Anyway, I am not concerned about making life easier. Life is easy enough, thanks be to God." Then, changing the subject, Hershel asked, "Have you thought more about Israel?"

Actually, Daniel had been thinking a great deal about the subject. Once again he was at one of those junctures, a fork in the road. In about two months he would need to return to teaching or find some other type of employment. He knew it was absurd to fantasize about retirement. Daniel wanted something to do that was rewarding; something he could feel good about at the end of the day, as if he had made a difference. That was proving more difficult to find than he had anticipated. He was fence sitting. He knew that, and the idea occurred to him that maybe he had met Hershel for a reason. Maybe it was fate or divine guidance. Perhaps Hershel was an angel sent to test Daniel's faith. He knew what Grace would say if she were here. "Daniel, you should be witnessing. How else are people going to learn about Jesus? They must know him before they can be saved. They need to learn God's plan for salvation." But Grace wasn't here. Grace was married to another man.

Sensing Daniel's hesitation, Hershel said, "Listen, Daniel. I know about a program. I can show you. You can live in Israel and study. There is no cost. You only have to pay airfare. You can study, travel, and learn some Hebrew. Who knows, when six months are up, you might find a job and stay."

Daniel thought, *I need a plan. I don't want to go back to teaching. My leg still hurts. I was lucky. That maniac could have killed me. I don't want to be an insurance adjuster again. Maybe this would be a good time to travel and see a little of the world.*

"I wouldn't have to pay for anything?" he asked. "The whole time I am living in Israel?"

"Nothing."

"It's free?"

"Subsidized, by the government of Israel."

"But isn't it dangerous in Israel? What about violence?"

"Well... yes," admitted Hershel, "there is some degree of danger. I would be dishonest if I said there wasn't, but you get in your car...it's dangerous. Detroit, now that's a dangerous city! No matter where you are, life can be dangerous. A meteor could fall on your head, God forbid." He pointed to Daniel's leg. "Even teaching can be dangerous."

"Yes, I know," Daniel replied. "What about food?"

"Meals are free. It's a good deal, Daniel. There is, however, one small thing..." Hershel appeared thoughtful, almost apologetic.

"What thing?" Daniel asked, suspiciously.

"You go as an immigrant—an oley."

"A what?"

"You say that you are planning to stay in Israel—to live there. You don't have to. They can't make you. But who knows? After six months, you might like it. You might want to stay."

"You mean I lie?"

"No… of course not. You go with an open mind, accepting the possibility that in six months you may come to appreciate your heritage and become part of the dream."

"You think?"

"It's possible. Why not? It's your homeland."

"My homeland?" He paused to think about this. Daniel had never thought much about Israel. Could it really be his homeland? He actually knew very little about his father's heritage or religion. *Maybe,* Daniel thought, *that is why I feel conflicted.*

Daniel had learned more about Judaism from Theophilus College than he previously knew in all the twenty years he had lived in New York. The faculty of Theophilus was preoccupied with Judaism. His teachers talked about Jews all the time because, for them, Jews were the key to Biblical prophecy.

Daniel wondered what his mother would think of Hershel Kirzner. Hershel was the first Hasid that Daniel had ever met, but he didn't seem like a stranger. In fact, Daniel found him pleasant company. He enjoyed talking to him these past weeks and regretted he hadn't been honest about his mixed-up heritage. But if he had, would Hershel have been so friendly? Daniel didn't know, but he doubted it. Hershel seemed to sense Daniel's insecurity. Daniel wondered if there wasn't some way his two identities could exist in harmony together. Of course there was the option of being a "Hebrew-Christian," like Aaron Alexrod, but Daniel didn't care for Aaron or the term. At Theophilus, a Hebrew-Christian, or what was sometimes referred to as a Messianic Jew, was always treated as something special—an oddity. The individual was paraded around as if he were a trophy. The term seemed disingenuous. Maybe the two religions weren't compatible within one person. Like oil and vinegar, maybe they didn't mix well. Daniel wasn't sure, but he knew he didn't want to witness to Hershel any more than he had wanted to pass out religious tracts to strangers in his practical evangelism class.

Daniel wished he understood himself better. *Know Thyself.* Wasn't that what Socrates or someone had said? Maybe it was Confucius or Bob Dylan or Captain Kangaroo. Daniel wasn't sure, but it seemed like good advice. He knew his Protestant self, sort of—what he had seen reflected through the doctrine of Theophilus and the eyes of his love for Grace Spindler. Maybe it was time to meet his Jewish self. Daniel wondered, Am I a stranger to myself? *Is this my interfaith dilemma—almost chosen, nearly saved, always troubled?*

Daniel looked down at the copy of *The Autobiography of Malcolm X,* which he had just finished reading. He turned to Hershel. "Have you read this book?"

"No," replied Hershel. "I know who Malcolm X is, but I have not read his book. What does it say?"

"Malcolm talks about his life and how he grew up. In his book, he describes a process he calls 'conking the hair.' It's terribly painful. Malcolm puts all kinds of chemicals, including lye, on his head. The chemicals irritate and burn his scalp. He does all this is to get straight hair, or what some people call 'good hair.' But by whose definition is straight hair good? By the majority definition—white society. So when Malcolm X is willing to subject himself to all this pain so he can have 'good hair' that he believes is important if he is to be accepted by society, he has internalized that his normal hair is bad and that straight hair is good."

"Yes," Hershel said. "I see. That is a bad thing. He has accepted the fact that he has something negative about him. He has judged himself in terms of alien sources."

"Exactly," said Daniel. "By trying to fit in, he has hurt himself. I find this book to be troubling. I was just wondering if people do similar things every day without realizing it. After all, why should it be so important to be like everybody else, anyway? Why do some people have the need to make everybody like them? We should respect all people no matter how different."

"Exactly!" Hershel slapped his thigh for emphasis. "Now perhaps you understand why I dress the way I do." He continued, "It's an interesting topic. Very interesting. I will have to read this book by Mr. X. Look, let me give you my address at the Jewish Community Center. Give some thought to Israel, and if you want more information about the program, I can go over the material with you. There's a lot of information at the center. I can help you make a plan, Daniel; it could be a real adventure...a quest. It might answer questions you have. Who knows?" He stood up to leave. "But even if you don't call, I'll see you next week. We can talk some more and feed squirrels."

"Thanks," Daniel said, and he watched Hershel walk away. "And thank you," he said in a softer voice to the paperback book by Malcolm X. They are a strange pair, he thought, *Hershel Kirzner and Malcolm X.*

Yet together these two may have helped him stumble onto something important—who he, Daniel, was and who was going to define him. *Have I been conking my hair spiritually without even knowing it?* As he watched Hershel walk away, he felt genuine affection for this man. *He is at peace with himself.* Daniel thought, *How can he have such certainty? He reminds me of someone...?* Then he realized who it was. *Of course,* he said to himself. *He reminds me of Grace.*

And that was the day Daniel Fisher decided he would make aliyah— he would immigrate to Israel.

Chapter 10

Bad Hair Day

When Daniel left Chattanooga to go to Israel he had four thousand, three hundred and twenty-eight dollars. Before leaving he stored some of his favorite possessions at his grandmother's farm on Signal Mountain: his collection of cast iron cooking pans, a brass bed, and boxes of books and antique bottles went into the barn. The three musketeers wouldn't allow him to put his round oak table and matching chairs out there for fear the furniture might get scratched or warped. Instead, it was agreed the table and chairs would stay in their kitchen for safekeeping until Daniel returned, if he returned, from his mission to the Holy Land. Daniel's remaining possessions were sold, given away, or stuffed into his car to go with him to New York. He had three weeks on Long Island to visit with his family before his flight to Israel. It was shortly before Christmas, 1974.

When he arrived at his parents' house, Daphne and Abe were overjoyed to see him. He was given a corner in the basement to store the belongings he had brought in his car—more books, his record collection, clothes, and personal papers. Christmas was a week away, so Daniel helped Daphne decorate the house and trim the tree. Every day, Abe would look at his son and ask, "Why are you going to Israel?" Both Abe and Daphne had difficulty comprehending Daniel's thinking. One night during dinner, Abe said again, "What is the reason you are going to Israel?"

"To understand myself and discover my heritage… my roots."

"Your roots aren't in Israel," Abe stated, as much to himself as to Daniel. "Your roots are in Romania, and your grandfather would tell you, if he was alive, it wasn't such a nice place for roots to be growing. If you saw Romania you would understand why your grandparents came here."

"You have Irish roots, too," Daphne interjected. "Don't forget those. Why, you had relatives who fought in the Civil War, what about those roots?"

"I know," Daniel answered. "But I'm talking more about religious roots. I feel like a piece of the puzzle is missing. I've felt that way for a long time."

"But dear," Daphne said, "what about Theophilus? You are a Christian now."

"Mom, I need to know where I came from. I learned about my Protestant heritage at Theophilus. I think I should give my Jewish side a chance. I want to learn more about that part of me."

Dinners were hard to get through at the Fisher household without getting into family arguments. It had always been that way and things hadn't changed.

Abe shook his head. "If you ask me, I think it's a waste of time and money. Israel is dangerous. Don't you read the newspapers? There's always something terrible going on there."

"Of course," Daniel said, "but there are problems everywhere."

"You should be practical, like your brother. Look at Mikey and Kelly. They're doing great. He's got a terrific job—he works hard and earns a good living. He's a good provider. That's what life's about, Daniel, taking care of your family."

"But I don't have a family. I'm single, remember?"

"You're too old to be gallivanting around the world trying to find yourself. Your life isn't a novel. You need a wife and a good job." Abe continued, "You should grow up and settle down like your brother, Mikey."

"Mick, dear. Remember he doesn't want to be called Mikey any more. He says it sounds childish. He wants to be called Mick."

Since Daniel returned home, each night at the dinner table he had to listen to his parents go on about how well Mikey was doing. "Not like you," was never said directly, but it was obvious that was what they meant. Daniel knew he had been typecast as the black sheep of the family. He believed he deserved a different role in the family drama, but right now no other was available. Daniel wanted to protest this casting decision, but he realized the futility. So, he said nothing.

"You know, Daniel, success isn't a bad thing," his mother said, rising to clear the dinner plates from the table. "Did you know your brother is a deacon in the church?"

"Mikey's a deacon?" Daniel replied. He hadn't known that Mikey even attended church. He placed his silverware on his plate and handed it to her. "That's good, Mom."

"You should see how nice he looks when he goes to work," Abe said.

"Success shows. He takes pride in his appearance. And your mother is right, he doesn't like to be called Mikey anymore. He's Mick now. That's what he prefers—Mick."

Daniel nodded. "Mick," he repeated.

Daniel knew that Mikey worked as a buyer for Saks Fifth Avenue. He could picture Mikey—Mick—in a business suit with an expensive necktie and shoes so determinedly polished they screamed. As a child Mikey had always loved dressing up. He liked uniforms, especially if they came with a hat.

"Does Mick wear a hat?" Daniel asked.

Daphne looked up, momentarily confused, and then stated, "No, I don't think so, at least not to work. I don't think hats are in fashion."

His mother poured coffee and eyed Daniel appraisingly as she brought his cup to the table. He was wearing a favorite grey sweatshirt and frayed blue jeans. The sweatshirt had food stains on the front. Actually it seemed all Daniel's shirts had food stains. "You could stand to dress a little more like your brother," she said as she set the cup on the table. "You want to look successful, don't you?"

"I suppose, but I don't dress like this for work, Mom. I'm on vacation."

"Mikey carries an attaché case," Dad added.

Daniel suspected the attaché case was empty. He was glad he would be leaving for Israel soon, because these comparisons between him and his brother were tedious. Why couldn't they just accept the obvious: Daniel and Mikey were different people. It was more than just the four-year age difference. The two brothers had always had distinctive personalities and their own interests. They were not alike in any way. They hadn't parted on the best of circumstances, either.

Mikey liked to tease. His idea of a good time was to ridicule or berate someone until he made them show signs of discomfort. The more miserable they became, the better. He went for the jugular every time. With Anna he was vicious. He would focus on her weight. Their little sister was always slightly overweight but never what you would call obese. When she was a teenager she was especially sensitive, and Mikey would chide her. "You're fat," he would say, imitating Ed Norton from the "Jackie Gleason Television Show." If she were going out somewhere, like a date or to the movies, he would say, "You better take extra money with you. I hear they're charging by the pound." This would immediately result in a torrent of tears from Anna. Then she would scream at him, "I hate you. You're so mean." Her reaction delighted Mikey.

A week after Daniel's arrival in New York, he saw Mikey and Kelly in person. It was Thursday, and Daniel had been invited for dinner and to spend the night at their new home. He was told Mikey would have to work the next morning, but if Daniel wanted to visit he should come before leaving for Israel. Mikey said Daniel was likely to be blown up in Israel, and he would like to see his brother one more time before the funeral.

Mikey and Kelly lived in a working-class neighborhood, a couple miles from Daphne and Abe. The houses were older with small yards, but nicely maintained. Mikey's was a white two-story farmhouse style, with a tree in each corner to delineate the boundaries. The trees stood tall and leafless now, like gray fence posts to which Michael, the workhorse, was tethered.

The dinner started predictably enough. "Tell me again," Mikey said. "Why do you want to go to Israel?"

"Lots of reasons," Daniel replied. "To learn who I am, to understand what it means to be Jewish. As part of the Diaspora I thought it would be good to learn Hebrew."

"The what?"

"The Diaspora. The dispersion. It refers to the Jews and their descendents who were taken into captivity in Biblical times. As the psalmist said, 'by the rivers of Babylon we wept... If I forget thee oh Jerusalem, let my right hand lose its cunning'... or something like that. It also refers to modern Jews like us. When we're living outside of Israel, we're in exile from our homeland."

"We?" Mikey sneered. "Don't say we, brother. I'm not a part of this. Where do you get this stuff anyway?"

"I have a friend in Chattanooga. He's a Hasidic Jew."

"I thought you were baptized. Wasn't that part of the Theophilus experience? Aren't you supposed to be a Christian?"

"Well, yes, and no. It's complicated. There are some things that still puzzle me. Anyway, I am looking for something. Maybe I need to have God speak to my heart. I think that might happen in Israel."

"So, you're marching to Zion, looking for a burning bush? Like Moses?"

"Not exactly. I am looking for something, but... to be honest, I'm not really sure what."

Mikey shook his head. "I wish you could hear yourself: 'taken in captivity'… 'let your right hand lose its cunning.' Do you know what that means? You won't be able to masturbate! I'd weep too. You sound like a crazy person, Daniel. How long do you intend to stay in the Promised Land?"

Daniel shrugged. "I'm not sure, a year, maybe more. Maybe forever. It depends on what I find."

"I hope you find a K-Mart." Mikey smirked. "I can see that's where you buy your clothes. How much did that sweater cost?"

Daniel looked down at his sweater. "What's wrong with my sweater?" he asked. It was one of the few that didn't have a food stain. And what made it worse was that the sweater actually did come from K-Mart. But so what? Truth be known, Daniel was not above trying to catch the blue-light special whenever the opportunity presented itself. Daniel liked K-Mart.

Mikey waved his hands. "Nothing. Nothing's wrong with the sweater. It's lovely. What is it—virgin polyester?"

Daniel wasn't sure what Mikey meant, but he knew it wasn't a compliment. Mikey didn't give compliments.

"What kind of person cares so much about clothing, anyway? If it doesn't itch I'm happy with it. That's what counts to me. There are more important things than apparel."

"No," Mikey said. "There isn't! Haven't you heard that clothes make the man?"

"That's a cliché," Daniel said. "It's stupid."

"Now, boys," Kelly interjected. "No arguing at the dinner table. Remember you are brothers. Also, I cooked too hard to have dinner ruined."

"It's delicious, babe," Mikey said, taking a bite of his salad. "She's a great cook, isn't she Daniel?"

"Yes, she is," Daniel agreed. He was glad to focus on the meal. "This is just terrific."

Kelly had made a Caesar Salad and cooked t-bone steaks and twice-baked potatoes. A chocolate mousse was on the menu for dessert. The table was beautifully set with their wedding china and a white tablecloth. Candles were lit, and Christmas music played softly in the background.

"And she's good looking, too, isn't she?" Mikey inquired. "You have to admit, she's a good-looking wench. You should see her in fishnet stockings."

"Yes, she is," Daniel said, raising his wine glass and nodding at Kelly. "Kelly is very pretty. You're a lucky man, brother." Daniel took a sip of wine, feeling uncomfortable with the tone of conversation. Was there anything safe to talk about?

Kelly smiled and thanked him. Even in the candlelight, Daniel could see she was embarrassed as she asked him about his plans.

"What will you do in Israel? Will you really learn Hebrew? "

Daniel nodded, and swallowed more wine. Before he could say anything, Mikey began to chuckle.

"Now that should be interesting. You couldn't pass Spanish in high school. Remember Mrs. Gonzales, the Spanish teacher? She couldn't believe we were brothers. I got all A's in her class. She kept coming up to me and asking, 'Are you sure you are Daniel Fisher's brother?' She told me you had more difficulty with Spanish than any student she ever had." He leaned forward with his arms on the table and fingers interlaced. "Seriously," he said, "are you sure you need to go to Israel to find out who you are? Because if you really want to know, I can tell you and save you a lot of trouble. But it might hurt your feelings."

"That's just like you Mikey—always worried about the other person's feelings."

"It's Mick, not Mikey," his brother snapped. In an instant, Daniel was taken back to the moment at camp when Mikey had refused to run away with him. Daniel could clearly see little Mikey's face in the grown man sitting across from him—his narrowed eyes and barely concealed contempt.

"Mikey...Mick...what's the difference? By the way, Mick, do you still have your ears?"

"Ears?" Kelly asked. "What ears?"

Mikey leaned back in his seat.

"Go ahead, tell her," Daniel said. "She'll like this story."

But Mikey remained silent. He tried to yawn, feigning indifference, but Kelly looked interested.

"Come on," she pleaded. "This isn't fair. Will someone please tell me about the ears?"

"It's no big deal, really," Daniel assured her. "When Mikey was a kid he always liked hats. Anyway, for his fifth birthday he joined the Mickey Mouse Club and got a set of ears. You know, one of those mouseketeer hats with the big mouse ears? He loved that hat so much. He wore it everywhere. I think he even slept with it on his head at night."

"Oh honey," Kelly cooed. "That's so sweet!" She got up and stood behind her husband's chair. "I'll bet you looked adorable," she said, kissing the top of his head. Mikey seemed uncertain as to whether or not he should be angry. He gradually gave in to his wife's attentions, and Daniel watched as the grimace softened to a half smile.

"How about coffee?" Mikey asked, patting her arm.

Kelly kissed his head again and then took off for the kitchen.

The conversation didn't improve during coffee and dessert. They had so little in common to talk about. Mikey loved sports—a topic in which Daniel had no interest. Sports were on Daniel's list of boring topics, things he couldn't understand, like, Why do the British people financially support the Royal Family? Or what is the big deal about going out to celebrate New Year's Eve? But Daniel nodded and listened to his brother while Mikey discussed which teams won and which lost. Daniel wanted to say, "Who cares," but he was a guest in Mikey's home and felt such a remark would be discourteous.

Next, Mikey explained his exercise routine and lectured on the importance of physical fitness. "I jog five miles every day. You know, Daniel, you have to look good to feel good. I feel great. Now take you, for example. I see you're putting on a little flab around the middle. You have a spare tire. I'll bet your cholesterol level is sky high. You probably don't watch what you eat." Mikey stood up and held in his gut and patted his belly. "I'll probably outlive you by twenty years. Did I tell you I'm a deacon in the church?"

"Mom told me," Daniel answered. "Good for you."

"Church is good for business."

When the conversation reached a lull, Mikey would return to the subject of Daniel's clothes. "Don't you have any pride in your appearance? Where did you say you buy your ties?"

"I didn't. I don't buy ties," Daniel replied. "But if I did buy ties, there's nothing wrong with a discount store. I'm a teacher, remember? I worked at a school where I got shot with an arrow. What do I need a tie for?"

"I suppose there is nothing wrong with a discount store," Mikey said condescendingly. "They have their place. But have you considered how really shitty you look?"

Back and forth the conversation limped, like a wounded bird tormented by a cat. The bird suffered numerous blows until finally, exhausted, it expired in the middle of the dining room table. The two brothers got up and moved like fighters to their respective corners. They went into the living room to watch some television while Kelly cleaned up the table. In about thirty minutes, Mikey fell asleep on his back and began to snore. It was 9:45. Kelly gently woke her husband and explained to Daniel that Mick had a long commute in the morning and had to leave the house by 5:30 a.m. After locking the doors and turning everything off downstairs, the three said goodnight and retired upstairs to their bedrooms.

It was too early for Daniel to fall asleep. He lay in bed and listened to house sounds while his thoughts drifted. It had been a year since he had last seen his brother and that had only been for a brief visit. Daniel was surprised by the changes he saw in Mikey. His brother was different. He was more aggressive than Daniel remembered. Was Mikey changing or was Daniel seeing his brother in a different light? But Daniel thought Mikey, Mick, whatever his name was, had undergone some type of transformation. Maybe it was the marriage, or perhaps the commute to Manhattan every day. The challenge of work and the constant pressure to perform—these things must be bearing down on his brother and altering his character. Mikey was a man, but what kind of a man had he become? Daniel wondered whether or not Mikey was aware of the changes. Then Daniel wondered about himself. *What about me? What kind of man have I become? Am I as ridiculous as my family believes me to be?*

*   *   *

The following morning Daniel was awakened from sleep by loud voices drifting through the walls. He sat up in bed and remembered that Mikey had to get up early. He looked at the clock radio on the night table; it said 5:00 a.m. Daniel fell back into bed and pulled up the covers. The noise outside the room continued, and Daniel tried to make out what was being said. Was there a problem? An argument? Daniel sat up again, straining to decipher the words. Mikey was yelling something. Curious, Daniel got out of bed and crept toward the door. Then he cracked the door open and put his ear in the space. He heard Kelly's voice now, lower and calmer. Then he clearly heard Mikey again, loud and accusatory. Yes, they were having a fight. Apparently they forgot there was a guest in the house or they thought Daniel was asleep and wouldn't hear them. Or maybe they just didn't care.

"God damn it!" Mikey yelled. "The collar's not right. It doesn't fit."

"I'm sorry," Kelly whined. "I worked all night on it. If it doesn't fit, I'll fix it later."

"I need it *today,* damn it! I'm making a presentation to the Midtown Rotary Club. I need it now! These are important people."

"Now?" Kelly sounded hysterical. "I can't fix it now. The stitches have to come out." There was calm for close to a minute, and Daniel imagined Mikey frantically searching the closet for a different shirt.

The silence was broken again by his brother. "Shit," he yelled. "Where's the goddamn hair dryer?" Muffled noise, then a desperate announcement to the universe, "I can't find the fucking hair dryer!"

"Wait...Mikey." Kelly's voice was frantic. She was pleading. "I left the dryer at your mother's house."

This admission elicited an explosion of epithets. "You did what? You left the hair dryer at Mother's? Damn it! What am I supposed to do? What about my hair?" Daniel imagined a volcano erupting with sparks flying and lava overflowing.

"Selfish bitch. Do you know how selfish you are?"

"I'm sorry." Kelly was crying now. "I'm not selfish. I just made a mistake. How can you call me selfish when you know I stayed up all night working on your shirt?"

"Yeah. You did a fine job on the shirt, didn't you? A great fucking job. What's the first thing you did this morning when you got up?"

There was silence. "Well, Kelly"—he drew her name out slowly—"the first thing you did when you got up was go to the bathroom. You know I need the bathroom to get ready for work. My appearance is important—it's what pays the bills. So, you're pretty goddamn selfish, if you ask me."

"Mikey!" Kelly screamed. "I had to go to the bathroom, that's all. I had to pee and take my pill. My God, that can't be bad. You sound crazy, you know that?"

She shouldn't have called him crazy, Daniel thought, shaking his head—*even if it was true.* As expected, Mikey sounded even more infuriated.

"Fuck you!" He hurled the insult at her as if he were Zeus throwing a thunderbolt.

He hasn't changed, Daniel thought. *He's still the biting baby. He just bites a little harder.*

"Fuck you, too!" Kelly screamed back.

Daniel smiled. He was rooting for Kelly.

A door slammed, and when he heard Kelly's voice again, it was muffled. *She must be in the bathroom,* he thought as he strained to hear. "Do your own fucking hair. I'm not doing it any more," she yelled. "I'm finished doing your hair, Mikey."

This threat was followed by a pause. Then, in a much calmer voice, Mikey began to plead with Kelly to open the door.

He said, "Come on baby. Open the door. I'm sorry I overreacted. It's just that this presentation is important. Management will be watching. I got a lot of pressure, that's all. You understand. No one can do my hair like you can. I need you to help me with my hair, sweetheart." His voice was consoling and gentle. "We can use your hot comb. I'm sorry I said you were selfish, I know you work hard. But no one is perfect. It was a mistake, that's all. You shouldn't have left my hair dryer at Mom's. That was thoughtless, you know, but I forgive you."

This calmer, more rational man succeeded in convincing Kelly to open the door, but he had failed to calm her down.

She was even more hysterical now, both crying and shouting at the top of her voice, "All right. All right. I'm selfish, and I'm stupid. I left your damn hair dryer at your mom's. Why can't you just get a second hair dryer—one for your mother's house and one for here? But, no… that's too easy. It's much better if I'm responsible for remembering your hair dryer as well as everything else around here. I do the housework, the cooking, entertain your relatives, and make your custom shirts. Do you even care how much I work? I can do a hundred things right and you never notice, but God forbid, I make one mistake and you come all unglued. Like you never make a mistake! Really. You're so perfect. All you really care about is your stupid hair and your custom made shirts. Why don't you just buy a shirt from Saks? You are the one who orders them for the department store. Hell, I can't even piss in the morning!"

"All right, I'm sorry, Kelly. Listen, I'm going to be late for work if you don't do my hair soon. I'm really sorry I got so angry. But remember, Kelly, I do it all for you. Have I ever missed a paycheck? *Please* Kelly, do my hair before I'm late? We'll pick up a second hair dryer later. Okay, honey?"

It was quiet after that. The fight was over. Daniel peeked out and saw his younger brother facing the hall mirror. He wore a black suit, with a white shirt and red tie. Daniel watched as Mikey straightened the tie and smoothed his jacket. Then, satisfied with his appearance, Mickey picked up his attaché case and descended the stairs.

He looks successful, Daniel thought, as he closed the bedroom door. *He looks good. He looks like...Mick.*

Chapter 11

The Challenge

The program that Daniel had applied to from Chattanooga under the guidance of Hershel Kirzner was called WUJS, an acronym for World Union of Jewish Students. Despite Hershel's explanation, Daniel was only dimly aware of what the program was about when he submitted his application. The thing that was most appealing to Daniel was the costs were subsidized. What little money Daniel had with him would last a long time. At least, that's what he thought. Now, aboard the long flight to Israel, he took out the brochure he had received from the program and began to read it carefully.

According to the pamphlet, immigration to Israel was referred to in Hebrew as *aliyah,* which meant to go up, or ascend. A Jew had the right to immigrate to Israel under Israel's Law of Return, which was passed by the Knesset on July 5, 1950. Under this law, Israel admitted any Jew from any country who expressed a desire to settle there, no matter what his or her circumstances. The Jewish Agency, the unit of government responsible for *aliyah,* operated several absorption centers where *olem* (immigrants) could learn about life in Israel with the goal of eventually being absorbed into Israeli society. WUJS, located in the city of Arad in the Negev Desert, was one such center. It also housed an *ulpan*—a place where *olem* could undergo intensive study of Hebrew.

The brochure described the program of study. In addition to Hebrew, the classes included seminars in Jewish history and the cultural and religious traditions of Israel. Excursions throughout the countryside and an assortment of interesting speakers were included in the curriculum. Daniel would learn about peace and justice, have social events, and even learn some Israeli folk dances. It sounded exciting and he looked forward to his adventure.

When Daniel arrived in Israel it was January of 1975. He had not expected winter in Israel to be cold so he didn't bring appropriate clothing. Now, wearing his usual T-shirt and jeans, he sat chilled in the orientation center among a group of about fifty new arrivals; some were from England, others from South Africa, a few from Scandinavia. Like Daniel, they had all indicated they were ready to make the commitment and begin a new life in Israel. But unlike Daniel, most knew enough to bring a winter coat. These college students were friendly, but not overly friendly. It was obvious they were serious.

The speaker was a longtime resident of Israel who had come from the United States more than twenty years ago. He looked at the faces of the enthusiastic young people who filled the conference room.

"Welcome to Israel," the man said in English. He paused and looked around the room. "It is a difficult place to live—this Israel of ours. I don't know if you had time to realize that yet. You're just getting started. Believe me, it's a hard place to live. I can't justify to you or anyone else the crazy shenanigans that go on here. Some of us come thinking we will stay. But you should never tell anyone you're coming to stay because you could be wrong. When the commitment is too strong, you will probably fail. And, I don't say this in jest. You wander long enough in this wilderness of bureaucracy, and you can get lost."

Daniel fidgeted. *Hershel hadn't said anything about Israel being a difficult place to live. He said it would be an adventure. I would like it. I might want to stay. Come to think of it, Hershel made it sound like a Land of Milk and Honey.* Daniel had a strange feeling, a sense of foreboding. *I am having doubts already? At the orientation session? This is not a good sign.*

"You know," the speaker continued, "there is pride in this country. Even the tourists come here and in three days, they say, 'It's ours... our country.' But live here three weeks, they say, 'Who the hell wants it?'" Pause. A chuckle from the audience. "That's because they haven't come for a mission. They're not different. And if you're not different, then be a tourist. Enjoy. Stay a while. Then, go home. If you don't want to meet the challenge of this place, don't hang around and let Israel discourage you. Don't live here and then go back and hate us. If you've come here and told everybody you're going to stay, then, with such a commitment, maybe you made a mistake. When you return home, you're going to need an excuse. And what's your excuse? The Israelis are no good. Because, if it was so good in Israel, then why the hell aren't you there? Why did you return home?

"So don't tell people you're coming to stay. And when the relatives come to visit for the next twenty years, tell them you'll stick around until Pesach.

"It's like the last war when one of the soldiers said to his buddy, 'Yitzoch, it's only a matter of days before we get released...one hundred days...two hundred days...'"

More laughter from the audience.

"So, you're sticking around until Pesach…this Pesach…next Pesach… every Pesach. You'll find that it will be easier to live here because you'll have a way out. And, while you're waiting, you can fight and win. But believe me, winning is not easy. It is a long and slow process. But it can be done.

"Look, there's this story I tell. A guy is stranded on an island. He gets rescued and the rescuer sees that the guy has built two synagogues on the island. 'Why,' he asks, 'are there two synagogues?' The man replies, 'That one, I don't go.'

"Let's go one step further. A guy like you or me, we come to Israel. We have a dream, and we've made a commitment. We stick around a few years. We beat our heads against the wall…suffer unbelievable problems and say to ourselves, 'if there were two Israels, this one I wouldn't go.' But since there's only one Israel, and I want it to be a good Israel, I'm sticking around. And that's the challenge—making this country the kind of place we would like it to be."

Daniel was beginning to perspire. He felt a tingling in the palms of his hands as if he had been sitting on them for a while and cut off the blood supply. He remembered feeling like this once before. It was in high school, and the doctor said he was having an anxiety attack. Daniel was acutely aware of the pounding of his heart. He could feel himself getting clammy. He wondered, *Am I having another anxiety attack? Maybe I am having a heart attack.*

The speaker continued. "We have a terrible emotional climate now. Many people have been killed in wars, the intifada, and the terrorism.

It's a tragedy. To add to the difficulty, they raise the prices of goods and services every day. Inflation. So, what's new? Economically, it's a tough time. Militarily, it's tough. No matter what they tell us is a great line of defense, the Suez Canal is the best line of defense.

"Okay, so we're put in a bind. We're here. If you're single, you'll go into the army, and though that will be difficult, it will be one of the best experiences you will have. You'll feel like you're participating in the life of the country. In spite of the troubles outside, the bureaucracy in the army still works. You do get your gun."

Army? Go into the army? Hershel didn't say anything about an army. Daniel's mouth was dry. He needed a drink of water. He felt completely out of place. *What am I doing here? I don't belong here.* He wanted to bolt, to run away. But he knew if he did then Mikey would be right. Even Sarah would have been right. He remembered he had felt this way before, the first few days he attended Theophilus. He didn't run away then, and he wasn't going to run away now. He wasn't a loser—not any more.

"To sum up: If you hear the Israelis say, 'We don't want you,' nonsense. Believe me, we want you. The Americans and the English, the South Africans, and the rest of us who are here making the fight—we all want you. Not because we think it's imperative that you live here with us. We won't tell you it's essential that you stay, but we would like you to stay. If you really believe in the challenge of this place and if Israel is your mission and your dream, then we want your help. Otherwise, be a tourist. Don't come thinking, this is the only place to live. It isn't. But to stay here, you've got to be ready to make the fight.

"So, if you're ready, if you're here to help us meet the challenge, to help us really make this The Promised Land, then with all my heart, I welcome you to Israel."

The speaker was finished. Daniel thought about his words as other people from WUJS were introduced and took their place on the stage. Some were there to talk, others to entertain. One girl, a student from South Africa, took out her guitar and sang about Jerusalem, the city of gold. The students were enthusiastic, the music uplifting. There was a sense of brotherhood in the air. This was a new beginning, and the experience reinforced Daniel's decision to come to Israel. Hershel had been right. Daniel was an oleh, an immigrant. He was making aliyah, and here he was in Eretz Yisra'el, the land of Israel.

But although he felt inspired by the events of the afternoon, he still wasn't sure about his decision to come to Israel. He recognized this was serious stuff. *These people mean business. This isn't fun and games.* He knew he wasn't ready or willing to go to war. He hadn't known exactly what he expected when he made the decision to come, but he was quite sure it wasn't to join the army—any army. After the orientation session concluded, he remained in his seat in a sort of daze, thinking, *I might have made a big mistake. Maybe Dad was right, and I should have bought a suit and been practical like Mikey. Maybe Mikey was right, and I am just a ridiculous man. I am a dreamer who isn't even sure what my dream is.* Then Daniel thought of Hershel sitting on a park bench feeding the squirrels. He couldn't help but smile when he thought of his friend and wished Hershel could see him now sitting here with these young pioneers. He remembered Hershel's words, "They can't make you stay. You can always leave." And Daniel thought of something else. He remembered those words that flapped on a banner outside of the tabernacle building: "To the weak and the timid, all things seem impossible."

Chapter 12
Ulpan

After a week at the WUJS institute, Daniel's overriding impression of Israel was that it was cold. Arad was a planned city in the Negev Desert. Daniel had never been to a desert, but from all he recalled from school and television, he thought deserts were supposed to be hot. He was wrong, because in January, in Israel, the Negev Desert was cold. A dusting of snow currently fell from the sky.

The word *apartment* didn't begin to describe Daniel's living arrangement. It actually was more like a dorm room, which made those at Theophilus seem luxurious. The buildings in the city were constructed to withstand the extreme desert heat which apparently was due to arrive sometime later. The cement walls and floors trapped cool air that was so needed in summer. A grille in the bottom half of the apartment door allowed ventilation and represented to Daniel a promising hint of the heat to come. In the meantime, Daniel and his roommate taped cardboard over the grille and huddled around a kerosene heater, the only source of heat. Two or three times a day they opened the front door and fanned the air to clear out the kerosene fumes. It would be ludicrous, Daniel thought, to come to Israel and die from carbon monoxide poisoning.

Daniel realized his life was now sparser than it had ever been before. Food and heat were the main concerns of each day. He dressed for warmth by wearing several layers of clothing and berated himself for not planning better before coming. Some of the students were prepared for the cold with heavy coats and sweaters. The Russian immigrants were the best dressed for the climate, although they had very little in material possessions. *Who ever heard of snow in the holy land?* Daniel wondered. *Wasn't Jesus always walking around in sandals and sleeping under olive trees?* All his time at Theophilus, Daniel never saw a picture of Jesus dressed in a snow suit. And where were the olive trees? Aside from the city itself (which was only a few square blocks of housing, stores, and the absorption center) there was nothing here—absolutely nothing for as far as he could see—except rocks. The students had been warned not to wander into the desert because it was easy to get lost in the nothingness. The wadi's could fill up with water and become treacherous. If it rained, a wadi, which Daniel learned was a dry stream bed, could become a raging torrent that could easily sweep someone away. Then there was the matter of the other inhabitants out in the desert, Bedouins who shared the nothingness and weren't friendly. If they came upon students walking in the desert, they would throw stones at them. It was best, the students were warned, to walk in groups and stay within sight of town. For Daniel, that wasn't a problem. He didn't want to go anywhere except to the dining hall for meals.

Meals were reduced to a basic level. Herschel, he mused, was right; food was provided free—three meals a day, but who wanted to eat this stuff? The menu was sparse. There were eggs, toast, and grits for breakfast. Lunch was usually soup or mystery-stew with lentils or beans, rumored to be made from camel or goat. There was bread and sometimes fruit. Meat was occasionally served at dinner. Sometimes, if there was no fresh fruit, dessert consisted of one small square of chocolate with coffee. It was a pathetic desert. Daniel hadn't been expecting gourmet food, but

Hershel had created the impression it would be better than what was being offered. Some students cooked in their rooms using a hot plate. Daniel owned two aluminum pots which were left behind by previous students. The pans worked with the large jar of instant coffee he had brought with him. Grocery items at the ulpan were limited and expensive. Daniel had purchased a few cans of soup and a box of saltines, making a dent in his budget. Perhaps his mother would send some of the items he had requested in his letter. Peanut butter and Ritz Crackers were at the top of the list. His roommate had already received a box of goodies from home, which Daniel coveted.

Daniel's assigned roommate was Norman Silverman, an intense young fellow from Philadelphia who was always reading. Norman, like many of the WUJS students, was fresh out of graduate school. He was younger than Daniel by six years, filled with idealism, but light on practical experience. At thirty years of age, Daniel felt old and somewhat out of place. Of course, Daniel had always felt out of place, so in this regard things weren't that unusual. The ulpan was a part of a resettlement program that housed a diverse group of refugees, all trying to learn Hebrew and gain their foothold in the promised land.

Norman was a big complainer against the Russians and their table manners—or lack of manners. Russians took more than their share of food, leaving others at the table with empty plates. In fact, Daniel usually sat next to Norman in the dining hall to be assured he would get a fair shot at filling his plate. Norman was a large, burly man who wouldn't tolerate being short-changed at a meal. Unfortunately, a shared interest in the equitable distribution of food was about the only thing Daniel and Norman had in common. Imagine plaids and polka dots on the same outfit. That was Daniel and Norman, constantly clashing and colliding. Although

Daniel didn't like Norman, he liked to taunt him because Norman didn't have much of a sense of humor, and he was so damn serious.

"You're a racist, Norman. What did those Russians ever do to you?"

"You can't trust them, and they steal food."

"You probably hate Black people, too."

"No I don't."

"They're Russians, for heaven sake. They're impoverished. Look what they've been through. Where's your compassion?

"Yeah, you're right. I'm going to do better," Norman apologized.

Norman was a larger man than Daniel, but not much taller—just beefier. With his lumpish frame, thick coarse hair and round face, Daniel thought he resembled a sheepdog crossed with a horse's ass. Norman held his head high, with his nose slightly elevated as he walked and looked down at the world through tortoise-shell frames. He reminded Daniel of the way peafowl walked around on his grandmother's farm. The birds heads bobbing up and down. Daniel could imagine how the bird evolved from a dinosaur like a velociraptor. Norman probably did, too.

Norman's side of the bedroom was filled with preppy clothes: Van Huesen button-down shirts, sweaters, and corduroy slacks. Mikey would have been proud of Norman's wardrobe, although Daniel thought it was like putting a suit on Bigfoot. Norman and Daniel each had a cabinet to serve as their closet, positioned in the middle of the sleeping area so as to afford them each some privacy. As a result, the quarters were cramped, and when Daniel lay down to sleep on his single cot, he felt like he was tucking himself into a bathtub. There was no actual bathtub in their flat (which is how the Australians and South Africans referred to the living quarters). The bathroom was a cement room completely lacking in beauty or comfort. It was Daniel's least favorite room. Against one wall stood a toilet and a sink; a shower-head sprouted out of the opposite wall. Everything was gray and dingy except for the white towels on either side of the sink and the face that looked out from the mirror when Daniel shaved or brushed his teeth. The shower drain was in the middle of the floor, and whenever someone showered, the whole floor flooded and the toilet got wet.

In the living room/study area there was a small dining table with chairs, two study desks, shelving, a couple of foam-covered platforms for lounging, and a coffee table. Norman had filled the living area with his personal belongings. He was a philosophy major who fancied himself a poet. He explained to Daniel he needed his books—couldn't live without books. "They are the air I breathe and the blood that flows through my veins."

Daniel was impressed with Norman's collection and couldn't help but wonder how he managed to bring so much stuff with him. The clothes, books, posters, French cigarettes, candles, flashlights, expensive after-shave, and the never ending supply of Kipper snack tins and crackers—it was enough to make Daniel wish he actually liked his roommate. Unfortunately he found Norman to be an intellectual phony. But Norman was serious about Israel and Zionism in particular. He loved to talk about the Holocaust and the next catastrophe that would inevitably befall the Jewish people.

"Only constant vigilance," he said, "will keep another holocaust from happening again." Norman was suspicious of the Russians. He suspected the ones at the ulpan might be part of an espionage ring whose goal was to infiltrate and undermine Israel's security. Norman also suspected some Scandinavian guy who was studying Hebrew with Norman's class. He believed the Scandinavian probably worked for the CIA. Norman's face actually glowed when he speculated about the supposedly secret nuclear plant at Dimona and what plan of action should be taken if the ulpan came under attack by Arabs. He had drawn a diagram of the city and ulpan with various paths of entry and vulnerable points coded in red. He already knew Hebrew, so while Daniel struggled in class trying to learn the most basic words, Norman sailed into the advanced group and spent most of his days either wandering around town or lounging with his books and charts, bugging Daniel and anyone else who would listen.

Norman reminded Daniel of the zealots he had encountered in Theophilus—those who considered themselves soldiers in the army of God, fighting the forces of evil. *Which was fine,* Daniel thought. He had no problem with zealots except that they always wanted to recruit others and draw them into their paranoia. Norman was no different. He craved affirmation and sought fellow travelers. But mostly he was just a big pain in the ass who wanted an audience for whom he could play out his vision.

Beware of zealots, Daniel thought as he glanced at his bookish roommate. It was then he realized that most of the other students were more like Norman than they were like him, Daniel. Not that they were zealots, but they were committed. They had come to Israel to take a stand—to be part of something bigger than themselves. They believed, and they were on a mission. Under the circumstances, Daniel had to admit Norman was behaving appropriately; it was he, Daniel, who was the odd man out. Not, that Daniel wasn't serious. He wanted to be serious, but he had come for an adventure, not a mission. He had been bored and unemployed, looking for something to do. Daniel thought, *What is the difference between an adventure and a mission? It must have something to do with commitment versus entertainment. Do I have the commitment for a mission? Probably not.* It had only been two weeks and Daniel was already having second thoughts. Last night he had awakened, needing to urinate, but feeling too cold to get out of bed. So he lay awake suffering. *Boy, did I make a mistake in coming to this place.*

* * *

It was Sunday and snowing outside. After breakfast, Daniel and Norman returned to the flat. There wasn't anything to do until later in the afternoon when a showing of the movie *Shaft* was scheduled in the recreation hall. The apartment as usual was cold, and Daniel cursed the heater as he prepared coffee.

"It doesn't put out any heat! All it does is make everything smell bad," he complained. "I can't get the smell of kerosene off my hands or clothes."

"I hope you didn't come to Israel to smell good," snapped Norman.

"No," Daniel replied, "I came for the cuisine. I like eating cardboard."

"This is an *ulpan*," Norman continued, "not a hotel. What did you expect?"

"I don't know," Daniel whined. "Not this. I didn't expect this. Look at me. I've lost five pounds. My clothes are getting baggy, and I'm always hungry."

Norman returned to the book he was reading in Yiddish by Isaac Bashevas Singer and nodded, "You need to lose weight. Maybe you should practice some Hebrew. Then you could go to town and buy some new clothes and a falafel."

Clothes again. First Mikey, and now this asshole. What is it with me and clothes? I can't look that bad. There was no question about it, Daniel was not having the rewarding experience he hoped for. The bad food, the uncomfortable living conditions, and a roommate he detested all contributed to his miserable situation. But the worst part was his inability to learn Hebrew. Norman was right; he should be practicing Hebrew. Not that it would do any good. He was totally confounded by the language.

At the ulpan they used an immersion, or sink-or-swim technique in which the instructor would only speak Hebrew. The problem was if you didn't understand what was going on you sank. There were no Jewish Indians like Big Chief Six Cats at Camp Thunder Bay to explain Hebrew, and no Grace Spindler to offer emotional support or encouragement. He tried asking Norman for help, but every time he did, Norman would simply turn the request into an opportunity to spout off about what would happen if Israel was attacked or some gibber-jabber he gleaned from the Kabala. Daniel was beginning to panic. Even among "his people," he didn't feel he belonged. It wasn't that he felt weak or timid as much as just plain stupid. He couldn't remember feeling more alone or more inept.

By the third week of language class, Daniel was wondering how he let that crazy Hasid talk him into this misadventure. He sat in Hebrew class feeling anxious and sorry for himself. His heart raced, and he felt the perspiration run down his forehead. He remembered something the speaker from the orientation session had said: "Don't come to Israel to live a normal life. This isn't the place to be normal."

Why not? He wondered. *What's wrong with normalcy?* All Daniel ever really wanted was to fit in and be normal. But he couldn't be normal here, not in this place.

He came to Israel to find his people. But after three weeks in the Land of Milk and Honey, he thought he might be lactose intolerant. Could Norman really be "his people?" He didn't think so.

Daniel sat in class and began to contemplate an escape plan. What would he say to everyone if he returned home? He could see Mikey in his mind's eye, saying, "I told you so, Daniel. You went to Israel and learned you were a shmuck. I could have told you that and saved you a lot of time and trouble."

While Daniel was thinking about Mikey, he noticed a girl on the other side of the classroom. She had brown hair, shoulder-length and curly. Her eyes were large and dark, and she had sensuous, full lips. Her olive complexion looked tanned, like she spent a lot of time outdoors. Most interesting to Daniel, besides her good looks, was she seemed to be struggling as much as he was with Hebrew. She kept making faces as if to say, "What is this? I don't understand?" The other students ignored her, as did Rebecca the Hebrew instructor who smelled so unpleasant. But Daniel found the girl's expressions adorable, and he became completely distracted by her antics. He felt himself relax as he watched her grimace and squint.

They had been in class together for three weeks, but Daniel had not paid much attention to her or anyone else because he was trying so hard to be serious-minded and learn the language. But now he was discouraged and ready to go home. He had all but stopped expecting to learn anything. Just watching this girl and knowing he wasn't suffering alone made him feel better. After class he approached her and introduced himself. She was friendly and smiled. She said her name was Mia Murphy.

"I don't know what I'm doing here. I just graduated from U.C.L.A. Coming to WJUS seemed like a good idea, but now I have my doubts. What about you? Where did you go to school?"

"I went to Theophilus College," Daniel replied.

"Was that named after a falafel? Is it like McDonald's Hamburger University?"

"Theophilus, not falafelous. The name is Greek. It means friend of God."

"Oh, I see. I don't believe I've ever heard of that school," Mia said.

"It is a church supported college… like Xavier or Tulane."

"My father went to Xavier." She seemed satisfied with Daniel's answer.

"Are you getting this language stuff?" Daniel continued.

Mia shook her head and looked pained. "Not really. I had no idea Hebrew would be so difficult to learn."

"That's the way I feel. I'm from Tennessee, but I grew up in New York. I'm not good with languages," he blurted out. "In fact, when I was in high school, I failed Spanish."

Mia smiled. "That's an achievement," she said.

"Yes, I wasn't very good. We were reading dialogue one day in class, and the teacher asked me which person was speaking. I had no idea what she was talking about. She glared and demanded, 'Is it the first person speaking? Is it the third person? Who? Mr. Fisher, which person is doing the speaking?' I panicked. I didn't know what to say, so I guessed 'fourth person?' Well, the whole class started to laugh, and I thought Mrs. Gonzales was going to throw an embolism right then and there. She probably thought I was being a smart-ass. To make a long story short, I failed Spanish. I always thought it was because I had a bad teacher. I never liked Mrs. Gonzales, and she never liked me, but now I think maybe languages just aren't my thing."

"What *is* your thing, Daniel—since you find yourself in a language class again?" Mia seemed to be teasing him, but her smile was warm and friendly, and it made him feel good.

"I'm not sure. But I'm in trouble if I don't do better here than I did in high school Spanish."

"I guess so. But you're not alone. I am having a terrible time. You know what they say about misery loving company."

Daniel inquired, "Mia, can I ask a personal question? Isn't Murphy an Irish name? I mean, it's not a Jewish name, is it?"

"No, it's not," she replied. Smiling, she gathered her study materials. "If you're asking whether or not I'm Jewish, yes, I am. My mother was a Feldman—that's certainly Jewish enough, isn't it?" Then she turned and walked away.

Damn. I must have offended her, Daniel thought. Then, *I like this girl. She is perky and cute.*

Hebrew wasn't any easier after he met Mia, but it was a lot more tolerable. He no longer sat in class and thought about going home. The two quickly established a bond based on failure, frustration, and a feeling of being out of place. They had been assigned to Aleph class, named for the first letter of the Hebrew alphabet because this class was for beginners, people with no prior knowledge of Hebrew, or those who were having an exceptionally hard time learning the language. That included a few others like Mia and Daniel who just seemed incapable of learning. They would have been reassigned to an Aleph-minus class if there had been one.

As he struggled day after day with Hebrew, Daniel wondered how he would be able to live in a country where he couldn't even speak the language. During breaks, he and Mia talked, mostly about food. "I dreamed I ate a cheeseburger last night," Mia would confess, "at McDonalds," and then describe the condiments on it. Daniel would counter with a description of some other culinary delight. Sometimes after class they would go off together to town looking for something to eat. Mia joked that when she left the institute she was going to get rich writing a book about The WUJS Diet. "You're guaranteed to lose weight."

Daniel enjoyed Mia. He had never known another girl quite like her. They were very similar. She had a weird sense of humor, and often when she shared her thoughts and ideas, she was expressing exactly what Daniel was thinking. She was also a consummate whiner—almost as good as he was. Mia's sense of smell was keen, like a bloodhound. Whenever they went to town together, she could sniff out food. Together they discovered a place that served French fries and another that made a bizarre tasting pizza that had eggplant topping. Mia noticed immediately whenever Daniel smelled of kerosene. She also observed that the language teacher, Rebecca, perspired profusely when the students frustrated her with their inability to comprehend the language.

"Have you noticed how badly Rebecca smells?"

"You mean her perspiration problem?" Daniel answered. "It's hard not to notice. She's strong...pungent."

"It's only February," Mia continued. "Can you image what it's going to be like in June?"

"In June?"

"Yeah. If she's pungent now, she's going to stink in June. It won't make learning Hebrew easier."

"Nothing will make Hebrew easier. It's hopeless. A stinky teacher won't make a difference. But, thank you, Mia, for sharing you observations concerning Rebecca's odor."

They both laughed.

By March, the two students were inseparable. They attended all the afternoon discussion sessions, which were designed to fortify the determination of the new immigrants. Many of the guest speakers referred to the problems of living in a new country and being frustrated by the bureaucracy, the language, the food, the people—everything. The talks were filled with humorous anecdotes about immigrants who nearly lost their sanity trying to adjust to the living conditions of their adopted homeland.

One lecture focused on finding future employment in Israel. After class as they walked to Daniel's apartment, he and Mia discussed what the speaker had said—"In Israel, you can't make a living, but you can make a life."

"What the hell does that mean? 'You can't make a living, but you can make a life.' What kind of life can you have if you can't make a living?" Daniel asked.

"A bad life," Mia answered. "But, remember, you shouldn't come here if you want a normal life. A life of poverty and hardship is an inconvenience, a trifle, to a person on a mission. Are you on a mission, Daniel?"

"I suppose. I have to keep reminding myself that's why I'm here."

When they reached Daniel's apartment, Norman informed them they were out of kerosene. Deliveries had been delayed because the army needed the fuel.

"Oh shit! What about us? Don't they know its cold outside?" Daniel was wearing several layers of clothing. Because of the temperature, he slept fully dressed. He wasn't even sure when he last changed. "When's it going to get warm?" he asked. "I thought it was supposed to be hot. We're in the desert for heaven's sake."

"You're always thinking about your creature comforts," Norman observed. "This isn't a resort, you know. You're not in the Catskills. Some people come here for serious study. They come to immerse themselves in the Jewish state, remember? What kind of a Jew are you?"

"A cold Jew," answered Daniel.

"Yeah, and hungry. You're always walking around town looking for food when you should be attending class. You missed yesterday's talk by Meir Kahane."

"Who's that?" Daniel asked.

"Only the most important Jew in Israel today. He is the rabbi from Brooklyn who founded the Jewish Defense League."

"What's that?" Daniel asked.

"Christ, Fisher. Your ignorance never fails to astonish me."

Fuck you, too," Daniel answered, taking Mia by the hand and walking out of the apartment.

The next day the water heater died quietly, and now there was no hot water. Daniel hadn't been showering frequently because of the cold weather. But knowing that he could shower if he wanted to was reassuring. Now he was really discouraged.

"You never know what you have until you lose it," he said.

Norman just shrugged. Mia, who was there again visiting Daniel, took him by the hand and said softly, "Daniel, you could use a shower."

Daniel should have realized that with Mia's nose, he couldn't escape detection indefinitely. "I could? You mean the kerosene?"

"No, the goat. Actually, you're beginning to compete with Rebecca and, as you know, she's in the process of decomposition. I should have told you earlier, but I didn't know how to do it without hurting your feelings. I was waiting for the right time. Maybe this is it, one of those teachable moments I learned about in college. I majored in education. Why don't you come to my flat and use my shower until your water heater is repaired? And I can wash your clothes. That would help. I plan to do laundry this afternoon."

"Thank you, Mia. You're very sweet." Daniel was so embarrassed he felt like crying. His eyes actually started to water.

"Not really. I spend most of my time with you. I'm only thinking of myself. I'm not fond of goats."

Daniel rubbed his eyes. He was thinking, *This is where my quest has led me. I'm cold, hungry, and I smell like a goat.* He looked over at Norman who had a stupid grin on his face.

"You could wash my clothes," Norman said.

Mia just looked at him without answering. Later, at Mia's flat after Daniel had showered and changed clothes, he and Mia decided to go to town to look for food. They shared a pizza with strange stuff on the top and walked back to Mia's apartment holding hands. When Daniel arrived at Mia's door, he kissed her.

She returned his kiss and gave him a hug. "I hope you have a better day tomorrow," she said. "Try and get some sleep… think positively."

Chapter 13

Reluctant Pilgrims

In April, the weather in Israel changed, and suddenly it was warm. Daniel and Mia began skipping Hebrew class and going on excursions or studying together while soaking up sun. They carried their pocket dictionaries with them, and in the town they found enough people who spoke English to get by. The two learned the words in Hebrew for "peace," "toilet," "ice cream," and the number "seven-and-a-half," all words important for survival.

Norman remained totally frustrated with Daniel, complaining that Daniel didn't study enough. "If you spent as much time studying as you do chasing that woman, you'd know Hebrew. I can't believe you let a woman lead you around. It's like you have a ring through your nose."

"Lead me around? She doesn't lead me anywhere. Besides, I already know three words of Hebrew. Would you like to hear them?"

"Look at you. You're pathetic. You can't speak. You cut class. All you want to do is hang around with Mia and whine. The two of you are Mr. and Mrs. Whiner. You're given this wonderful opportunity, and you piss it away."

"Oh gee... you think so? I'm sorry."

The name caught on, and as Daniel and Mia would enter the classroom or dining hall, other students would call out "Hey! It's Mr. and Mrs. Whiner." Daniel and Mia would smile and bow and say, "We are foraging for food."

"If you had lived during the Holocaust," Norman said, "you'd know suffering. Then you'd have something to complain about. Your attitude disgusts me."

"I understand," Daniel said. "I'm sure I'll never know suffering like you do Norman, with all your designer clothes and snack food. Why don't you share with us how much you've suffered?"

"Fuck you," Norman hissed. Daniel sometimes felt a guilty sense of pleasure for provoking Norman. *I'm getting like Mikey,* Daniel thought. But it seemed vulgar that Norman would exploit the Holocaust to make some mundane point. Daniel realized he didn't know what real suffering was. He wasn't that cavalier, but not having the right topping on a slice of pizza was a good place to start. Feeling dirty and incapable of learning the language helped—or sharing a flat with a horse's ass like Norman.

In a perverse way, Daniel enjoyed his role as part of the team of Mr. and Mrs.Whiner. It was a dubious distinction, but it set them apart and gave them an identity. He finally knew who he was. Daniel confessed to Mia that the two of them were probably the best complainers in the absorption center, maybe even the whole community of Arad. And that was saying something, because there were some Russian immigrants who were really adept at complaining. Anybody could see these people were truly unhappy. Daniel might not understand them, but he could tell they were plenty pissed off.

One day as Daniel and Mia walked to their favorite falafel stand, they saw a man waving his arms and talking to himself. As they got closer to the stand, they heard him rant in English. He was obviously upset. Daniel and Mia assumed he was American since he was talking in English. They stopped a few feet away, and when the stranger seemed to have calmed, Daniel asked, "Is something wrong?"

The man stared at him for several seconds. "Wrong? What's wrong? I was trying to explain something to this falafel salesman, but he doesn't speak English. And why should he? This isn't America, this is Palestine. So it's not what's wrong, because everything is wrong. What you should be asking is what's right."

"Okay," Daniel said, "what's right?"

"Nothing. Nothing is fucking right."

The stranger took a sip from his canteen and seemed to regain some composure.

Then he put the cap back on the canteen and introduced himself as Harvey. Daniel offered to buy Harvey a falafel, and after he did, the three sat down at one of the outdoor café tables. After eating, Harvey began to tell his story.

He was born in New York, but his parents were from Finland. As a young adult, he had moved to the Republic of Finland where he met and married his wife, Olga. They settled in Helsinki, and he became a Finnish citizen.

"Last September," he continued, "my wife and I decided to immigrate to Israel with our two-year-old son and our year-old daughter, so that I could expand on my international resume. Like all Finns who have never been here before, I tended to romanticize Israel almost to the point of hallucination.

"As an inducement to come to this place, we were told we would be given free land in Arad, if only we would build a house on it. A house, incidentally, they said we could furnish tax-free at any time within three years of our arrival."

"You were committed," Daniel said. "You were on a mission."

Mia brought three coffees back to the table.

"Yes, I suppose you could say that." Harvey nodded an acknowledgement to Mia and took a sip. "Anyway, it all sounded marvelous, even if none of it was true. Relying on this pack of lies, I quit my job, sold our house, and came to Arad with my wife, my children, my car, and enough clothing and other crap to start a new life, not to mention a couple thousand pounds of house-building tools."

"Boy," Mia said. "How do you get a car to Israel?"

"You drive," Harvey said sarcastically. "By ship, of course. Anyway, our first shock on arriving was to learn that there is no free land and hasn't been for years. What land is available is for sale at prohibitively high prices.

"As it turned out, it was all moot, anyway. The law had been changed retroactively, so we wouldn't be allowed to bring in any tax-free goods after December 31st, even if there had been free land to build the house on.

"And then, of course, our papers weren't in order—at least Olga's weren't—which is why we...my family...my precious children ended up occupying a tent in the middle of the Negev."

Harvey paused and took another long sip of coffee. He looked like he might cry. "You see, I'm classified as an immigrant, but my wife and children are classified as tourists. So while I'm allowed to live in one kitchen-less room, my family must stay in a *plastic tent,*" his voice started to rise again, "where the temperature in winter rises to fifty degrees centigrade during the day and drops to sixteen degrees at night."

He slammed the cup on the table.

"The fact that our papers weren't in order because of the Israeli bureaucrats' stupidity is of no apparent importance. That I have given up my job, sold our home, moved my family from Helsinki to this development town in the middle of the desert and exhausted our savings by relying on misinformation from government officials is of no apparent importance."

"How awful," Daniel said.

"Well, yes. I became angry...bitter. In fact, I was losing my will to live. So I started writing letters to everybody, especially to the newspapers— most of which they won't print. That's how the rumors that I'm a spy got started. People began saying, 'He came here to stir up discontent so the Russians would leave.' Of course, my letters are all in English, in the English-language newspapers, which the Russians don't read anyway, but that's a minor point. I'm a secret agent now, and the fact that I don't speak Russian just shows how clever I am."

"Wait a minute," Daniel interrupted. "Have you been studying Hebrew at WUJS?"

"Yes."

"You're the spy! I heard about you from my roommate. You're the Scandinavian spy he's been talking about!"

"Your roommate must be a clever fellow."

"Not as clever as he thinks he is."

"I'm sure. Anyway, my wife got a magazine in the mail from her mother. It was one of those women's magazines that have fashion and home decorating articles. We were actually reading it and discussing ways to decorate our tent. Our tent! Just think of it—we are beginning to think of this tent as home. I tell you, if I stay here much longer, I'll go crazy."

He continued, "I write letters. I keep saying, 'Dear so-and-so, do you have any idea how really bad it is here? I'm sure none of your Sabra friends will tell you. You might, however, reflect on the thought that a person who has spent his whole life in Israel simply doesn't know any better. And I'm also sure that a few Eastern immigrants will tell you it's not so bad. Of course, to someone who has spent his life conversing with goats, Israel must look pretty good. What I'm suggesting is that you have a little chat with a Western immigrant or two—especially one with a college education. However offended I may be by the insolence, arrogance, and stupidity of your bureaucracy in general and the Ministry of Absorption in particular, this is nothing compared with how I feel about the way I was systematically misled and misinformed by both the Israeli Embassy and the Jewish Agency in Finland.

"And that's why, at the first opportunity, I'm taking my wife, my children, my education, and myself away from my sweltering tent and this desert as soon as I can. I'm finished." He looked at Daniel and Mia and in a calm voice said, "My advice to the two of you is to do the same thing before you can't get out. This country is the tar baby."

Having ended his story, Harvey stood up and shook their hands. "Thank you, people, for the falafel and the company, and for giving me the opportunity to express my rage." Then he turned and headed off across the desert in the direction of his tent. Daniel and Mia were silent as they watched Harvey disappear behind an outcropping of rock.

"Wow," Mia said. "I've never seen a better whiner. He's an artist."

"I'll say," replied Daniel. "I wonder if anything he said is true. How do you think he supports himself and his family?"

"I don't know, but talking about employment," Mia asked, "have you thought about finding a job when the institute is over? You know, it won't be long now, and we will be finished with our course of study."

"I have an interview at the Dead Sea Works next week."

Mia smiled a broad smile and chuckled. "To do what?"

"I'm not sure. Something. Shoveling salt or whatever one does at the Dead Sea Works."

"How long do you think you'll last in salt?" Mia was laughing now.

"Maybe a long time. Salt is a good preservative."

"If you're a codfish! I don't think it's going to preserve you, Daniel. I can't see you doing manual labor...in salt, pepper, or even oregano."

"To be honest, I can't either, But I'm desperate. Jobs are scarce, especially when you can't speak the language. What else can I do?"

They got up and began walking toward the town square. The sun felt warm and comforting on their backs and cast long shadows making them look like giants. Then Mia said, "You know Daniel, you can't speak Hebrew at all. You can't really get by on three words."

"I know," Daniel replied. "It's a problem. Can I ask you something?"

"Sure."

"Remember when I first met you. I asked about your last name being an Irish name? You said your mother's name was Feldman. So your mother is Jewish, but your dad isn't?"

"That's right. My father's Catholic. I used to go to Mass with him when I was little. My mom is Jewish."

"You went to Mass with your dad, but you think of yourself as Jewish?"

"Yes. Technically I am Jewish. Judaism uses matrilineal descent. I'm Jewish because my mother is Jewish, even though I went to Mass instead of synagogue. I was raised in an interfaith family."

"Did you consider yourself Jewish as a child?"

"Sometimes yes, but other times I didn't. Like I said, I went to Mass with my dad. Those were happy times."

"Why did you come to WUJS?"

Mia shrugged. "I don't know. I guess I always felt part of me was Jewish. When I attended college at Berkeley, I saw some anti-Israel sentiment, and it bothered me. I thought maybe it was time to take a stand and make a journey of self-discovery. I really wasn't into the immigration thing so much, but I figured who knows? I could change my mind. I thought the institute would be a good experience. My parents weren't too crazy about the idea, especially my dad. But I was sort of floundering, and it was something to do. What about you? Why did you come?"

"It wasn't to expand on my international resume, like that Harvey fellow. I don't have an international resume. In fact, my resume isn't impressive. I was an insurance adjuster and a teacher, and I didn't do those jobs very well. Like you, my parents also had a mixed marriage. My father is Jewish, but he doesn't practice Judaism. As far as I know, he never has. But I did have a bar mitzvah once. I figured that should count for something. So I reasoned it gave me the credentials to say I was Jewish when I applied to WUJS. I might not have been completely honest."

"What type of synagogue was your bar mitzvah held in?"

"A reform synagogue on Long Island."

"I don't think that counts. I mean here in Israel. I don't think they would recognize a ceremony done by a reform congregation. It needs to be done by an orthodox synagogue. But even so, that alone wouldn't make you Jewish. Since your mother isn't Jewish. You would need to convert. To be a valid conversion in Israel, it would have to be an Orthodox rabbi who performed the ceremony. I'm afraid you're out of luck, Daniel. You're not Jewish. But I suppose you can say you are and be a secular Jew."

"I don't know what I should do. I was on leave from my job and was recovering from an injury. I had a little extra money, and it seemed if I ever was going to travel this was the time. I met this Hasidic man, and he told me about the institute. He got me all worked up. Said it was a great opportunity and convinced me I would find my people. I thought it would be sort of like going to the Caribbean, like taking a cruise. Only this one would have more purpose."

"Did he know you weren't technically Jewish?"

"Not really. I told him my dad was Jewish and that I had a bar mitzvah. I didn't mention my mother."

"So naturally he assumed…"

"Yeah, I suppose. I also told him I had been conking my soul, spiritually speaking."

"You had been doing what?"

"It's a little hard to explain. It's a theory I came up with when I was reading *The Autobiography of Malcolm X.* It's about making straight hair from curly hair using lye."

"That's interesting. So now what? Do you plan to stay and make *aliyah?* Are you really going to take a job at the salt works? You're not that crazy, are you?"

Daniel turned toward her and smiled. There was a little crease right between her eyebrows, and she looked earnest and concerned for his welfare. He felt warm inside, just watching her.

"Seriously, Daniel. Do you want to stay in Israel?"

"I don't know. Probably not. Hershel, my friend the Hasid, may have talked me into coming—and I'll always be grateful for that—but I don't think I found what he was expecting me to find. I certainly didn't find my people or my homeland like he thought I would." They stopped walking and both looked around, deciding which way to go. Then they turned left, and began walking toward the small park in the center of the plaza.

"Actually, to be honest," Daniel continued, "what I found here in Israel is something better than I was looking for."

"What is that?" Mia asked.

"You."

Mia stopped in her tracks and looked at Daniel. "Me?"

They locked eyes, and Daniel nodded. "Yes. If I hadn't come to Israel, I never would have met you. And then I never would have the chance to marry you."

"Marry me?" Mia looked a bit uncomfortable. "Is this before or after you go to the Dead Sea Works?"

"I'm serious, Mia. I've never met anyone like you. You're the best. Being with you feels so natural and easy. I can't imagine not being with you. I think I'd feel empty. What I'm trying to say, Mia, is I love you. Will you marry me?"

She paused as if to give the matter thought. Daniel wondered if she was really thinking or just delaying giving him bad news. But then she looked up and smiled. "Yes, Daniel, of course I'll marry you." And she threw her arms around him, almost knocking him over. "Where should we get married? Do you want to marry here or back home?"

"That depends." Daniel asked. "Where do you want home to be? Do you want a normal life or are you still up for the challenge?"

"To be honest, I think I prefer a normal life—a normal life with my parents in attendance at my wedding. And with normal pizza. I don't care for eggplant on pizza, and I'm not too crazy about falafel, even if I don't show it. I don't know about you, but I feel like I've done enough of the pioneering thing. I love Israel, but I don't want to live here, not permanently. I really don't think I'm strong enough for that challenge."

"Me, either," Daniel confessed. "I've had enough adventure. Let's go home and get married. Let's have a good, old-fashioned, pepperoni pizza."

"That's a terrific idea," said Mia. "But I was looking forward to the trip to the Northern Galilee that's scheduled in two weeks. Do you think we could stay and visit that region before we return to the states?"

"Of course," said Daniel. They circled around the garden once and then headed back. Daniel took Mia's hand. "The weather is getting very warm," he said.

"You mean hot," Mia replied. "It's either too cold or too hot here."

"Israel is a country of extremes."

"Yes," answered Mia. "It is. You know, Daniel, it's a good thing we're both terrible at Hebrew. Otherwise we never would have met. Then who would we have complained to? There would have been no Mr. and Mrs. Whiner. I think we should name our firstborn, Alef, after our class.

Daniel laughed and stopped walking. He pulled Mia close and kissed the top of her head. Her hair had the warm tangy smell of an exotic fruit, and he nuzzled his nose a moment before he started walking again.

"Coming to Israel was the best thing I ever did. I didn't find myself... I found you. You are my people, Mia...my people and my mission. I love you."

Chapter 14

Mia's Fear

It was Friday, and Mia was running late. There had been an emergency meeting after school regarding funding, and then a trip to the grocery store because as far as she could recall there was no food for the cats in the house for the weekend. Next, there were items to pick up at the dry cleaners and then another trip back to the grocery store because she forgot to buy toothpaste. Finally, she filled the car up with gas and headed home. She would have barely enough time to rush inside and take a bath before Daniel arrived. *At least it's Friday,* Mia thought. *Thank goodness for that.*

Home for the Fishers was a stately, old Victorian, situated on the side of Missionary Ridge in Chattanooga. Their home had been neglected and in bad repair when they purchased it, but Daniel was thrilled because it was the ugliest house in a prestigious neighborhood.

"This is exactly what I've been looking for!" he proclaimed after he and Mia saw the house for the first time. "If we fix this up, we can't lose. We'll make a bundle when we sell it. Location is everything in real estate." That was two years ago, and it was the second house they bought in Chattanooga. Their first home was the one they bought after their wedding.

The wedding had been a glorious affair in Brooklyn on a cruise ship.

From one side of the ship the Manhattan skyline was visible. You could also see Ellis Island, where so many thousands of immigrants had their first glimpse of America. The wedding guests could see the Statue of Liberty off the bow. The Fishers were married by the captain of the ship, and the honeymoon was a seven-day cruise to the Caribbean that followed the ceremony. It was a gift from Mia's parents.

Shortly after their return, Daniel and Mia decided that Tennessee was the place to start their life together. They moved to Chattanooga and both landed jobs—Daniel in real estate as a salesman, and Mia as a teacher. Two years ago when they bought their current home, the plan was to fix it up and sell it for a profit. But Daniel had been right; the house was a gem. It now stood proudly beside its neighbors, as attractive as any on the street. They would show a substantial profit when they sold it, but now they couldn't bear to let it go. Most of the work they had done themselves, and it had been a labor of love. Besides, they didn't really need the money. Daniel was doing well in real estate—he was a natural—and Mia was happy teaching art at a private girls' school. Money was not a problem.

Mia pulled into the driveway and parked at the back of the house. With her arms full she entered through the back door into the large kitchen. All was quiet, except for the ticking of the grandfather clock, which they had purchased at an estate sale right after buying the house. She and Daniel loved seeking out old and unusual items for their home. They enjoyed furnishing their Victorian house with authentic period pieces to recapture the splendor of another time. But with their work schedules, it was hard to find time to relax together; weekends were usually busy for Daniel with clients calling day and night to look at houses. It was, as they say in the business, a hot market.

The grandfather clock chimed five times, and Mia glanced at her watch to confirm it was really five o'clock. As she unpacked the groceries, Rose and Henry, her two cats, wandered into the kitchen and rubbed against her legs. Rose was a delicate orange, black, and white calico; Henry had black and white fur and large white feet—he looked like he was dressed in a tuxedo with high-top sneakers. They were an attractive pair, feline counterparts for her and Daniel. They all got along well, except that Daniel didn't like sharing the bed, so whichever cat settled too close to his feet usually wound up on the floor. The animals had learned to steer clear of Daniel, and they slept entwined at Mia's end of the bed. Their affectionate greeting and sweet upturned faces brought tears to Mia's eyes. *Damn hormone pills,* she thought, as she leaned over and rubbed the top of their heads. *Better go start a bath so I can have a good cry before Daniel comes home.* Rose and Henry trotted after her, up the stairs and past the open doors to the far end of the hall and into the master suite. Mia didn't look to either side at the empty guest rooms. The term "guest rooms" was actually a euphemism. They were supposed to be children's quarters. For over a year they had been left empty. "Ghost rooms," she had complained. She and Daniel waited for children that never came. Finally, in an admission of failure, she decorated them as guest rooms. It made things less awkward.

The master suite was painted yellow and white and was usually filled with sun from the south-facing windows. Its soothing glow was always a comfort to Mia. But there was no sun today, only a stubborn grey sky that threatened rain. The bathroom was also yellow and white, with black and white floor tiles and a large claw-foot tub which befitted the Victorian décor. As Mia started her bath, Rose and Henry settled on the end of the bed and watched. She believed cats could sense sadness, because whenever she cried, they rushed to her side as if to offer assistance. The two felines stared at her intently and started to purr. *Of all days to start my period,* she thought, throwing her clothes into the hamper. Wrapped in Daniel's bathrobe with her hair gathered up in a top-knot, she headed for the tub and closed the bathroom door behind her. She knew Rose and Henry would wait, patiently watching the door until she was done and reentered the room.

When the tub was full and the air fragrant with the smell of jasmine, Mia slid her body into the warm water. She leaned back gazing, at the mountains of her kneecaps as they poked through the froth of white bubbles. It was then that she let the tears loose. The first tears were quiet and left glistening tracks on her cheeks. But this gentle flow was soon followed by a fierce cloudburst that wracked her body and contorted her face with anguish. The violence she felt inside used to scare her—it reminded her of the upheaval the earth must experience when a volcano erupted. Mia carried within her a volcano of tears. She was becoming used to these eruptions. Eventually her body would settle, and when it was over she would sooth her face with a warm washcloth. Released of tears, she would be devoid of any feeling other than the emptiness left behind—emptiness inside as vast as the canyons of time.

Today was a little worse; she was having bad cramps and she suspected the new hormone pills the doctor had prescribed were wrecking havoc with her body. The past few weeks she had cried more than usual. Anything set her off—a song on the radio, dog food commercials, even a smile from a stranger in the grocery store. She worried she might be losing her mind. What did she want more, a baby or sanity? Did she really want a baby if the process of becoming pregnant drove her nuts? Maybe. More than anything in the world she wanted to have a baby with Daniel, but she wasn't sure how much longer she could hold on.

More and more her thoughts wandered to a place she didn't want to go, to a time in the future when they would have to accept that the in vitro procedures weren't going to work—that she and Daniel would not have a baby. Quite possibly, no one would ever call her "Mommy" or Daniel "Daddy." Her heart ached with the weight of this thought. And just beyond the ache was fear. What would this mean for her and Daniel? How could they ever be complete without a child? How strong was their bond, truly? In some cultures she could be abandoned or divorced for failure to produce a child. She would be considered barren, a woman without value. She knew Daniel loved her, but was it fair to hold him to their marriage vow if she couldn't bear his child? Did she love him enough to offer him his freedom? They needed to talk, seriously, about adoption, but she couldn't bring herself to ask the question out loud, "What do you think about adopting?" She knew once the words left her lips and she looked into his eyes, she would see the answer more clearly than any reply he might give. She hoped he would say yes and that he would be sincere.

There was one more in vitro procedure left, and Mia prayed each day it would succeed. She never told Daniel about her fears or prayers. They made her feel dishonest and hypocritical. She didn't even know who she was praying to—was it the mysterious God of Israel, the One they left behind when they left the land of their forefathers? Or was it Mary, the Mother of God, whom her father prayed to? Maybe it was Jesus Christ Himself? She wasn't sure, and she didn't care. Whatever name you called God there was only one God. Of that much she was sure. After each prayer, she quickly said another prayer asking for forgiveness of her ignorance. She knew this whole ritual was ridiculous and compulsive, but she didn't know what else to do. When all else failed, pray.

Mia pulled the plug so the tub would drain and she directed her attention to tomorrow's big event. It was the ten-year reunion of Daniel's class at Theophilus College in Nashville. He was excited about it, and she didn't want to spoil the weekend for him. Grace might be there, the saintly girlfriend she had heard so much about. Grace was the perfect woman with the "laughing" eyes—whatever that meant. *Grace probably has children,* Mia thought. *She probably has a baker's dozen.* It seemed practically every female on the planet could have children except her.

Mia wished the reunion wasn't this weekend. She felt so tired that all she wanted to do was crawl into bed with Rose and Henry. Instead, she got back into Daniel's robe and headed downstairs to the kitchen, considering what to pack. She wondered if she would be meeting Grace—the one who got away. The first woman Daniel wanted to marry. How would Daniel feel? Would a small part of him still belong to Grace? Mia felt the need to make some kind of statement, to somehow demonstrate that she was a worthy and formidable woman who should be taken seriously—not the vulnerable failure she feared she might actually be. Tomorrow she must shine and make Daniel proud. It was something she could do. But first she needed just a little something from the cabinet above the dishwasher.

The kitchen was Mia's favorite room in the house. Daniel had turned it over to her, and she filled it with lots of glass and white cabinets. Almost everything in the kitchen was white, with red and black added for accent colors. The floor (tiled with black and white squares) felt cool beneath her feet as Mia moved across the room. She grabbed a small jar and shook out three aspirins, which she downed with a shot of Southern Comfort. Then she took a second shot to ready herself for her adventure.

* * *

It was a three-hour drive from Chattanooga to Nashville. Daniel and

Mia arrived Saturday afternoon and rented a room at the Holiday Inn. After a brief rest, they headed to campus for the reunion. A conference room had been prepared, and it was crowded with smiling, well-dressed people who appeared to be Daniel's age—in their early to mid-thirties. They all looked conservative; there were no flower children or bohemians. There was no alcohol, either, only red punch or coffee to drink. Mia opted for punch, which Daniel fetched and brought back to her. She stood by his side as he nodded and made small talk with a few people, while he scanned the room for familiar faces. He had told her that Grace was his only real friend at Theophilus, and it was Grace he had come to see. For about thirty minutes, Daniel and Mia wandered around, replenishing their drinks, and feeling generally uncomfortable. Then Grace appeared. Daniel stiffened and grabbed Mia's arm, pulling her with him across the room toward a single woman with drab blonde hair who was pinning her name tag to the front of a white sweater.

"Grace!" Daniel called as they approached.

The woman looked up, somewhat startled, and then smiled.

"Daniel," she spoke softly. For an instant Mia could see a flicker in her eyes and a softening of the face. But then it disappeared, and the face that greeted them seemed guarded. Plain was the first word that entered Mia's mind, and she was ashamed at the relief she felt. *What did he see in her?* There were traces of former beauty. Mia saw that Grace could still be attractive if she wanted to, but evidently she didn't.

Then Daniel put his arm around Mia and held her close. "Grace, this is Mia, my wife."

Grace smiled and took Mia's hand. "I'm so happy to meet you," she said, squeezing Mia's hand with affection. "Your husband and I are old friends."

"Is Tommy here?" Daniel asked out of politeness.

Mia watched the smile fade from Grace's face as she shook her head. "No," Grace answered. "I'm sorry, he couldn't make it. He had to stay in Guatemala on program business."

"Maybe he's at the movies," Daniel joked.

Mia wondered what he was talking about and waited for Grace's response. But if Grace understood what Daniel meant, she didn't acknowledge it.

After an awkward moment, Daniel inquired about her life. Mia listened and watched as the two caught up. Grace explained she was visiting her grandparents in Alabama, and it was only by good fortune that the reunion was being held at the same time she was in the U.S. She was spending the weekend in Murfreesboro with two friends from school named Karen and Mark. She explained that her grandparents were elderly now, and she tried to make three or four visits a year with her children to see them.

Daniel asked about the children.

"Yes. I have three children," Grace said. "Two biological children: a boy named Sam and my daughter, Evie. I adopted my other son, Joshua, after the earthquake. His parents, like so many others, were killed. They had worked at the mission where we live in Guatemala. Tommy is Assistant Director now and a program administrator. Anyway, I couldn't bear the thought of Joshua living in an orphanage, so Tommy and I adopted him."

"Wow," Daniel said. "You really did what you said. You became a missionary. So you and Tommy are serving the Lord, just like you planned."

Mia's eyebrows arched slightly. This was a side of Daniel she was unfamiliar with. She didn't say anything.

"Well," Grace paused a moment, "We are trying."

"What's it like being a missionary? What's Guatemala like?" Daniel asked. Mia could tell Daniel's enthusiasm was genuine. But Grace's responses were tepid, as drab and predictable as the clothes she was wearing. Mia thought there was a haunted, disinterested quality to Grace, and as she listened she found herself intrigued by this seemingly sad woman. There was something familiar about Grace that Mia couldn't put her finger on.

"It can be rewarding. Guatemala has lovely people and beautiful geography. Did you know about the earthquake?"

"No. What earthquake?"

"We had a terrible earthquake three years ago. That's when Joshua lost his parents. Josh is thirteen now. The country is still recovering."

"And you were there? That must have been a life-changing experience!"

"Yes, it was. In more ways than you can imagine. The earthquake affected all of us. As I said, we are still dealing with the aftermath."

"What about your other children? How old are they?"

"Sam is nine and Evie is eight."

"Amazing," Daniel said, shaking his head. "Time really flies." Then he changed the topic. "Mia and I met in Israel. We were there almost a year. It was an incredible experience, but the food wasn't very good. You know, Grace, you can't get good pizza in Israel, at least not in Arad."

"I didn't know that. Are you telling me you went to the Holy Land for pizza?"

"No, of course not. But I think it's an interesting point. The pizza in Israel is not good. They put eggplant on it. Anyway, I'm in real estate now, in Chattanooga. That's where we live."

Grace nodded. "The pizza is better in Chattanooga?"

Mia smiled at Grace's attempt at humor.

"I envy you having children, Grace. Mia and I have been trying for several years now…" His voice trailed off.

Grace glanced from Daniel to Mia, and back to Daniel again. "Don't give up," she said. "It will happen. I'm sure it will."

Daniel shrugged. "I hope so. We both checked out fine with the doctors. They haven't been able to find anything medically wrong. But here we are, just the two of us alone in our huge house. We're trying in vitro fertilization now, but so far haven't had any luck"

Grace nodded and looked concerned. "I'm sorry," she said. "I'll pray that you're successful."

"Thank you," Daniel said. "Prayers from a missionary probably work better than ordinary prayer. I hope so. Anyway, it's great seeing you again, Grace."

"Yes," Grace said, smiling at both of them. Mia thought it odd that even though Grace was smiling, there was a pained look about her face. Her eyes seemed sunken and her voice remote. It was as if she were communicating with them from a distance. And at that moment Mia understood as she was smacked full force with the shock of recognition. Like Mia, Grace was locked in her own canyon of misery. She was a woman suffering alone. *Odd,* she thought. *She is married and has children, and still she is empty.* Mia shuddered, vowing to herself that she would not let herself become lost like Grace. Whatever happened, she had Daniel. He was her husband, and he loved her. Of that she was sure. Somehow they would work things out together, children or no children. Obviously, from Grace's condition, children weren't the answer to everything.

Grace and Daniel said farewells. There was an exchange of phone numbers and talk of getting together if she had time on one of her visits home. They held hands and kissed one another's cheeks. Then Grace turned to Mia, and they kissed cheeks, too.

"It was nice to meet you," Grace said.

"The pleasure was mine," Mia replied. "I do hope you'll visit us sometime. I'd like to become friends."

Grace smiled and nodded. Then she turned and walked into the crowd.

"Do you want to stay for more refreshments?" Mia asked.

"No," Daniel answered. "There's no point. I've seen enough. I'm ready to go."

They walked back to the car in silence. Then Daniel sat a moment behind the steering wheel, as if deep in thought.

"Was Grace the way you remembered her?" Mia asked.

"Not at all. I can't imagine what happened to her in ten years to make her so... so different."

There was more silence and stillness. Then Mia said, "Tell me about Theophilus, Daniel. And what's the business about serving the Lord?"

Daniel laughed. Then he started the car and all the way back to the motel he talked—as if a dam had been broken.

"I was a lost boy, Mia. My soul was not at peace. I had failed at school and was into drugs. I guess you could say I had failed at everything. And then I found Theophilus or to be more precise, Theophilus found me. I didn't learn until years later that it was my mother who had applied on my behalf. It didn't matter. Theophilus was the best thing to ever happen to me. Until I met you—then you became the best thing. But when I was at Theophilus, I almost quit. Then I met Grace, and she befriended me. She gave me support and encouragement. She was always there for me."

The following morning on their drive back to Chattanooga Daniel continued his conversation about Theophilus. Daniel told Mia about Grace's advice that the wine mentioned in the Bible was really grape juice. He laughed when he told Mia that story. He even confessed how Grace encouraged him to become born again. Mia felt like a bridge was being constructed between the two of them, and Daniel was moving some of his memories over to her side. She welcomed his memories. They would help fill the emptiness.

Later when Daniel was all talked out and they had arrived home, Mia asked Daniel to sit in the kitchen. She had something she wanted to say. "I've been wondering about the in vitro."

He looked at her and cocked his head to one side. She loved this expression. It was the one he used when he wasn't sure what was coming next, and he was braced for the unexpected.

"What if it doesn't work?" Mia continued.

Daniel didn't respond. He just sat there with his head tilted. Thinking. Waiting.

"What about the idea of adopting?" Mia asked.

Then she saw it. His face held the answer she had prayed she would see.

Daniel smiled. "I've been wanting to talk about adoption."

That night before going to sleep Mia said one simple prayer: "Thank you Lord—whoever you are."

Chapter 15

Choices

After the last in vitro fertilization failed, Daniel contacted the state adoption program. Mia was grateful. She wanted to adopt and had no doubt that a child was waiting for them somewhere, but she was discouraged. They looked over the paperwork that arrived from the adoption unit, and Daniel announced he was ready to send in the application and begin the process. All it needed was her signature. She glanced at the form that Daniel had meticulously completed. Her eyes hovered over his handwriting, neat but manly. Over the question **REASON FOR ADOPTION** he had answered: *We are unable to have biological children.* She loved him for that, for the We, rather than saying "She" or "My wife." Daniel didn't blame her, although she suspected that somehow she was responsible for the problem. Under the section **CHILD DESIRED**, Daniel wrote: *Healthy baby of either sex, under two years of age.* That sounded good; it summed everything up. Their problem and their dream, side by side on a single form, off in the mail to strangers—another plea for professional help. The first professionals, the doctors, had failed. Now it was the social workers' turn. *Who would be next,* Mia wondered?

On the upside, their sex life improved. They were no longer slaves to the calendar, basal temperatures, and other ovulation predictors. It was a relief not to have to record her temperature anymore or have to lie still after intercourse so as not to impede the progress of Daniel's sperm. She still silently cheered the little fellows on and hoped one day one of them would reach its target, but in all likelihood they were doing the best they could. Bad swimmers? Whatever the problem was, it was nice once again to enjoy sex as love making and simply lose herself in Daniel without concern for the science of conception. The payoff, their baby, would come some other way, something more understandable. Like one day opening the door and finding the Publisher's Clearing House people standing outside with a grin on their face and a check in their hand. Until then, you waited. It was, Mia felt, an act of faith.

After Daniel sent the application, Mia decided to make one of the guest rooms into a nursery—the nursery for their baby. She painted the walls yellow, like the walls in the master bedroom, with white trim and a white oval rug in the middle of the wood floor. There was an oak dresser and an old rocking chair. This was as far as Mia got before the first visit with their social worker, Diane Gamble.

Ms. Gamble was the worker assigned to their case *(problem)*. She would investigate their situation *(problem),* and write a report called the Homestudy *(a description of their problem)*. A committee would review the Homestudy and decide their fate—whether or not they could place a child with the Fishers and *fix the problem once and for all.*

Diane Gamble was an important person; Mia knew this, and that made her nervous. Could it really come down to this—that their fate and future rested in the hands of this woman? Mia suspected Diane Gamble did not like her. First impressions. Mia sensed they weren't exactly in harmony. Diane, as she asked to be called, looked about twenty-one years old, though she was probably older. She was a woman with a large frame and bad acne. She was coarse in appearance and seemed distant and noncommittal. She wore her hair short, not much longer than a man's haircut, and she resembled a man who was making a bad attempt to pass as a woman. Diane was without poise or femininity. To make matters worse, she totally lacked a sense of humor. She tried to make Daniel and Mia comfortable by assuring them they didn't have to be saints.

"The department" she said "isn't looking for perfection. You don't have to be an Albert Schweitzer, Daniel. And Mia, you don't need to be Mother Teresa. Just be yourselves. The department wants to see you are everyday people. Ordinary folk who just want the opportunity to parent a child."

Mia and Daniel nodded and smiled. *How reassuring,* Mia thought. *We don't have to be perfect.*

"Now I have a few questions to ask you, and please remember that there are no right or wrong answers. Okay? Remember, be yourselves."

Mia and Daniel nodded and smiled. *We must resemble a couple of those head-bobbing dolls,* Mia thought. *The ones you see in the back of people's cars.* She pictured little statues of herself and Daniel looking out the rear window of somebody's car, their little heads bobbing up and down.

"All right, then. Have both of you accepted your infertility?" Ms. Gamble asked. Mia and Daniel looked at one another, uncertain how to answer, and then looked back at Diane.

She continued, "We have to be sure a couple has accepted their infertility before we place a child with them. It's for the sake of the child. You aren't still trying to become pregnant, are you? You can't adopt if you become pregnant. There is a minimum waiting period of one year following a pregnancy." Diane looked at Mia intently, waiting for an answer.

"We both realize we won't be biological parents," Mia replied. It was a lie, because deep inside she still carried the small kernel of hope that someday, somehow, she might become pregnant. But she sensed this was something she must never admit to the social worker. So she would hide this hope and guard it against the harsh scrutiny of Diane Gamble.

Diane tried another approach. "I see you've been married for five years. Have you considered the impact a child will have on your marriage?"

Improve it, Mia thought. *It will bring Daniel and me together in a whole new way. It will complete us.* Instead she said, "We know we will have to make adjustments, but we're ready. We've had plenty of time together, and we've traveled. Both of us are ready to settle down with a family."

Diane's face remained impassive as she wrote down answers. Mia noticed Diane's fingernails were bitten down to the quick. *A little makeup wouldn't hurt,* Mia thought. *Maybe the acne prohibits wearing makeup.* Daniel was starting to fidget, and Mia hoped this meeting would end quickly. She felt like she was taking an exam that she hadn't prepared for. Besides, she worried about Daniel. She knew he was trying, but she also knew he was easily frustrated. He could go off at any time. Then, too, was his weird sense of humor—the sarcasm and irreverence. He might respond to a question with one of his "cute" answers, which Ms. Gamble would fail to recognize as a joke. The humorless social worker would be alarmed, and the Fishers would be out of luck.

"What about religion?" Diane asked. "I see you left that section blank. Don't you belong to a church?"

Before Daniel could say anything, Mia jumped in. "We're looking. We think religion is important and plan to join a house of worship soon. It's a big decision, so right now we're narrowing it down."

Then Daniel interjected, "I am a graduate of Theophilus College. That's a religious school in Nashville. You've probably heard of it. Any child Mia and I parent will have a good religious upbringing."

Diane looked at them rather skeptically, Mia thought, and wrote something in her notebook.

"That's good," she said. "But no, I don't believe I ever heard of that school."

"Excellent school," Daniel replied. "High standards...associated with the church."

After the first meeting, Daniel and Mia both let out a sigh of relief.

"I think we passed, don't you?" Daniel asked.

Mia didn't answer. She immediately ran to the bathroom to lock herself in and start drawing a bath. On the way she heard Daniel say, "Not a good sign," as he talked to himself.

*   *   *

As time passed, the interviews didn't improve. "You must prepare yourselves for a significant wait," Ms. Gamble said. "You can't be impatient. Eventually, it will work out, but it's likely to take a while. You might want to consider adopting an older child. With your background in education, Mia, this might be a good option for you."

"You mean...a teenager?" Daniel said. "Exactly how old do you mean?"

"He's kidding, Ms. Gamble. My husband sometimes has a rather strange sense of humor."

Diane didn't seem to know what to say.

"Maybe later," Mia continued, "if we adopt a second child. But to start with, Daniel and I would like a baby. It's our dream."

Diane sighed. "It's your decision, of course. But you need to be patient."

"She's so encouraging," Daniel remarked after Diane left. "Sometimes I just want to scream at her. She's younger than you are, Mia. She doesn't have any children—she's not even married. God, who would marry her? Talk about the blind leading the blind. Yet here she is judging us and our marriage. What gives her the right to decide whether or not we get a child? She still has pimples, for heaven's sake!"

Mia sighed. "The State of Tennessee—that's who gives her the right. Acne or no acne."

Diane had advised them they would need to childproof their kitchen cabinets. When Mia pointed out to her there was currently no child to proof the cabinets against, Diane smugly replied that a willingness to prepare in advance for their child would demonstrate a cooperative attitude.

"Are those indoor cats?" Diane asked, nodding at Rose and Henry.

"Yes," Mia replied.

"They could be a problem. Sometimes pets and children don't mix."

Giving in to Diane's steady gaze, Mia stated, "My mother will take them if there's a problem. But I'm not too worried about it. Both cats are old, and you said this would take a while."

Mia was used to succeeding. The only thing she remembered failing at was her attempt to learn Hebrew while living in Israel. She blamed that failure on love. Once she met Daniel, learning Hebrew seemed superfluous—especially when she realized how inept Daniel was at the language. She knew intuitively she would probably not be staying in Israel, so the whole language thing ceased to be important. This baby problem was different. It was significant, and it had her stumped. All she wanted was what came so easily to everyone else—just to be a parent. Half the girls at her high school could become pregnant just by smiling at a guy on prom night. It was simple, a piece of cake that any bimbo in the world could accomplish, except her. Fine. She would be happy to adopt. But now, even that seemed too much to hope for. *Is there some kind of conspiracy against me? Am I being punished for leaving Israel or for something I did in a past life?*

Lately Mia was feeling sorry for herself. She couldn't keep running to the bathtub every time she had a bad day. There were so many bad days: homestudy days, parenting class days, days when coworkers had baby showers, days when friends had babies, holidays, and on and on. Daniel was patient. He'd pull down the bed covers and stretch out with Rose and Henry to read a book or magazine. Sometimes he'd just listen to the radio until Mia emerged in her pink pajamas, still warm and damp. Then he'd pull her under the covers beside him and hold her close until they both fell asleep.

For over three years Mia and Daniel waited without even a hint of a referral—nothing, only those wretched visits from Diane Gamble. There were lots of baths during that period of time.

"Mia," Daniel said one day. "I know cleanliness is next to Godliness, but don't you think you might be over doing it?" Then Mia began to cry and ran to draw another bath.

At the end of each year, Diane came with new forms to complete, so their file would be current. She updated their homestudy twice, noting any significant changes. Child locks had been installed on all kitchen and bathroom cabinets. Mia added two white bookcases to the nursery, and they were now filled with books that she hoped some day to share with their child. She added a desk and filled the drawers with items she intended to pass down—pieces of jewelry, old photos, a teacup and saucer from her great grandmother, and Daniel's old baby spoon were some of the items that found their way into the desk. Daniel never lost his temper with Ms. Gamble, although by now he detested her and referred to her as "the beast." Occasionally he was sarcastic or made a bad joke, but Ms. Gamble just ignored him.

There was an antique rocking chair that Mia hand-painted red, blue, and green and placed by the window. She often sat there and slowly rocked. She didn't actually pray anymore, that was too much like nagging. She didn't want to be a kvetch. Instead she communed. Her mind wandered and she daydreamed, opening herself to whatever thought might come. Her heart ached, but she could still feel the kernel of hope hidden there. *No Ms. Gamble, I haven't accepted my infertility, and I never will. And you can go to hell.* She did all she could to nurture her hope and keep it alive.

One day, Mia got up from the rocker and began rummaging through the desk drawers. On top of the desk she placed a baby bonnet that had belonged to Daphne, Daniel's mother. She took it across the hall to the other guestroom, which was also Mia's workroom. In one corner there was a table and a storage cabinet where Mia kept her surplus teaching and art supplies. After several days work, Daphne's bonnet was the centerpiece of a collage with photos, buttons, and paper items from Daniel's past that Mia had held on to. The perimeter was outlined with flowing gold calligraphy, noting personal data for Daphne—date and place of birth and the names and dates of significant people and moments in her life. In large cursive writing, the name Daphne was positioned inside the perimeter under a favorite photograph of Daphne holding her baby, Daniel. Mia was pleased, and after the collage was framed, she hung it in the nursery.

"I love it," Daniel said when he first saw it on the wall. He stood, gazing transfixed. "What made you think of this?"

"I don't know. I guess I didn't want to keep important stuff like this hidden away. It didn't seem right. I wanted to make something to really show who Daphne is. It's her homestudy. Only this one is a visual homestudy. Do you think she'll like it?"

"She'll love it," Daniel said. "Are you going to give it to her?"

"I'd kind of like to keep it…for the nursery, if you think that's all right. It's as if Daphne will be here watching over the baby, whenever the baby comes."

During the next months, Mia delved into her art projects, experimenting more and more. Each piece focused on one particular place or person. Each was different. They were part decoupage, part collage, and sometimes part sculpture. One day she came home with an old pair of cowboy boots she had bought at a thrift shop. She made a plaster cast from one of the boots and used it as the base of a collage in remembrance of Daniel's grandfather who had raised horses on a farm in Tennessee. The outside was painted to look like old red leather over which she applied decorative detail, vintage photos, rodeo tickets, bits of denim, and horse paraphernalia. She then covered the boot with an antique glaze so the collage items appeared to fade into and out of the boot leather—like memories. The inside of the plaster boot was hollow with a cactus planted inside. The boot was titled "Memories of Signal Mountain." She entered it in an art contest, and it won first place in the mixed media category. There were offers to buy her work, but Mia couldn't part with any of the items she made. They were too personal and represented people or places she loved.

It was May when Mia learned that she was losing her job. The school had lost some of its funding, and art was considered expendable when money was tight. She became occupied with writing letters, developing a resumé, and going on interviews. After she sent job letters to all the area schools, she began going to the library and reading newspapers from different cities as well as perusing professional journals. Mia was desperate to find another job. She wouldn't accept losing another piece of her identity. If she couldn't be a mother, she had to be something. Besides, her income was important. For the past few years they had been investing in real estate, and much of their savings was tied up in land. The investments would eventually pay off, but not immediately.

Daniel encouraged her to aim high in her job hunt. "Apply everywhere," he said. "Use a shotgun approach. Look at the awards you've won. You're a great teacher and artist now. They will be lucky to have you."

They could move if necessary. He could work in real estate and manage his investments anywhere. So Mia applied for a variety of positions and went on interviews as far away as Florida and California. But no one was more surprised than she when she received a job offer from a community college in Oakland, Michigan. They had flown to Michigan in July when Daniel had encouraged her to take advantage of the free trip that was part of the school's selection process. He paid his own way and accompanied her because he had never been to Michigan. While Mia spent the day on campus, he rented a car and explored. Mia was impressed with the college, but neither expected the trip would result in a job.

Two weeks after the interview, Mia received a phone call offering her the position. She had one week to decide. The job would be challenging, with good pay and excellent benefits. Mia wanted to accept it, but she wasn't sure how Daniel would feel. To her relief, he was supportive. Daniel started calling her Professor Fisher, causing Mia to laugh and blush. Before making the final commitment, Daniel called Ms. Gamble to explain their circumstances. Mia was out buying donuts when he made the call. Later, when she returned with the Krispy Kremes, he shared the news.

"She said there might be a baby boy, but there is no guarantee."

"Really? When?" Mia asked.

"Don't get too excited, honey. It's several months down the road. And it's a maybe at best, not a sure thing."

"What about the move?" Mia asked. "Is that okay?"

Daniel shook his head. "No. She can't place a baby with us if we move to Michigan. She was emphatic on that. She says we'll have to start over."

Mia was still holding the bag of donuts. "What should we do?" she asked. "We've waited so long. How did she sound? Tell me everything she said, Daniel!"

"She sounded like a beast—a big, fat beast with zits on her face. When I told her about the move, she said 'Oh, that's unfortunate. There might be a baby boy becoming available soon. I was thinking he might go to your family.' When I asked what she meant, she said she couldn't say anything for certain, but there was a mother whom she thought would have her rights terminated in two or three months. I asked her if there could be some sort of guarantee that if we stayed here that the baby would be placed with us, and she said 'No.' The operative word she used was 'might.' It's all a big maybe."

Mia opened the bag and took out two donuts. She listened as Daniel continued.

"Then I asked her if she could place the baby with us if we moved to Michigan, and she said 'No.' She said they can't place a baby outside of Tennessee because they only work with Tennessee families. I reminded her that we were one of those families and that we had been waiting for four years. We would still be a Tennessee family, only temporarily living in Michigan.

"She told me that she was sorry, but she wasn't paid to worry about us or about Michigan. She only works for Tennessee and Tennessee families. If we leave Tennessee then we're no longer a Tennessee family. She's a beast, Mia. We're not going to get any sympathy from her or cooperation, for that matter."

Mia stood still, letting this news sink in. "What did you tell her? I mean, how did you leave it?"

"I told her we'd discuss it and get back to her in a couple of days to let her know what we decide."

Mia and Daniel agonized over the decision. In the end it boiled down to how much faith they had in Diane Gamble. Not enough. They weren't ready to gamble their future on her. She made it clear she had no allegiance to them. She was just a worker doing her job. *At least she has a job,* Mia thought. *That's more than I have if I stay here.*

Mia doubted they would ever become parents. But the new job was real and good, not a pipe dream. She could finally teach students who actually wanted to learn about art and art history.

While they were discussing their options, Mia confided to Daniel, "You know, I think I am finally accepting my infertility. Ms. Gamble would be proud. The thought that we might never succeed at adoption still frightens me, but not as much as before. If I can't be a mother, then I'll just throw myself into my career. I'll be the best art teacher I can be. I've come to accept that if it's meant to happen it will."

Mia called Diane Gamble and informed her of their decision to move to Michigan.

Ms. Gamble sighed and said, "All right then. I'm sorry. Now you'll have to start all over."

When Daniel and Mia left Tennessee, Daniel was forty years old, and Mia was thirty-three. It was 1984, and Israel was fading in the way dreams do. They had been two kids on an adventure who fell in love. It seemed so long ago. They weren't kids any more. They were two adults—happy, successful, but incomplete. The puzzle of their lives was missing a piece right in the center. They would need that piece for their lives to have the meaning they craved.

On the day the Fishers left Tennessee, the sky was clear and blue.

As they drove the U-Haul truck over the foothills and through green valleys and mountains, the weather grew cooler. By the time they reached Michigan two days later, the sky was overcast. It was a gray day and chilly, and the terrain was completely flat.

"It's not very pretty here, is it?" said Daniel.

Mia didn't answer. She was deep in thought, wondering if she had made the right decision.

In my life I've had three big loves: Sarah Koppleman, Grace Spindler, and Mia Murphy. Sarah was my first girlfriend. What led me to her was an abundance of hormones. Sarah was sexy, beautiful... full of juice. As they say in Yiddish, she was zaftig, a ripe fruit ready to burst into a cornucopia of earthly delights. With her effervescent personality and sensual lips, peeking out from behind that curtain of auburn hair, Sarah was a living Mardi Gras... a festival. When Sarah was with me, I was King of the celebration.

When I think of Grace Spindler, I think of Mother Theresa with a pretty face. Grace was an angel helping others. She was so pure she had a halo. I'm not sure why Grace chose to befriend me when I needed it most. It wasn't my good looks. And I know it wasn't her hormones. I don't believe she had hormones because I don't think angels do. Maybe an angel needs someone to save, and I was her assignment. Grace was my fantasy. She was a sparkle I didn't deserve and would never possess. I knew it from the beginning, but I tried to pretend otherwise. All my efforts with Grace failed. I would have followed Grace down any path, even to become a missionary. She preferred to travel without me.

Mia was the best of all—the gold ring. As a kid, riding the merry-go-round at Coney Island, I would grab a ring each time I passed the ring machine. The rings were all silver—except one. Only one person on each ride got to possess the ring. It meant they could ride again for free. That was a big deal. If life were a ride on a merry-go-round, then Mia was the gold ring. She was the total package, with personality, intelligence, and good looks. Quite simply, Mia was always essential to my happiness—but that may not have been enough. Mia and I had one major obstacle in our path. We couldn't have children. That may not seem like such a big deal—especially if you have kids. To Mia it was everything. It was all she ever wanted. So when we couldn't have them, we had a problem.

It sounds like I'm being fickle to think of all these women at the same time. I know. My point is I've had relationships with three interesting and really fine women. One wouldn't have me, another dumped me. But one chose me and gave me unconditional love. I have been fortunate.

Chapter 16

Children's Hope

During a committee meeting one April morning, Mia sat next to Kathleen Brown, an instructor of English. They were chatting while waiting for other committee members to arrive and take their seats. Mia shared that she and Daniel were thinking about adoption.

She described her discouragement. "I've been told the wait is seven to ten years. I've called Lutheran Services, Catholic Family Services, and other adoption agencies. They all say the same thing. It's discouraging."

"Have you thought about adopting internationally?" Kathleen asked.

"No," Mia replied, shaking her head. "I mean, we've thought about it briefly, but not seriously. There's so much that can go wrong. I just read about an adoption program in Missouri called the Mission of Mercy. The acronym was MOM. What could sound more wholesome? But some families lost a lot of money—not to mention their emotional investment. They sued, and the agency eventually lost its license, but I don't think the families got any of their money back. Then, just the other night, I saw a program on Romanian adoptions. The kids had been warehoused in institutions and were badly damaged. I just don't think Daniel and I could deal with something like that."

"But it's not always like that," Kathleen said. "My brother and sister-in-law adopted a baby girl from Central America about a year ago. Everything went smoothly for them, and the entire process only took about six months. Lisa is precious. You should see her. Everyone in the family loves her to death. She's spoiled rotten, you understand, but not from anything that happened before the adoption. Lisa is my brother's little princess."

"What agency did they use?" Mia asked, trying to hide her excitement. "Do they live in Michigan?"

Kathleen smiled and nodded. "Yes, my brother lives in Flint. The agency they worked with was Children's Hope. It's in Shepherd, a town just south of Mount Pleasant."

"Where is Mount Pleasant?"

"It's in the center of the Lower Peninsula, right in the middle of the mitten. Mount Pleasant is the home of the Chippewas and Central Michigan University. You've heard of the Chips, haven't you?"

Mia hadn't heard of Mount Pleasant, the Chippewas, or Central Michigan University, but she was curious about the adoption program. A few days later, she called Children's Hope and requested an application and literature. After studying the material together, she and Daniel made an appointment for an orientation.

On the day of their meeting, they drove north on Highway 127 for almost three hours. The further north they drove, the sparser the countryside appeared. Once they passed Lansing, the major cities were behind them, and the highway seemed almost deserted. They drove past farms and acres of empty land.

"There's a lot of vacant land around here," Daniel said. "There's certainly not an overpopulation problem." Forty-five minutes north of Lansing they began looking for the Shepherd exit heading west. Before coming to the exit, they saw a billboard: *Shepherd—The Sweetest Little Town Anywhere Around.* As they turned off the highway and drove west through the town they discovered that Shepherd was having its annual Maple Syrup Festival. Suddenly they encountered traffic and had to be rerouted around the outskirts of the town.

Children's Hope was located approximately six miles west of Shepherd, and although the directions sounded simple enough, Mia and Daniel drove right past the agency twice. They were at their wits' end when Mia finally spotted a small wooden sign saying "Children's Hope" in front of a house trailer next to a horse paddock. As they reached the end of the driveway, a smaller sign read, "Eggs for Sale."

"You're kidding," Daniel mumbled to himself. "People actually have a business here, in this place?"

Mia ignored the question. She had been telling Daniel about the latest adoption horror story she had seen on television. "The children were from someplace in the Far East, Vietnam or Cambodia... someplace like that. Anyway, they weren't really orphans. An American woman had bought them! The birth mothers were poor and uneducated, and they thought the orphanage was just a temporary place to keep their children until times got better and they could come back for them. It was a sad story."

Now, looking at the peeling sign, Mia continued, "You don't suppose these people are doing something illegal, like I saw on television? This looks a little suspicious."

Daniel was studying the mobile home. Several brightly colored chickens roamed the yard. "I don't believe this," he said, ignoring Mia's question. "There must be something wrong. How did you hear about this place?"

"On the television show," Mia continued. "The lady who ran the program made thousands of dollars selling children. After she was convicted, she had to forfeit her business, her home, and her income to the U.S. government."

"No. Not that place, Mia—this place. This…trailer house."

"Oh. Kathleen Brown from the English Department told me."

Daniel looked incredulous. "Mia, do you think the government would want this place? Look at it! Would you want it? You'd have to pay someone to haul it off for salvage. And to be honest I don't think you would get much. They can't be making any money at all. They're selling eggs, for goodness sake. But we've driven all this way. We might as well hear what they have to say. At least we can use their bathroom. That is, if they have indoor plumbing!"

At the door, they were greeted by a couple who introduced themselves as Cheryl and James. The mobile home looked better inside than outside, but it was cramped. The living room and dining room were converted into an office and meeting room. As they entered, the kitchen was to the right. Straight ahead was a large round table with four chairs. To the left were a couch and love seat. A television set and bookshelves lined one wall. Beyond the couch was a hallway leading to the rear of the trailer.

They all took seats around the kitchen table, where reading material had been arranged for Mia and Daniel. As Cheryl brought coffee for everyone, Daniel and Mia sat facing a window. Outside, Mia noticed three horses, their heads resting on a paddock fence, staring in at them.

Chickens, horses, what's next? Mia shifted her eyes to the walls, which were covered with pictures of children and smiling couples.

James began the orientation while Daniel and Mia sipped coffee. "We started this agency five years ago because we wanted to help other adoptive families," he explained. "We adopted two children from Guatemala ourselves and learned the hard way how the system works. A lot of people began asking how we did it. So, we decided to share our knowledge and help others. The only way we could really do that effectively was to start our own agency. So here we are."

Mia guessed the couple to be in their late thirties. They didn't look like social workers, more like farmers. Both were dressed in jeans—clean but casual—and they were nothing like Diane Gamble.

James explained that in Michigan, an adoption orientation was required by law in order to inform a family about the process and fees before getting too far into the process. "It's for your protection, so you don't get involved emotionally and financially without first knowing the facts. It also gives us a chance to learn about you and whether our agency can help you. Think of this as an informal get-together where you get to ask any questions you might have about adoption."

James glanced at Cheryl, and she took over. "We want you to leave with answers, so please don't hesitate to interrupt if there is anything you don't understand."

Mia and Daniel nodded. Cheryl picked up a questionnaire and a pen from the table. "To begin with, Mia and Daniel, can you please explain why you want to adopt?"

Before Mia could respond, Daniel blurted, "Because we can't have children. That's a no-brainer."

If Cheryl was offended by Daniel's abrupt response, she didn't let it show. "Actually, many of our adoptive families are already biological parents. They would like additional children, and for a variety of reasons feel adoption best meets their needs." Cheryl spoke in a soft, reassuring voice.

"I'd like to ask you a question," said Daniel, emphasizing the word "you" for effect. He shifted in his chair and leaned forward with his elbows on the table. "What's with this trailer in the middle of a field? It seems a strange place to have a business. It's not very reassuring."

Mia could feel herself blush. *Why,* she wondered, *does Daniel have to be so abrasive?* She intuitively liked James and Cheryl and was embarrassed by Daniel's attitude. But the agency couple chuckled good-humoredly.

"A lot of people wonder that," James replied. "I guess coming from the Detroit area, this does seem remote. Actually, it's a matter of convenience. We live across the driveway in that farmhouse. The trailer was here when we bought the farm, and for a while we rented it out, but we didn't like being landlords. When we started the agency, it seemed a perfect setup to have the office here. We don't have to rent a facility in town, which saves money, and we can just walk across the lawn when we need to. The phone rings in both places, so we are always accessible, which is good because a lot of families, and lawyers, need to reach us at odd hours. Cheryl can work here or at the house, so she can also spend time with our kids. It's convenient and efficient for us and saves on expenses for adoptive families. It's the main reason we can keep our fees low."

"I saw a show on television where families were paying thousands of dollars to agencies, but they never received a child," Mia interrupted. "They just lost their money and had their hearts broken."

James nodded. "That's unfortunate. Like anything else, Mia, there are good adoption programs and bad ones. It's not always easy to tell which is which. And, if you make a mistake it can be costly."

"Right. So how do you tell?" Daniel asked. "I mean, how do we know you aren't the bad guys? No offense, but you seem kind of small and, well…look around. You can't be typical. How many other adoption agencies are selling eggs?"

"A good point," James replied. "But our eggs are exceptional. Many of them have two yokes. I call them double-headers."

Mia observed that James didn't seem put-off by Daniel's skepticism.

"Seriously though, I don't expect you to know who the good guys are right now—you're just starting this process. But I will tell you how to find out."

"How many children have you placed?" Daniel asked.

"We've been a licensed agency for five and a half years and have placed close to three hundred children. Our waiting list is limited to fifty families at any given time. We don't want to work with more families than that because we don't want people waiting too long. Cheryl and I decided when we began Children's Hope that we weren't interested in becoming a big agency. I don't earn my living from Children's Hope; I serve as an unsalaried administrator. Our bylaws state I'm never to receive any money for adoption work."

Daniel looked at James skeptically. "If you don't get paid for this work, James, why do you do it? How do you earn your livelihood—selling eggs?"

James smiled while Mia shot Daniel an angry look.

"Please," he said, "call me Jim. I do it because adoptions are good. I believe in adoption. It's brought so much joy into our lives. I can't imagine not parenting our two girls, and I don't want to imagine what might have become of them if they had stayed in an orphanage or on the streets of Guatemala. Adoption isn't for everyone, Daniel. I'll be the first to admit that. It's a difficult process and can try the patience of even the most resolute would-be parents. And, for your information, I earn my living teaching at Shepherd College."

"We saw the Maple Syrup Festival as we drove into town."

"That's not run by the college," Jim said. "The festival is sponsored by the community of Shepherd. You see," Jim continued. "The school is named after the three shepherds; the Good Shepherd, the shepherd's pie, and the German Shepherd."

Daniel looked at Mia and rolled his eyes. He couldn't decide whether Jim was making a joke or not, but he was pretty sure he was.

Then, after a pause, Cheryl said. "There is a Shepherd College but it has nothing to do with three shepherds. My husband likes to tell that story to all the people that come here. I think each time he tells it he believes it is funnier than the last time. I don't know why. Let me refill your coffee mugs and we can continue with the serious business of your orientation."

After Mia and Daniel watched an international adoption video, it was starting to get dark outside. Mia glanced at her watch and was surprised to see that over three hours had passed. After all the questions had been asked and the Fishers were getting ready to leave, Cheryl handed them their handbook, along with a sheet of paper that listed the name and telephone number of their licensing consultant and several adoptive families who were willing to speak to prospective clients. "Call them," she said. "Ask them to tell you about their experience. And by all means, call our licensing consultant. He has a unique perspective and oversees many agencies."

As they headed toward the door, Jim said, "Whatever you decide, it's been a pleasure meeting you. You'll receive a letter from us next week confirming we had this orientation and instructing you on how to proceed if you want to continue working with Children's Hope."

Daniel and Mia said good-bye and left for home. As they headed south on highway 127, Mia remarked, "That was an interesting experience. It almost seemed like they were trying to talk us out of adopting."

"I know," Daniel said. "I noticed that too. They didn't seem eager for business. I don't know what to make of it—whether it's a good or bad sign."

"I think it's a good sign and we should let them do our homestudy," Mia said. "I have a good feeling about them. They're not judgmental or self-righteous like Ms. Gamble."

"You mean they don't seem like assholes. I agree, but appearance can be deceptive. I think we should check their references before we spend any more money. I don't want to end up on a television exposé like that show you were telling me about."

Mia leaned back in the car seat, clutching the handbook and papers from the orientation. She felt safe and secure beside Daniel, cruising toward home in the early evening. Slowly she became aware of another feeling growing inside—a sensation she didn't recognize at first. Familiar, like a whisper from the past, it was an emotion she had not felt for a long, long time. It was hope.

Chapter 17

When Manna Falls

I t was late in the afternoon when the telephone rang. Daniel answered. "Hello." He heard an operator with a heavy accent, stating it was a person-to-person call from Guatemala.

"Yes, this is Daniel Fisher," he answered, wondering who could be calling.

There was scratchy static followed by a woman's voice. "Hello, Daniel?" The voice sounded familiar.

"Yes."

"Daniel... This is Grace. Grace Tuttle."

All of a sudden Daniel put two and two together. Grace lived in Guatemala! He felt a surge of warmth. "Hi Grace, how are you? Is everything all right?" He was happy to hear from her, but concerned. It had been five years since he last saw her at the reunion in Nashville. Grace was little more than a memory.

"I'm fine. Listen, Daniel. I have a question. I was wondering whether or not the fertilization treatments worked. Did you and Mia have a baby?"

"No, Grace, I'm sorry to say, it didn't work."

"Then you never had the baby you were hoping for?"

"No. But we're on an adoption list. Since we moved to Michigan we had to start the process all over. It's been discouraging. Why?"

"Well… I have a baby for you… if you want her."

"Her?" Daniel felt his stomach knot.

"Yes! She's a beautiful baby girl. She was born last week. Her mother abandoned her, and there's no father—I mean no father of record. He's unknown."

"Grace. Hold on. Let me get Mia."

Daniel called Mia to the phone and quickly explained the situation. Mia stood transfixed, as if her feet were nailed to the floor, and vigorously nodded her head. She seemed unable to speak.

"Yes, Grace!" Daniel yelled into the phone excitedly, as he watched Mia. "Of course we want the baby."

"Good. Then I need a name for her."

"A name? Okay, we'll think about it and get back to you. How can I reach you?"

"No, Daniel. You don't understand. I need a name now. The doctor is here filling out the birth certificate as we speak. He's already late with the paperwork. It should have been completed two days ago. It took me a while to track you down. We need a name, immediately."

"Okay…" Daniel stalled. "Just a minute…"

Mia stood frozen and mute, probably not in a position to help. He felt his mind reeling, as if a hurricane was unleashed in his head. *A baby...a baby...* like a mantra the words spun round and round. *A name...female... a girl's name...* suddenly in his mind's eye he saw the Quetzal bird—his old friend. It was the same bird he had written about so many years ago when he was a child. It was elusive and beautiful. Without hesitation, he heard himself say, "Quetzal. We'll name her Quetzal."

"Quetzal? You mean like the bird?"

"Yes," Daniel said. "Name her after the bird, Quetzal Maya Fisher. Maya is spelled M-A-Y-A."

Mia's eyes were growing bigger, and he thought he detected a smile forming at the corners of her mouth. She still didn't say anything.

"Now tell me, Grace. What do you want us to do?"

"Do you have passports?"

"Yes."

"Good. Then one or both of you should come to Guatemala as soon as possible to take care of Quetzal."

"Okay. We'll make arrangements and get back with you. Give me a number where I can reach you."

"Daniel?"

"Yes."

"You're also going to need an adoptive homestudy. It has to be current. Do you know where you can get one?"

"We already have one, Grace, from the agency here in Michigan. It was completed just a few months ago."

"Great, then I think you have everything you need to get started. But whoever comes is going to have to stay here a while—maybe five or six months. It's going to take that long." Daniel began scribbling down Grace's address and telephone number, forcing his mind to slow down and concentrate on what she was saying. Her final words were, "Let me know as soon as someone can get here. We'll be at the airport waiting."

"Thanks, Grace. Thank you so much. You're an answer to our prayers. And thank your husband, too. We've been waiting so long. It's a miracle."

As Daniel hung up the telephone he stared at Mia in amazement. Fate had just handed them a winning ticket; it was difficult to comprehend what had happened. He turned to Mia and noticed she was crying. He reached out and pulled her close.

"Imagine," he said, as he held her tightly, "out of the blue…just like that."

When Mia asked Daniel about his choice of name, he explained about the quetzal bird and the Maya of Guatemala. "I've always loved that bird, ever since I did a report on it in fourth grade. You know, the currency in Guatemala is called *quetzales*. Their money is named after the bird. But, if you don't like the name we can change it later. I had to think fast, and I wanted something special… something unique, befitting this extraordinary event. It was all I could come up with. You don't mind, do you?"

To his surprise, Mia said, "I never heard that name before, but I like it. And it's certainly different. It's probably a good thing, though, that you don't have a special feeling for guacamole. Of course, you might be saving that name in case Quetzal ever has a brother."

They both laughed, basking in the joy of the moment. "Pinch me," Mia said. "This can't be happening. I feel like I'm dreaming."

"It's not a dream," Daniel said, looking into her radiant face. Mia was beaming with joy, and it melted his heart to see her so happy. "Unless, of course, I'm having the same dream," he said. "Maybe we should pinch each other!"

Mia smiled and shook her head. They settled on a kiss.

The next day, Mia booked a plane ticket. Then she met with her department head and arranged for an emergency leave of absence. It was summer, and she wasn't teaching for two months, but she didn't know when she would be back. It could be Thanksgiving or Christmas before she returned. She didn't care how long she stayed, she was getting a baby, her baby. She packed, shopped, got her course materials in order for her replacement. One week later, Mia was flying to Guatemala to meet her new baby, Quetzal Maya Fisher.

Daniel remained behind to manage things at home. Not knowing how long the process would take, they couldn't afford for both of them to be absent from work. While legal procedures ran their course, Mia and Quetzal would stay with Grace and her family in a village called Canoguitas. Daniel would join them later.

It was a good thing Daniel remained behind, because he soon learned that there was plenty to be done. As soon as Mia left for Guatemala he called Children's Hope to let them know what had happened, and a meeting was quickly arranged with Jim and Cheryl.

"I don't know how it happened," he told them excitedly as he sat down in their office. This time the agency was easy to find, and he felt like he was meeting with old friends. "Out of the blue, just like that, we have a baby waiting for us in Guatemala! Mia is already there, taking care of her. We named her Quetzal Maya Fisher."

Jim and Cheryl smiled. "That's great news, Daniel. Tell us all about it. Do you have an attorney in Guatemala?"

Daniel shrugged. "I don't know. I didn't ask. But our friends have lived in Guatemala for years. The Tuttles have their own lawyer."

"Tuttles?" Jim looked at Cheryl with a curious expression, as if he recognized the name.

"Yes, Grace Tuttle. I went to college with her. In fact, she was once my girlfriend—before Mia of course. You don't know her or her husband Tommy, do you?"

"I don't know Grace, but I think I might have met her husband once in Guatemala. I recall he was interested in adoptions and asked a lot of questions about fees."

Daniel changed the subject. "Jim, I was wondering about the legal fee we'll owe to Children's Hope."

"You won't owe a legal fee to Children's Hope," Jim explained. "You will just pay the lawyer you work with directly. It would be a good idea to check with the Tuttles about this and see if they already have an attorney. If not, I know several honest lawyers in Guatemala. I'll be glad to give you a name if you need one. If the Tuttles already have a lawyer, try and be sure you're working with someone who is honest and experienced in adoptions. Unfortunately many attorneys are sharks. They're greedy and see adoption as a way to make a lot of money. Others have good intentions but little experience. In that case, you'll be waiting forever because you'll get bogged down in paper work and red tape. Find out, up front, how much money the attorney is going to charge, and don't pay it all at once. You should only pay about half the fee when you start, and the final half when you are cleared to leave the country with your baby."

Daniel listened and took notes. He needed to gather various documents and have them authenticated and translated. He also had to notify the Immigration and Naturalization Service to forward their Orphan Petition to Guatemala City. Jim and Cheryl estimated the whole process would take four to six months! *What will I do without Mia for six months? Of course there is baby stuff to buy, and a room to prepare.*

Before the meeting at Children's Hope, Daniel had been dizzy with excitement, but talking with Jim and Cheryl had sobered him. There was a lot to do before Mia and Quetzal could come home. And there were so many things that could go wrong. As he drove home that evening, he thought of Mia and the little baby he could only imagine. They were so far away, staying in a place he couldn't even pronounce. And all of this was occurring because of a phone call from someone he hadn't seen in five years. Grace had once given him a graduation present. It was only a memento, but at the time he hadn't even thought to offer such a small gesture to her. Now, here was Grace again, but with the present of a lifetime. Suddenly the dream he and Mia were so eagerly chasing seemed obtainable. He remembered Mia's face as she blew him a kiss before boarding the plane. *She looked so beautiful, so hopeful, and vulnerable. Where was she now? Was she safe? Of course she was safe. She was with Grace. Grace would be her protector. Grace was still Daniel's angel.* He tightly gripped the wheel of the car and did something he hadn't done since leaving Theophilus. He prayed.

* * *

Mia also prayed. In fact she prayed several times a day her first weeks in Guatemala. There was so much to do and learn, so much to hope for, so much to get right, and so much that could go wrong. Every morning began with a prayer of gratitude as she awoke and gazed at baby Quetzal. Quetzal was always awake first, cooing and stretching. She slept in a crib right next to Mia's bed, and when Mia awoke Quetzal would look at her and smile.

Quetzal, she was told, was two weeks old when Mia arrived. However, two weeks later Mia was told Quetzal's birthday, which would add an additional two weeks to Quetzal's age. Mia asked about the discrepancy, but everyone looked at her as if she was crazy and ignored the question. Mia noticed that time was not precise in Guatemala. Dates, deadlines, and appointments were not to be taken literally. They were simply estimates and generalizations, nothing more. So, if Mia couldn't be certain about Quetzal's age or the exact day she was born on, so be it. That was the way things worked here. Nothing much surprised her. After all, she was not in the real world any more, but in Guatemala. This was the country the tourist board referred to as the Land of Eternal Spring. Except in Mia's case, it was the land where dreams come true. It was a place so exotic, vibrant, and lush that Mia could imagine babies sprouting in the fields or dangling plump and ripe from tropical vines.

Once awake, Mia's day revolved around Quetzal from morning until night. There was bathing, dressing, feeding, changing, napping, and on and on. Quetzal didn't sleep through the night, so Mia dutifully stumbled in the dark through the courtyard to the kitchen for a bottle. If she happened to make too much noise, a startled peacock would shriek admonitions. The first two weeks Mia was exhausted and lost her sense of time. *Where does the time go*, she wondered each night as she fell into bed. It was then, at the end of each day, that she would think about Daniel and wonder about his day. She missed him so much that it felt like a big ache she carried around in counterbalance to the joy that Quetzal brought her. She wished she could call him every day, but that wasn't possible. The expense was too great for international phone calls, and the adoption was going to be costly. Each time she met with her attorney, she learned of a new expense, and even though Grace was housing her without charge, Mia still contributed to food, transportation and miscellaneous expenses. It all added up.

On weekdays, Grace was frequently gone during the day doing volunteer work. Often she and Mia would have coffee together in the morning, but then Grace would leave the house, either gardening or volunteering, until evening. Marta, the maid, was left in charge of the home, and she had been assigned to assist Mia. Marta spoke no English, so Mia began learning Spanish, which she found to be much easier than Hebrew had been. She actually learned a few Spanish words. Marta showed how to care for the baby, and checked on the two of them throughout the day. Mia was advised never to leave the compound without Grace. And whenever she did go out with Grace, Marta accompanied them with the baby.

"You must never hold the baby in public," Grace advised. "Many Guatemalans are suspicious, and they resent North Americans adopting their children. There are rumors that rich Gringos want children to use as domestics or to extract their organs for medical treatment."

"What?" Mia asked horrified by what she heard.

"I know it's ridiculous," Grace said, "but people are superstitious here."

Although Grace was away much of the day, her three children buzzed in and out as they pursued their busy lives. Mia was impressed with their politeness. They always took time to say hello and tickle Quetzal, especially Josh the oldest boy. Tommy, the husband, was usually not to be seen until the weekends. He left the compound before anyone else each day and worked long hours into the night. Sometimes he was away for days at a time.

Mia had dinner each evening with Grace and the children. Meals were served by Marta in the large dining room amidst much laughter and conversation. Quetzal slept right through the meal in a playpen beside Mia's chair. If Quetzal woke up, Evie and Josh would vie for turns holding her. Sam was too interested in soccer to think about babies, but occasionally he would rock Quetzal while she took a bottle. After dinner, the children scattered while Grace and Mia had evening coffee in the courtyard. Slowly the two women shared the details of their lives. Gradually, they found a friend in each other.

The weekends were more hectic. Tommy was usually home, which meant a constant stream of visitors and workers seeking him out. Also, he prepared for the church services. The lazy, mellow weekday pace quickened to a frenzy of activity on weekends. The noise and commotion seemed to agitate the baby, so Mia spent a lot of weekend time in her room playing with Quetzal or working on her project.

The project was a way to pass time and to document things to be shared with Daniel. Throughout the week, Mia collected items—mementos associated with some activity or event. These would wind up on the dresser in her bedroom. Mia reflected on them while writing letters to Daniel because they served as a catalyst for ideas. Since Daniel couldn't come to Guatemala, she wanted to send a sense of her experience to him.

One of the first items to make it to the dresser and into her letters was a peacock feather. White as well as blue/green peacocks wandered around the compound. Mia found them beautiful to look at, and at night she took an odd comfort in their presence. Like invisible sentries, they positioned themselves in trees high above the house and warned of any suspicious activities below. With their loud honks and haunting calls, they guarded the night. During the days a peacock would occasionally find its way into Grace's courtyard and have to be chased away. One such peacock left a feather behind, which Mia picked up and put on her dresser. Later, in her room, the feather inspired two pages describing the compound and the peacock patrol. Eventually Mia cut the feather to fit into an envelope, and sent it to Daniel. Other items wound up in a cardboard box under her bed. She planned to take her collection home. Each Sunday and Wednesday night, Mia sorted through the treasures on the dresser. There was a small rock from the little zoo where Mia and Quetzal strolled with Marta and Grace. There was a leaf from the banana tree that grew outside their bedroom window. There was also a poem that Mia had found in one of Grace's magazines. The magazine said the author was unknown, but Mia knew the emotions the writer was feeling when she put her thoughts to paper. Mia would read the poem out loud:

Patchwork Quilt

Our family's like a patchwork quilt,

With Kindness gently sewn.

Each piece is an original,

With beauty of its own.

With threads of warmth and happiness,

It's tightly stitched together.

To last in love throughout the years,

Our family is forever.

Sometimes Mia would gaze at each item she collected and jot down notes and then determine what to keep and what to let go. About half of the items made it to the boxes under the bed. These she would bring home to use one day in her artwork. Until then they remained precious artifacts, valuable treasures that documented the most extraordinary experience of her life.

Although Mia started the project for herself and for Daniel, she came to realize she was also doing it for Quetzal. It was a way of capturing for her daughter the magic of these days and this time they shared together in the guestroom at Grace Tuttle's house at the Evangelical Friendship Mission of Guatemala. She wondered if Quetzal would ever appreciate it when she grew older. Grace learned about Mia's project, and one morning over coffee Mia was presented with a leather-bound notebook filled with blank pages. *Quetzal and Mia in Guatemala* was printed on the front cover. Inside were the first photographs of the new mother and daughter. The pictures had been taken outside the airport when Mia first held Quetzal in her arms. Mia was so moved by the gift she started to cry. In the months to come, Mia filled the pages with more photographs, drawings, thoughts, poems she composed, and personal observations. There were also recipes, dreams, and prayers. Each page was a glimpse through the window of Mia's heart, revealing her transformation from a woman into a mother.

That first day at the airport when Mia held Quetzal and claimed her as her own was the most wonderful day of her life. Quetzal was proof that magic existed, and Mia's faith in all things good was restored. Mia looked at the beautiful baby in awe; Quetzal had skin the color of honey and almond-shaped eyes as dark as olives. Her face was round and so bursting with hope and innocence that Mia was brought to tears. Then she noticed the hair, thick and abundant, that sprung from Quetzal's head in all directions like a dandelion crown—only it was black, matching her eyes. In a letter to Daniel, Mia described the moment when she first laid eyes on Quetzal: "It felt as if something inside me leapt in recognition, and then I felt my soul smile."

Chapter 18

Adoption

Each day Daniel waited for the mail in hope of finding a letter. If a photo was enclosed, he hit the jackpot. He missed Mia and their life together. Once he finished the paperwork requirements for the adoption and immigration, Daniel concentrated on the house, a three-bedroom ranch located in the suburbs. It was a nice comfortable place, but lacking the charm of the Victorian mansion they had once owned in Tennessee. He traded charm for convenience. The house was close to town and to Mia's school. Daniel mowed the grass and fenced in a play area for Quetzal. He painted her room pink and had matching carpet installed. Then he painted the shutters, built a barbecue, and watered the roses.

When he felt lonely, he pulled out the pictures of Mia and Quetzal and imagined life when the three of them would be together. He kept a peacock feather Mia had sent on the table by his bed. In moments of doubt, he questioned whether or not having Quetzal was worth the aggravation. After all, he and Mia had been happy without her, hadn't they? Mia was his best friend, Mrs. Whiner from Zion. It was Mia who made his Holy Land adventure memorable. Without her he would have returned home with another failure experience. Yes, Mia completed him. Then he looked at the tiny face in the photos, trying to conjure up the feelings Mia expressed in her letters. He thought, *who completes us? As a couple, we are missing something.* Looking at the photo, Daniel wanted to see the magic and beauty Mia assured him were there. He wanted to feel what Mia felt. But all he really sensed was he missed Mia and wanted her home. *The baby is cute, but aren't all babies cute?*

By the time November arrived he was frustrated and needed to see for himself what all this effort was for. Finances were another matter. There seemed to be a stream of surprise expenses, which he hadn't anticipated or budgeted for. These were stressful, and he wondered if the whole adoption could be a scam, like the ones Mia had told him about from the television show. *No,* he told himself, *not if Grace is involved.* Daniel had faith in Grace. Angels don't let people down. But this adoption seemed to be taking forever. So, early one morning he called a travel agent and made arrangements for a visit, even though Mia had told him by telephone it would only take two or three more weeks to complete the adoption process. Daniel couldn't wait.

It was a beautiful day when he arrived in Guatemala. When he got off the plane he felt tired, but excited. He hadn't slept well in two days. Mia and Grace were waiting for him outside the airport after he cleared customs. He saw Mia waving, and then she ran toward him like a charging lion. She threw her arms around him and wouldn't let go. They walked to the car huddled together. It felt reassuring to know Mia had missed him so much. Once in the car, he saw Quetzal for the first time. Even though he had seen pictures of her, he wasn't prepared for the sheer impact of her presence, and he felt dizzy as his eyes took her in. She looked Asian with big brown eyes that were almost black and thick black hair that sprang straight out from her head. His first thought was that she looked like a cartoon character—a cross between a baby and a porcupine.

"Wow," he said. "What a head of hair. Does she stick to Velcro? Because we could put a piece on the ceiling and if she cries too much we could toss her up and leave her hanging for awhile."

"Daniel," Mia squealed. "That isn't funny. Quetzal is precious. How can you talk of sticking our baby to the ceiling?"

"Just kidding."

He couldn't help but smile at the sight of such an adorable little person. Her skin was the color of caramel, and as smooth as a flower petal. Daniel was mesmerized by the sight of her. She looked at him quizzically as he poked his head in the car, and then gazed past him seeking out Mia's face. Quetzal smiled pure joy at the sound of Mia's voice, and Daniel knew in an instant the two were utterly in love.

After greeting Grace and thanking her for all she and her husband had done, Daniel and Mia climbed into the backseat of the car. Grace and Marta rode up front. In Mia's lap Quetzal relaxed, kicking and cooing and holding her toy elephant. All was well with the world. During the ride to Canoguitas, Quetzal settled back, staring intently at Daniel while he and Mia talked. Her expressions changed constantly: curiosity, confusion, annoyance, amusement, joy, and awe. Toward the middle of the trip he believed Quetzal was—in her baby way—flirting with him. She would gaze at him and then smile broadly when he looked back. He touched her tiny hand, and she grasped his thumb. He was surprised by the strength of her grip. Quetzal refused to let go and tugged it close to her chin. Even after she fell asleep, she held on to his thumb firmly, claiming it as her own. This was how Daniel was initiated into fatherhood. By the time the car pulled into the compound he was hooked. He was Daddy, and there was nothing he wouldn't do for this baby, his child.

That night as Daniel held Mia in his arms, he felt such contentment and joy. It had been a perfect day. As he lay in bed, he listened to the sounds of his surroundings. Mia was softly snoring on the side of him next to the wall. In a crib on the other side was Quetzal, breathing loudly for such a tiny thing. He couldn't see Quetzal, only her form under the blanket, but he felt her presence so strongly that it was difficult to remember what it felt like not to be with his baby. She was the missing piece of the puzzle of the Fishers' life together. With his eyes closed, he could still see her bright beaming face and astonishing hair. He thought of Grace and her children. They had shared dinner earlier, but he couldn't recall anything that was said. He just remembered his surprise at how much older Grace looked. Mia had said it was because Grace didn't wear makeup. Still, Grace seemed pleasant and content, almost otherworldly. Tomorrow Tommy would take him on a tour and show him the compound. Daniel would rather be with Mia and Quetzal, but maybe they could all go on the tour together. Monday he would talk with the lawyer, a woman named Francisca Sanchez. He was anxious to have some time alone with Mia, when he wasn't so tired. There was so much to catch up on.

Daniel felt himself floating off into a delicious, irresistible sleep when his thoughts were interrupted by the scream of "A-hoe…A-hoe" in the distance. *The peacocks,* he thought, too tired to open his eyes. He remembered the peacock feather Mia had enclosed with her first letter.

"Mia warned me about you," he whispered. "Everything she said is true."

When Daniel opened his eyes, the morning sun was streaming into the room. He looked around and saw Mia and the baby were not there. Cheerful chatter drifted from somewhere below in the house. There was the clanking of dishes and the smell of food. He stretched lazily for a moment, then dressed and dashed out to find his wife and child. Breakfast was being served in the courtyard on a table surrounded by brilliant red and pink flowers. Two young women dressed in cloth as bright as the courtyard flowers scurried around the table moving dishes and pouring coffee. Mia was feeding Quetzal a bottle across from Grace and Tommy. Tommy looked much as Daniel remembered him from school, only slightly older and a little heavier. He hadn't aged as much as Grace. Their children were also present. Tommy stood with his hand outstretched as Daniel neared the table. The two shook hands. Daniel felt the old resentment from college days, but masked it. He was acutely aware that Tommy was part of the adoption solution. Daniel was grateful.

Grace prepared a place for Daniel, and even before he was comfortably seated two young maids fluttered to his side, bringing coffee and a plate of fruit. One of the girls asked him something in Spanish, and he looked around helplessly.

Grace came to his rescue. "She wants to know how you would like your eggs cooked. Would you prefer ham or bacon?

He was barely done eating breakfast when Tommy reminded him about the Saturday morning rounds. He wanted to show Daniel the compound. By now Quetzal was snoozing, and the women were sipping coffee.

"Go ahead, honey," Mia said. "I'll be busy for awhile. I have to bathe and dress Quetzal when she wakes up."

Reluctant but gracious, Daniel rose and followed Tommy outside into the glorious day that awaited them. The temperature was warm and comfortable, with a slight fragrant breeze. The paths before them were dappled by sunlight that filtered through the canopy of trees surrounding the compound. Everything seemed so bright. The entire area was like a little village, a world within a world, something that should be painted and captured forever.

In the middle of the compound was a beautiful garden area with flowering shrubs and flowerbeds. It was bisected by paths, and there were several benches for sitting and relaxing. Surrounding the garden were various buildings, each serving some purpose. At the far end, opposite Grace and Tommy's home, was the church. The house and church appeared to be a matched pair, both being two-story structures of beige and white stucco with red tile rooves and dark ironwork trim. Atop the church was a steeple, and Daniel could make out the bell that hung within. The church was simple but classic in appearance and added a sense of dignity and timeless beauty to the setting. Around the perimeter of the compound, Daniel caught glimpses of huts and dwellings scattered throughout the greenery. Lush vegetation and mountains stretched beyond the perimeter. Far in the distance he could see smoke from one of the peaks—a volcano.

"That's Valcan Pacaya," Tommy said, following Daniel's gaze. "It's still active, but hasn't erupted in ages."

"Your father started this place?" Daniel asked, impressed by the size and beauty of the enterprise.

"He came here when I was a child. There was nothing but jungle when we arrived. For almost a year we lived in a tent under these trees. Eventually he built a church and then a house. Gradually the place just grew."

"I remember him speaking at Theophilus. Where is he now?" Daniel asked. "I'd like to meet him."

"In Florida. He recently had a stroke, and he's recovering in Miami. His wife Lila, my stepmother, visits with him regularly. She lives in the house next to the church."

From where they stood Lila's house was partially hidden from view, but Daniel could make out enough to see that it was a structure similar to Tommy and Grace's home, but grander.

"She doesn't stay with him in Florida?"

"No. She would like to, but she's very busy. Technically she's in charge of the program now, so there's a lot for her to do. Besides, there's not much she can do for him. They have nurses for that kind of stuff."

"I'm sorry to hear about your dad's illness," Daniel said. "What exactly does Lila do?"

Tommy smiled. "She's mainly in charge of fundraising. She manages the business side of all this and keeps the books. She's a remarkable lady. You'll be meeting her later. I believe she's coming to dinner tonight."

As the two strolled around the grounds, Daniel noticed all the attractive young women. Each would smile at them and lower her head as she passed. Tommy definitely seemed to be held in high regard, like a head of state amongst commoners. He smiled and acknowledged each by name, occasionally stopping to exchange a few words in Spanish. He was clearly in his element, and Daniel thought he might be showing off. Daniel mentioned this to Mia later when the two were alone with Quetzal in Grace's garden.

"What I have been able to put together," Mia said, "is that Tommy works alongside Lila, coordinating and supervising various projects, which accounts for why he is frequently away from home. He helps Lila with the sponsorship program and its letter writing campaign. He also hires preachers for Sunday services and Wednesday prayer meetings. Elmer used to preach, but obviously he can't now. Tommy doesn't seem to be religious. He oversees the school, feeding center, and emergency housing programs. But what Tommy seems most interested in is the adoption work. When I arrived," Mia continued, "he said he began working on behalf of orphans in 1976 after the earthquake when so many were left without families. But he didn't place these children for adoption. Instead he placed them with relatives or in foster homes. Grace told me Tommy has only recently become involved with international adoption. She says she doesn't know where all these children are coming from or going to, but Tommy seems to be the driving force. Grace supervises the foster home. I don't know if there's more than one. She says the children will be going to families in the United States, Israel, Italy, and other countries. And yes, I think I know what you're thinking. Tommy does seem to have an eye for the ladies."

"What about Grace? Doesn't she mind all these young girls flirting with her husband?"

"I'm not sure," Mia replied. "She might not. She and Tommy seem to live separate lives, except on weekends. She's busy with volunteer work, and he with whatever he does."

"What kinds of volunteer work?"

Mia shrugged. "Besides supervising the foster home and helping Father Martin, the local priest, I'm not sure. But she manages to find a little time every day for her garden. I know she does charity work."

"For the mission program?" Daniel asked.

"Some," Mia replied. "But I think it's her own stuff, mainly with children. She's busy most days until dinner."

"Do you think they're happy?" Daniel asked.

"As a couple? No, not really. But Grace seems content and satisfied. She adores her children and her home and garden. She's serious about her religion and prays frequently, which made me uncomfortable at first. But then I realized she's not pushy or preachy. I can understand why you liked her so much in college. She's a kind, gentle person. I think she is one of the nicest people I've ever met."

"She's changed a lot since college. She doesn't even look the same."

"We've all changed, Daniel. Remember Mr. and Mrs. Whiner? Look how much we've changed."

"She was always opinionated with me in school. She had her own ideas about everything. Remember I told you how she said Jesus turned the water into grape juice? I think she may have even said it was Welch's Grape Juice. When I said that was ridiculous, she scoffed. 'How would you know? Were you there?' You couldn't argue with Grace back then, but she was always nice. I hope she's happy."

"I didn't say happy," Mia said. "I said satisfied. There's a difference."

Daniel was holding Quetzal in his lap, and Mia snapped a picture of the two of them. The baby was relaxed, leaning back into the crook of his arm, examining a spoon.

"I suppose. But it seems weird seeing all those pretty girls following Tommy around like the Pied Piper."

"That's nothing," Mia said. "Just wait till you meet the step mom. Talk about a piece of work."

Later that night Lila joined them for dinner, and Daniel saw what Mia meant. Initially, he was taken aback because he had never met anyone like her. He had no idea how old Lila was. She had a quality that transcended age, and it was obvious that in the full bloom of youth she must have been a knockout. She could still stop traffic, in Guatemala City or anywhere else. Lila was petite with a voluptuous figure and long black hair pulled back from her face and twisted into an intricate knot. She exuded sexuality. Against the white dress she was wearing, her bronzed skin gleamed, smooth and firm as polished teak. Tommy sat at the head of the table, with Grace on one side of him in all her plain simplicity and Lila on the other, a human fireworks display.

During dinner Daniel expressed his sympathies about Elmer's stroke. "I hope your husband has a speedy recovery," he said.

Lila leaned toward Tommy, placing her hand over his as she turned to Daniel. "Thank you," she said. "God willing, everything will work out."

"Yes," Grace said, from the other side of Tommy. "I pray for Elmer every day."

* * *

On Monday, Daniel had an appointment to meet with the adoption attorney, Mrs. Francisca Sanchez. It was an entire day's event in Guatemala City. Their car was crammed with Grace, Marta, and the driver in front, and Quetzal, Daniel, and Mia in the back. They left before daylight so they could get into the city early, and at 8:00 a.m. they were waiting in line outside the U.S. Embassy. The attorney had advised them to check in with the embassy about their visa petition for Quetzal, and stressed that they should show up with the baby. After waiting an hour, they learned their clearance had arrived and a note of the visit with Quetzal was put in the embassy file. The official they spoke with was harried and unfriendly. Upon hearing the nature of their visit, he immediately expressed his disapproval of adoptions. Daniel hoped he and Mia would never need help from the embassy, because he doubted they would get it.

After the embassy visit, they headed to the attorney's office. No one was there, even though they had an 11:00 a.m. appointment, so they settled on the benches outside the office door and waited. It was 11:50 before Mrs. Sanchez arrived. She was a middle-aged woman dressed stylishly, with white gloves and a matching white hat. She carried herself like a professional and apologized for being late. Then she shrugged.

"Guatemala time," she said, as if that excused her lateness.

Inside her sparse but practical office, Daniel heard about all the possible delays and the need for patience. Grace interpreted. Apparently there was a document missing, a "critical document." However, with a little extra money, a trip to Mazatenango could be arranged to obtain the document. For $500 the lawyer would personally retrieve the paper and then finish the proceedings. The whole adoption could be done in ten days. Otherwise, it might be a month or more. Attorney Sanchez shrugged, as though everything were completely out of her hands.

"How far away is Mazatenango?" Daniel asked Grace.

"About two hours. It depends on the traffic, and if it's been raining or not. But it's not just the distance. It means dealing with the bureaucracy, standing in line, and basically spending the better part of a day waiting."

"Could we go and get the document ourselves?"

"I'll ask, but it's really not safe for Gringos, Daniel. There are robbers on the roads."

Grace turned to Mrs. Sanchez and rattled off the question in rapid-fire Spanish. The attorney looked at Daniel with wide eyes and a horrified expression. "Oh no!" she sputtered, waving her hands in front of her face, as if Daniel were an oncoming car ready to run her over. Then she turned to Grace, and Daniel watched as the two women conversed.

Mia sat beside him with Quetzal fidgeting in her lap. "Daniel," she implored, trying to keep her voice low so as not to distract the two women volleying in Spanish across from them. "If it can really be done in ten days, isn't it worth $500? We could go home together. Shouldn't we consider this? Please?"

Then Grace began speaking to them in English. "Francisca says it is a bad idea for you to go to Mazatenango, even with her. First, the officials will all try to get bribes from you because they think you are a rich American. Secondly, the workers will be mad because they think you are a rich American and deliberately slow things down just to be mean. It is best if only she goes and does it alone. It requires delicacy."

"Can we really be finished with the adoption in ten days?" Daniel asked.

"I don't know," Grace said, "but Francisca is reliable. She is not the attorney that Tommy uses for his program. His lawyer, Mr. Cantu, travels with two armed bodyguards because he says he represents dangerous criminals. But Francisca is different. She has good connections, and she is a Christian lady. She and her husband are prominent attorneys. They don't usually handle adoptions, but made an exception with Quetzal because we are friends. She is the one who helped us adopt Josh, and I completely trust her. Francisca says it is important to try to get everything done before December. Everything shuts down for the Christmas season. If the adoption isn't completed by the beginning of December it will probably go into the middle of January."

Daniel looked over at Mrs. Sanchez. She smiled and nodded her head. He smiled back, noticing that her front tooth had lipstick smeared on it. Before leaving the office, he peeled off five, one-hundred-dollar checks from his book of travelers' checks.

"Oh well," he said, "We will have faith." Then thinking to himself: *If any other expenses come up in the next ten days, I might not have enough money.* He worried about this on the way home. He was hoping he wouldn't have to use his credit cards. Mia and Quetzal dozed.

Finally he stopped worrying and gazed out the car window. Somehow it would work out. If he had to go into debt he would. He wanted desperately to return home, but not without Mia and Quetzal. He was growing tired of the beauty and brightness of this place. The country was too intense—it was an assault on his senses. Daniel longed for the simplicity of life in Michigan, where the landscape was bland and the temperature often too cold. He turned his head from the window and watched Mia. She was sleeping upright with her head against the opposite door of the car. Her soft, subdued tones soothed his eyes, and he felt himself relax. He closed his eyes and didn't look out the window again until they reached the compound.

Chapter 19

Root-Bound

At dinner Tommy announced he had a surprise for everybody. He had arranged a short trip to a resort that was a family vacation spot used by Guatemalans.

"It's not for Gringo tourists," Tommy said.

Daniel sensed Tommy wasn't fond of Gringos even though he was one himself.

"You'll love this place," he promised. "They have musicians and a swimming pool and lots of beautiful birds. We usually take the children, but they're involved with school activities, so they'll be staying home with Marta. I think it will be nice for you two to get out and see some of the countryside. We'll leave right after breakfast."

Grace looked surprised, but didn't say anything. She excused herself immediately after dinner, stating that she had a lot to do if they were going to take a trip. Mia and Daniel went upstairs early. Neither was excited about Tommy's surprise.

"I don't want to go. I am a Gringo tourist," Daniel said to Mia when they were alone. "I don't need a vacation. I'm on a vacation."

Mia giggled. "I know, but we *have* to go. They're our hosts, and look what they've done for us. We can't refuse. Tommy's trying to be nice."

"Maybe," he replied. "I guess we're obligated. At least we'll have the baby with us."

The resort, located on a stretch of beach in Tiquisate, consisted of bungalows situated around a beautiful, manicured lawn and an Olympic-sized swimming pool. Brightly colored parrots nested in trees that gracefully swayed to the marimba music playing in the background. Mariachi groups strolled the grounds, stopping here and there to perform for guests. It was indeed a tropical paradise, and as Tommy had indicated, the guests were predominately affluent Guatemalan families on vacation with their children.

To Daniel, Grace and Tommy didn't seem to belong in such a romantic setting. They were awkward with one another, certainly not like two people in love. They never teased each other or shared sweet nothings. They avoided touching and never held hands. When given a choice they sat opposite one another. Both were polite and civil, but there was no affection in their interactions. The overriding impression was one of benign indifference.

"This could be a great place to repair a broken marriage," Mia observed. She and Daniel were strolling the grounds on the way to meet Grace and Tommy for dinner. "But I think the Tuttles are beyond the point of fixing their marriage. Sometimes when I'm with them I feel guilty about how happy I am with you and Quetzal. I'm so lucky. It's ironic that they've done so much to make us happy, but seem so unhappy themselves."

During dinner at the restaurant, the Fishers saw a side to Tommy that disturbed and embarrassed them. Tommy flirted openly with the waitress and asked things like, "Where do you live?" and, "I'll bet you have a lot of boyfriends, don't you?"

Daniel thought the questions too personal and inappropriate. The waitress did the best she could to provide suitable service while acting indifferent to Tommy's questioning.

After having their order taken, Tommy turned to Daniel as the waitress walked away. "I told you they had beautiful birds."

Daniel tried to ignore Tommy by focusing his attention on Mia and Grace. Between dinner and dessert, the two women excused themselves to change the baby's diaper and fetch a warm bottle of milk. Daniel wanted to go with them. He felt the need to escape, even if only for ten minutes. Instead he stayed while the dishes were cleared and coffee was brought for the two men. Tommy continued to banter with the waitress.

When she left, Daniel asked, "Do you come here often?"

Tommy nodded. "Whenever I can. A few times a year. Usually I come without Grace. You know how wives can be. You can't be yourself when they're around."

Daniel sipped his coffee, and after a few moments of silence said, "It's beautiful here. Thank you for bringing us."

"It's my pleasure," Tommy replied. "Too bad you're not going to be here longer. I could show you the real Guatemala." He looked off into the distance. "I mean, you wouldn't believe the women here."

Daniel realized his discomfort must have shown because Tommy took one look at him and smiled sheepishly. "Don't get me wrong," he said,

"Mia's great, but Guatemalan women… they're special. They really know how to please a man."

Daniel looked around and wondered if this conversation was real or if Tommy was playing a joke on him.

"Actually," Tommy continued, leaning closer to Daniel as if the two were old buddies, "I know where there's a really good whorehouse. It's close by, and if you can get away in an hour or so, I'll take you there."

"You're not serious?"

Tommy shrugged and then sipped coffee. "A man needs a good wench once in a while."

Wench? What kind of word was that to use? Where have I heard that word before? Oh yes, Daniel thought, *from Mikey. That's how he described Kelly.* It was a long time ago, yet the scene remained indelibly fixed in his memory. *A funny word to use,* he thought, *then and now.*

"It sounds like you're talking about a Cuban cigar," Daniel said.

"They're worth about the same; a momentary distraction, a simple pleasure."

"I'm sorry," Daniel replied. "I can't do that. I mean I don't want to do that." He leaned back from the table. "I didn't come all the way to Guatemala to be unfaithful. I just want to spend as much time as possible with Mia and Quetzal before we return home."

"Suit yourself. I guess you still love you wife? I mean, you like being with her?"

"Being with her?" Daniel asked. "She's my wife. Of course I like being with her." He was annoyed with this conversation. Still, he dared not offend his host and risk saying anything that might jeopardize the adoption. So thoughtfully and slowly he answered, "I love my wife. Why would you think otherwise?"

"I don't know," Tommy said, looking down into his coffee cup. "It gets old, the same routine, every day. The thought of having sex with Grace any more makes my skin crawl. You know what I mean? Just look at her. She's cold...a block of ice. And she's so damn pious. Did you ever try making love to a saint? Believe me, a good whore is better. At least they've got blood in their veins. You know, Daniel, you should have married Grace when you had the chance. You probably would have appreciated her."

Daniel was angry. He wanted to hit Tommy, but knew that would be a mistake. Tommy was bigger and in better physical shape, not to mention he held his and Mia's dream in his hands. So Daniel tried to proceed as if he was having a normal conversation with a normal person, a Christian missionary.

"I never had the chance," Daniel said. "And I do appreciate Grace. I think she's terrific. I think you are fortunate to be married to such a fine woman. You should value her more. She's an inspiration."

"Yeah, yeah... if you say so. Anyway, we gave up on each other a long time ago. If it wasn't for the children, I'd be out of here, or she would."

To Daniel's relief he saw the wives returning to the table. Quetzal was gripping her bottle. *Finally,* he thought, *I don't have to be alone with this colossal shmuck.*

Tommy looked at Daniel and smiled. "If you change your mind, pal, you know where to find me."

Daniel and Mia retired to their room after dinner, claiming exhaustion. They stretched out in bed with Quetzal propped between them and the television turned on low. It was wonderful to be alone, just the three of them in their private world. When Daniel recounted his conversation with Tommy, Mia didn't act surprised.

"It's sad," she said. "It explains a lot. Tommy is gone so much. He's hardly ever home until late at night. And they have separate bedrooms."

"They do?" Daniel asked.

Mia nodded. "You know what Tommy said about not wanting to touch Grace? I think the feeling is mutual. I don't think Grace especially wants to be touched by Tommy—not any more. I'm surprised she ever did."

They remained silent for a few minutes while Quetzal practiced kicking and grabbing her tiny feet.

"I hope we never get that way," Mia said. "If we do, let's get a divorce amicably. I never want to be trapped in a toxic relationship."

"Don't worry," Daniel said. "I will always want to touch you. In fact, right now…" He leaned over Quetzal, getting ready to tickle Mia in the side, but she was too fast for him and leaped out of bed. Quetzal watched in bewilderment as her mother and father engaged in a pillow fight that ended with the two of them back in bed softly kissing Quetzal's feet.

After the weekend at the resort, they returned to Canoguitas, and life resumed as before. Daniel made the necessary arrangements to extend his stay, but left the return date on his ticket open. He and Mia spent their days relaxing with Quetzal and wandering around the compound. When Quetzal napped, they would walk to town, look around, and return with a cold Coca Cola in a plastic bag. Quetzal and Daniel bonded, and he took pride in the fact that he had become one of her favorite people—sometimes even preferred over Mia. Tommy and Grace went about their normal lives, so Mia and Daniel were on their own most days. Marta was with them in the house, and she seemed to magically know when to bring out a snack or fix a meal. In the late afternoon, the house filled with people, and the Fishers listened while the children talked about the events of the day. Daniel felt like a ghost on the outskirts of life, but strangely didn't mind. He knew it was temporary. Although he and Mia did little that could be called productive, they spent practically all of their time with Quetzal. That was all that was important, and the days went by fast.

One evening when Tommy was present for dinner, he explained some of the financial problems the ministry was having. "After the earthquake," he said, "everyone wanted to help. There was an outpouring of generosity from the United States. But that was eight years ago, and contributions have slowly been drying up. Without a major disaster, people just aren't willing to give."

"Please, Tommy," Grace interrupted. "It sounds like you're actually saying the earthquake was a good thing. Don't you remember how horrible it was? People died."

"Hey," Tommy said. "Life goes on. I'm being pragmatic. Of course the earthquake was terrible, but it did make people appreciate the mission and what we do here. The fact is, an occasional disaster is good for religion. We're not responsible for earthquakes or floods or acts of God."

Grace lowered her head and stared at her plate.

"The problem now," Tommy continued, "is the idea of indigenous missions. Some critics started saying, 'Why send money to an American couple in Guatemala? Guatemala has its own people to do mission work. Why not send money to the Guatemalans themselves?' So the trend now is to support indigenous missionary work. That's the buzz word, but it leaves us out in the cold. That's why we're developing our international adoption program. You wouldn't believe how many rich foreigners want to adopt Guatemalan kids. People are crazy for these babies. I wish I had realized this years ago."

"Tommy!" Grace sounded alarmed.

Tommy looked at his wife and then at Daniel. "Not you. I don't mean you and Mia. You're friends. That's different. Grace said you would be great parents, and I can see she was right. Quetzal's a lucky baby."

"We're the lucky ones," Daniel answered. "We're so thankful to Grace for remembering us." He looked at Grace, who smiled.

Tommy continued, "We already have a waiting list of clients—people from all over the United States, Australia, Israel, Italy. So many people want babies, and it's amazing what they are willing to pay. One of our lawyers, Jose Cantu, says he's grown rich off of adoptions, and I believe him. Adoptions spell opportunity."

"Quetzal is the answer to our prayers," Mia said. "She has made our dreams come true. And we have the two of you to thank for it."

"You two are the answer to her mother's prayers," said Grace, "and to mine."

* * *

Twelve days after the meeting with attorney Sanchez, Daniel and Mia had their wish granted. They had an appointment at the U.S. Embassy and received the visa for Quetzal Maya Fisher to enter the United States. At last they were free to go home.

Later that afternoon, Daniel found Grace in her garden.

"I can't thank you enough," he said. "Who would have thought it, all those years ago at Theophilus? You've been a wonderful friend, Grace. You have made our dreams come true."

Grace was watering some potted plants and turned toward Daniel and smiled. "You don't need to thank me," she said. "It was God who told me to give Quetzal to you. You and Mia are good people. I always knew you were a good man, Daniel—I just didn't realize how good. Quetzal is lucky to have such good parents. I can see how much you both love her, and it warms my heart. Enjoy Quetzal and give her lots of love. She's had a tough beginning, being abandoned by her poor mother. Did I tell you I knew her mother? Her name was Felicita, and she was the sweetest thing. A beautiful young woman. Her father...well, I didn't know him... not really."

"I thought her father was unknown. At least that is what it says on the adoption papers. That's what you said."

"Yes, Daniel. Her father is unknown."

"Grace? Is there something I'm missing?"

Ignoring his question, she lifted a potted plant that seemed to be doing poorly. "This poor little guy," Grace said, turning the pot. "Just look how much smaller he is than the others. He's the same age, but the pot is too small. I should have transplanted him a long time ago. Now he's root-bound. If he doesn't get a bigger pot soon, he'll remain stunted his whole life. We don't want that." Grace looked wearily around the garden, and Daniel was struck by how out of place she looked. He felt a stab of sadness at the thought of her remaining in this garden after he and Mia were gone.

Then Grace continued, "People are like plants I think. Sometimes we outgrow our environments. We get constricted, and we can't thrive. We become like this little fellow—root-bound. Unhappy little things unable to reach our potential." She put the pot back in its place and turned to leave the garden. "Come on," she said. "There's something I need to give you in the house." Daniel followed and waited in the courtyard while Grace went upstairs. A few minutes later she returned and handed him an envelope. "It belonged to Quetzal's birth mother Felicita," she said, as Daniel pulled out the Saint Christopher medal. "I don't believe in saints, but she did. She wanted her baby to have it. The medal was very special to her. So I'm entrusting it to you. She also left this book. I don't know if she left it on purpose or by accident."

Daniel took the writing book. It was just like one he had as a child in school. It was a Mead notebook—with a black and white cover and lined pages inside.

"It's Felicita's writings," Grace said. "Mostly recipes, but it also has a collection of *echizos*."

"Of what?"

"Magic spells. Incantations," Grace replied. "Typical Guatemalan folk beliefs."

"Oh," said Daniel. Thank you. I'll keep them safe for Quetzal. I'm sure she'll want them when she grows up."

The next morning Grace and Marta drove Daniel, Mia, and Quetzal to the airport. Mia and Quetzal stood by the suitcases with Marta, who was having a hard time saying goodbye. Marta kept asking to hold Quetzal and kissing her, and handing her back to Mia and wiping tears from her eyes. She smiled and nodded her head the whole time.

Grace took Daniel aside for a moment and in a soft whisper said, "God bless you Daniel. It's been so good seeing you again. I will continue to pray for you, Mia, and the baby. Take care of her. Quetzal is precious."

"Thank you, Grace. For everything."

On the flight back to Michigan, Daniel sat with his new baby in his lap.

Mia's voice brought him out of his reverie. "She's holding your thumb again."

Daniel turned to his wife, who was looking down at the baby, who was peacefully asleep and holding tightly to Daniel's thumb.

"I guess she's bonding with you," Mia said.

"We've already done that. She just likes holding Daddy's thumb."

Chapter 20

Michigan

It was an ordinary October day in Michigan. Snow threatened to fall. The sky was overcast, and looking out the window one could sense the cold. The leafless trees leaned to one side, pointing the way for the inevitable bone-chilling winds that would shortly arrive. Mia looked out her kitchen window and thought *I wish we lived in Florida*. If they had, the Fishers likely would have noticed a small item that appeared on page six of the *Miami Herald*. The story read:

> An American missionary in Guatemala was arrested in an alleged   kidnapping ring. Police raided a house operated by the Evangelical Friendship Mission of Guatemala and arrested the   directors, Mrs. Lila Tuttle and her stepson, Mr. Tommy Tuttle. Police seized six children ranging in age from one week to ten years. According to children's rights worker, Elida Hernandez, "Guatemala has ineffective laws regulating adoptions. Some people make money by trafficking in babies put up for adoption to foreign couples."
>
> The investigation of the Tuttles began when a 24-year-old woman claimed her son had been taken without permission and sold to Mr. Tommy Tuttle. Upon investigation, it was determined that many of the children housed in the facility lacked the proper documentation to satisfy legal requirements...

The Fishers were not in Miami. They would eventually see the story, but it would be weeks later when a friend sent them a photocopy. Now they were in Michigan and Mia was looking out the window. Suddenly she turned and began frantically waving her hands to get her husband's attention. Daniel was slouched in an overstuffed chair reading. He looked up.

"Look honey! Quetzal…She's walking. She's taking her first steps."

It wasn't the most momentous event in the world, and only two people in Michigan witnessed it. Moving like an uncoordinated robot, the tiny miracle with hair that was only now beginning to lay flat on her head waddled to the kitchen table and collapsed into the arms of her waiting mother. For Daniel and Mia Fisher, the moment was more than sufficient, and the grace of it would sustain them for a long time.

Chapter 21

Call of the Quetzal

*T*was the night before Christmas and all through the house not a creature was stirring, not even a mouse ... This had always been a favorite story of Daniel's, but never had he enjoyed it more than the night he read it to his wonderful little girl. Five-year-old Quetzal could hardly contain her excitement as she squirmed beside him in the big chair, turning the pages as he read the words aloud. When the story was finished, Daniel carried her upstairs, noting to himself how heavy she was. *Or maybe I'm just getting old. Not many more years of this,* he thought sadly. Mia met them at the top of the stairs, and she took Quetzal to brush her teeth and go to the bathroom. Then both parents tucked her into bed, watched her say her prayers, and kissed her goodnight.

"Do you think we'll hear the reindeer on the roof?" Quetzal asked.

"Maybe," Mia answered seriously. "But if you do, remember to be quiet. If Santa thinks you're awake, he might not land."

"Do you think Santa will bring me a Cabbage Patch Doll?"

Daniel smiled at the sparkling eyes and rosebud lips of Quetzal's face.

"I wouldn't be surprised," he replied. "You've been an awfully good girl this year." He kissed her forehead once again. "We all better get to sleep, before Santa comes. And remember, if you hear the reindeer on the roof or Santa downstairs, stay in bed. Okay? And remember to be quiet."

"I will, Daddy," she replied and pulled her stuffed best bear close to her.

Daniel and Mia left the room and closed the door partway behind them. Then they went downstairs to lock up, eat Santa's cookies and put out the gifts. They were experienced parents now, and performed their tasks quickly and quietly. Stockings were filled and then all the toys that had been hidden in the utility room were set in front of the Christmas tree. Several attempts were made at arranging their placement while the couple munched sugar cookies and sipped milk. What should go in front of the tree—the doll house or Nipper the large stuffed horse? For a while it was a tossup, but eventually Nipper was moved to the background, with his head peeking through the branches of baubles and tinsel. The result was magical. Daniel and Mia stood in the doorway under the mistletoe and admired their handiwork. No one could doubt that Santa had stopped for a visit. With their work complete, they turned out the lights and headed upstairs for bed.

*   *   *   *

The grandfather clock in the hall chimed twice when Quetzal heard the reindeer on the roof. Their hoof beats sounded like tap dancers. Then she heard jingle bells ringing, too. The deer must be wearing bells! She couldn't wait to tell Daddy! She stayed in bed, just like she'd been told to do. She was a good girl. She hugged her best bear tightly and stared at the ceiling, listening to the bells. From across the hallway she could hear her father snoring and hoped he wouldn't scare Santa away.

*   *   *   *

Daniel was indeed asleep, with Mia curled up beside him and the cat stretched lengthwise across the end of the bed. The cat twitched his ears, as if he might have heard the reindeer, too; then promptly slipped back to sleep. Daniel was aware of none of this except for the chiming clock. But what he heard wasn't a clock at all. It was the call of the Quetzal bird, "A-hoe, A-hoe." In his dream, the bird called to him twice as he chased it through a dark forest. He could only catch glimpses of the bird as it flashed ahead of him, leaving a trail of sparkling dust for him to follow. But darkness was beginning to close around him. The dust was fading, and there were no more bird calls. Just as Daniel felt overcome with a heavy sense of loss, he emerged from the forest into his living room where the bird was perched atop the fireplace mantle. *Thank goodness,* Daniel thought with relief. *I thought I'd lost you this time.*

Daniel liked this dream. It was one he had frequently. The bird now fluttered playfully around the room, and Daniel watched as it displayed its beauty. It flew so close to him that he could feel the breeze from its wings. Daniel reached out his hand and lightly touched the glistening green feathers.

You're real, he thought, as his body was flushed with pure joy. *It's true, you're real!*

Daniel stood in his living room basking in the radiance of the magical bird, and he vowed to himself he must share this moment with Mia. *As soon as I wake up, I'll tell Mia about you. You can stay here for as long as you want. We'll keep you safe, and I will never confine you. You can be as free as you want to be. I promise.*

But of course Daniel wouldn't remember any of this when he woke up. He never did. He never would.

The bird simply replied, "I know, Daniel. Thank you. Now, go back to sleep."

And that is exactly what Daniel did.

At one time, religion was the lens I looked through to interpret my world. The problem with looking through a lens, however, is it doesn't necessarily improve one's vision. Sometimes it distorts what you see. My parents' interfaith marriage was the excuse I used for my turmoil. Over time I've come to realize my problems had nothing to do with religion. I just needed something to blame for my shortcomings. But I had the same questions everyone has—where do I belong, and what kind of a person do I want to be?

I remember while in Guatemala adopting Quetzal I saw one of Grace's peacocks spread its feathers. I looked at the color pattern on the tail, with its blues and greens and the precision of the design. At that moment the thought occurred to me that this was one of God's masterpieces. I also thought this lovely animal is only one of the thousands of clues God has left for us to find. Then there is the Quetzal bird, the symbol of Guatemala, a delicate creature with iridescent colors. The bird that can't be confined. Yes, God leaves clues everywhere. All we have to do is open our eyes. And when we do finally open our eyes, all that remains is one simple question: Do you choose to believe or not?

The only words I remember from my Bar Mitzvah are: "The earth is the Lord's and the fullness thereof..." I spoke those words in English. Of the Hebrew words which I didn't understand and recited phonetically, I remember nothing. I might as well have been speaking in tongues. But I'm only now beginning to appreciate the impact of those English words; especially when I think of that peacock and the lovely Quetzal bird.

I am an alumnus of Theophilus College, and therefore, by definition, a friend of God. I like to think that is an accurate description of me. I am a spiritual person, and I will always cherish my memories of Theophilus and the few friends I made there, and the one special friend—Grace Spindler.

And, too, I am a friend of Israel. There have been nearly three million Jews who have made Aliyah and immigrated to Israel. I am not one of them. For a while I thought I failed as an Oleh, a new immigrant. I believed I left Israel to find an easier life, that I ran away. But that wasn't correct. I left to find the right life, the life that was meant for me. That life wasn't in Israel. So I don't feel guilty for leaving.

One of the speakers at WUJS, wisely said: "Some of you will not stay here. If you need to leave, then go. But before you do, get to know us. Become our friend and learn what we're about…" That's what I did. Now, I consider myself a friend of Israel, an ambassador of good will, a Zionist. If someone is selling Israel bonds, then I am buying. If a politician says he's behind Israel, he has my attention.

Maybe I didn't actually find "my people" while living in Israel. To be honest, I'm not sure I have a people. I am an American, a product of the melting pot and as such, rather nondescript. But in Israel, I did find Mia Murphy, and she is the best of any people. Or, as my grandmother would say, Mia is an easy keeper.

Quetzal is grown now. She is married and the mother of her own daughter, a fine child who has eyes as blue as the Caribbean Sea. Quetzal earns her living as a counselor. She specializes in adoption. She talks to kids with adoption issues, kids who say they are in-between, who fantasize about their "real" parents and wonder how such people could have given them up for adoption. These children aren't sure where they belong. I can relate to that. Adoption is the lens they see through when trying to make sense of their world. It distorts their vision.

Nowadays, when I see my Quetzal holding her baby and being the terrific mother that she is, I am moved—almost to tears. When we are together, Mia, Quetzal and her family, I realize I don't have a dilemma at all. I never did. That whole interfaith dilemma thing was nonsense, just an excuse.

So, I'm no longer wandering the dispersion asking, "Who am I?" I know who I am. I am a husband and father and recently, a grandfather. I look forward to the experience of watching my grandchildren grow up. I am complete within the richness of the tapestry of my patchwork family.

I don't have all the answers, only my answers. I don't know why some people are anti-Semitic or racists, or apparently born just plain evil. Sometimes I remember my mother's words spoken so many years ago. "We believe in tolerance." That's what she had said when I was a child, and she was right. I do believe in tolerance.

These days, when I look into my grandchild's blue eyes, I know I don't need to search for God any more. Fortunately, God has found me.

About the Authors

Jim and Cheryl Pahz live on sixteen wooded acres in the middle of Michigan, When not writing, they enjoy reading, spending time with family and friends, and appreciating nature.

Visit the authors' website at

www.pahz.net

www.ingramcontent.com/pod-product-compliance
Lightning Source LLC
Chambersburg PA
CBHW081149170626
46813CB00009B/3128